Murder
at
Marleigh Manor

Jay Palmer

All Books by Jay Palmer

The VIKINGS! Trilogy:

>**DeathQuest**

>**The Mourning Trail**

>**Quest for Valhalla**

The EGYPTIANS! Trilogy:

>**SoulQuest**

>**Song of the Sphinx**

>**Quest for Osiris**

Souls of Steam

Jeremy Wrecker, Pirate of Land and Sea

The Grotesquerie Games

The Grotesquerie Gambit

The Magic of Play

The Heart of Play

The Seneschal

Viking Son

Viking Daughter

Dracula – Deathless Desire

Murder At Marleigh Manor

Murder at Marleigh Manor Cover Artist: **Jay Palmer**

Website: **JayPalmerBooks.com**

To my beloved muse,
Partner in all things,
And joy of my life,
Karen Truong

1838 AD

Queen Victoria has ruled England for 1 year.

Map of Marleigh Manor & Grounds

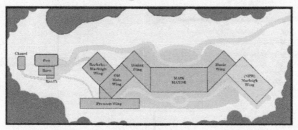

Rooms in the (New) Marleigh Wing

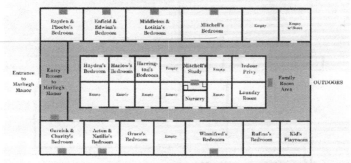

For full version, see:
http://jaypalmerbooks.com/MMM/MMM.html

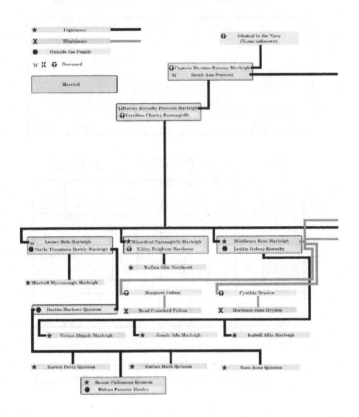

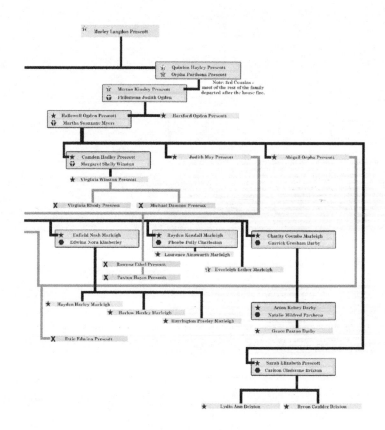

For full version, see:
http://jaypalmerbooks.com/MMM/MMM.html

Chapter 1

The burly, grizzled blacksmith whose name she'd already forgotten rummaged through her father's toolbox with thick, meaty fingers and a scowling sneer. He stank of smoke, ash, and sweat, and his smithy looked no cleaner than a coal scuttle.

"I don't think so, wench," the smith said.

"My name is Miss Adella Hester Cumberbatch," Adella said. "These were my father's tools, and a better man and carpenter God never made."

The smith frowned, lifted three wood-chisels out of her toolbox, examined them closely, and then set them back inside. He drew out a wood-handled iron drill and cranked it once.

"Four crowns and five shillings," the smith said.

Adella faltered in disbelief.

"Sir, these are worth pounds ...!" Adella insisted.

"I'm a smith. Metal is all I care for. If you want more, sell to a carpenter."

"There's not a carpenter in the city ...," Adella complained.

"They're all at Marleigh," the smith said.

"Where ...?"

"Marleigh Manor, ten miles up North Road, just south of Lake Prescott," the smith said. "Lord Middleton Marleigh is adding a new wing to his estate. Every carpenter in three districts is there, trying to beat the winter snows. They'll pay twice what these are worth, but it's a long ways from here."

"Sir, thank you very much," Adella said. "I'm sorry I wasted your time."

With one hand, the muscular smith lifted the heavy wooden toolbox and held it out to her. Adella needed both arms to take it.

"Can you cook?" the smith asked, eyeing her appreciatively.

Adella shook her head.

"My father was a carpenter," Adella said. "Everything I know I learned from him."

"Too bad," shrugged the smith.

Lugging the toolbox, Adella departed. She'd no interest in blacksmiths, especially one looking for a wife. She'd always had plenty of men wanting her that way, but she wanted a better life than a dumb brute's slave and whore. No man had ever been kinder to any woman than her father had been to her mother; she wanted such a man.

Yet marrying men were rare, especially as she'd followed her father from job to job, living out of their tent until he'd saved enough to buy his own tools. Less than a year ago, they'd rented a room and settled down, living under a solid roof for the first time since her mother had died of influenza. Then her father fell ill. She'd sold all they owned to purchase medicines that proved useless; Diphtheria left her an orphan. She was desperate; rent was due, her coin-pouch empty, and she had nothing left but her father's tools.

The chill morning was still fresh, so Adella began walking up North Road. Ten miles was a long journey carrying a heavy toolbox, yet she had no choice. She'd eaten the last of her food, and if she couldn't pay rent in two days, she'd lose her only shelter ... and soon it would start to snow.

Amid colorful fall leaves blowing in every direction, dropping from countless trees, North Road appeared briefly barren, then grew suddenly crowded with carriages and wagons. From each carriage stared clean faces, not deigning to speak to her. Wagons rolled northward laden with lumber. Some drivers were eating or drinking; Adella was hungry, yet she refused to beg. The stigma of begging would stain her reputation for life; she hoped to avoid begging as long as she could.

If she were a man, she wouldn't sell her father's tools. She'd helped her father since she was six, sorting nails, straightening them, waxing, sanding, and edging dovetails. She could haul, frame, and finish as well as the best, but no one would hire a woman carpenter.

Selling his tools would only delay her fate. No matter how much she got, to survive more than a month, she needed an honest job or a good husband ... and both were rare as diamonds.

Gritting her teeth, she constantly switched the handle of the toolbox from one arm to the other. Its burden cut into her thin arms, yet she trudged on, mile after mile.

A shrill, lewd whistle blew from a creaking wagon behind her; she kept her face averted. She was a mile from the last farmhouse, alone on an empty road surrounded by thin woods and grazelands; screams would die unheeded. Even looking at the driver might be considered encouragement ...

The heavy, creaking wagon pulled alongside her, and its horses suddenly slowed.

Adella silently cursed. She stepped farther off the road, into the leaf-covered tall, dry grasses that rose past her knees. Long skirts made pushing through tall grass harder, but ...

"Would the young lady care for a ride ...?" voiced a robust baritone.

Adella stepped away, pushing deeper into waist-high weeds.

"Now, I wouldn't call that friendly ...," the driver deepened his voice. "No one's a'harming anyone, is they

....?"

His horses stopped, and with scrapes and squeaks, his heavy cart ground to a halt.

Adella stumbled over rough, unseen ground, almost dropping her father's tools. Yet she righted herself and kept walking. She reached a line of thin trees, and slipped between their narrow trunks. Low bushes blocked her path, yet she crashed through them.

She risked a backward glance; the grimy driver, wearing a wispy beard, ragged clothes, and a leering smile, had dismounted and was following her. He didn't look much older than she.

Squirrels darted off, and tiny birds took wing as she approached. Wishing she could escape as easily, Adella followed their retreats. Even jumping grasshoppers evaded perceived threats better than she ...

"Leaving a lady helpless in the wild would be ungentlemanly ...!" he called to her.

She kept her eyes looking ahead into thickening wilderness.

"No gentleman would pursue a frightened lady!" Adella shouted, pushing through thick weeds and bushes, trying to avoid the thorns raking her long skirt.

Sarcastic laughter came from closer behind than she'd expected. Rapid footfalls; he was chasing her.

"A gentleman would teach you a lesson in manners!" Adella screamed.

"Maybe you need a lesson in kindness ...," the man was right behind her.

Adella couldn't outrun him, especially not while lugging the heavy box of tools, which she couldn't abandon. Adella reached into the wooden box, lifted out an adze, and turned to face her pursuer. She raised her weapon warningly.

His amused eyes frightened her. His laugh stabbed like icicles.

Adella screamed as loudly as she could.

He paused and spread his arms, smiling and showing empty hands.

"No one here but us," he said.

His long arm shot out overtop the small bush separating them. He grabbed her blouse roughly.

Adella swung like a carpenter ...!

Her adze struck hard and deep. Blood spewed, spraying both sickening red. He staggered and cried out, yet yanked her in close, right up against his chest, and knocked her toolbox from her hand; it crashed noisily upon leaf-strewn bushes. She struggled, but ...

Slowly his grip weakened. He fell against her, to his knees, looking up in horror as blood from his leaking skull trickled into his round, unseeing eyes. Horrified, she stumbled backwards ... onto dry leaves, fallen branches, and twigs ... and tripped, toppling onto a hard, spiky bush.

He fell with her.

She kicked to break free of his deathgrip on her dress ... her stiff shoes kicked against his face, but elicited no reaction. On palms and heels, she scrambled away.

She froze, trembling ...

He wasn't moving ...

Adella jumped to her feet, then startled to realize she was still tightly gripping her bloody adze. She'd never used one; her father had done rough cuts, yet she swung hammers with practiced expertise. She tried to drop the adze, but her bloody fingers seemed locked upon its handle.

His blood dripped from her ...!

She pried her fingers loose; her adze fell into a leafy bush. She staggered.

Had she killed the driver ...?

Sufficient blood painted them to assure he'd never rise again. Yet she foundered; she knew nothing about dead men ... except that lawyers hung murderers. If they found her, who'd believe her, a woman soaked in a man's blood ...?

No one had seen ...!

She had to get away ... far, far away.

But she had no ...!

A horse snorted.

Adella glanced at the wagon.

It was her only hope ...!

She dared not touch the corpse; if he weren't dead, then he might awaken. Wiping her hands on a dry spot on her skirt, she hesitated just long enough to retrieve her adze and wipe the blood off it, then she dropped it into her toolbox, and picked up her other spilled tools. She couldn't leave evidence behind; she checked to make sure no other tools had spilled, and then hurried back toward the wagon.

She kept glancing behind her, assuring herself that he wasn't following.

She lifted her heavy toolbox onto the driving bench and climbed aboard. Without hesitation, she grabbed and flapped the leather reins, watching the still woods. The dead driver was hidden by weeds, yet she knew he was there, and someone was sure to find him when crows gathered.

The horses whinnied, but she shook the reins repeatedly, and eventually the beasts began moving. The creaky cart resumed its journey, rolling slowly away. Adella didn't dare urge the two horses faster; she'd seldom driven a cart ... never without her father sitting beside her.

Minutes passed like prison terms, yet slowly she departed the site of the attack. She was still trembling, but she was getting away ...

Painted in blood ...!

His blood ...!

Anyone who saw her ...!

Her few remaining clothes and everything she owned, even her comb and brush, lay back in her room in town. The road was too narrow to turn the horses around, and if she tried, she might get stuck. *She was still too near the corpse ...!*

A strange bag lay at her feet. Wiping her hands

again, telltale blood still accusing her, she leaned down and opened the bag. Half a loaf of brown bread, some apples, and a flask lay on top. Pushing those aside, she felt underneath.

She pulled out a thin, oiled leather half-cloak; drivers wore these in the rain. Wearing this, with its hood up, she could disguise herself slightly, but the bright red wetting her hands and skirt would easily reveal her crime. She dug deeper, pulling out a ragged, torn man's shirt and dirty breaches.

Adella glanced about. Seeing no one, she began pulling off her bloody dress and chemise. As the horses pulled her along, she redressed in the dirty driver's clothes and hooded rain-cloak. After she wiped her hands clean on the back of her dress, she ran a finger across her forehead, unsurprised to see blood on her finger tip. Using a clean spot on her dress, she scrubbed with her own spit, and scraped at her face until no more blood came off, wiped her hands one last time, and then balled up her dress and stuffed it under the seat.

Lastly, she pulled the hood of the thin, oiled leather half-cloak as low as she could, her long hair tucked inside.

Disguised, she urged the horses along. She glanced back at the cart's heavy load of lumber, doubting if these two horses could pull it faster, and certain it'd be dangerous to try.

Eventually a fancy carriage appeared on the road ahead, coming toward her. Adella didn't know what to do; *how would they pass?* The road wasn't wide enough for two. *Should she pull off to the side?*

Fortunately, the other driver knew their business. He pulled off to the side, and her horses squeezed to the side of the road without their wide wheels going off, as if accustomed to traffic. She kept her head low and didn't look at the driver or his passengers.

Shortly afterward, she came to a fork. She'd no idea which road led to Marleigh Manor; she didn't dare go there. Finally she chose the right fork, and hoped it would take her in the opposite direction. The last thing she wanted was to arrive where somebody would recognize the cart.

She rode a ways farther, and saw a small stone bridge ahead.

A stream ...!

Adella halted her horses and jumped off the wagon. The stream was wide and strong, and she knelt before it and washed as best she could. The underbrush pressed against her, yet she scrubbed vigorously, face and hands, and ran fingers through her hair, washing off every trace of blood.

Dripping, she ran back to the wagon, unhampered by a full skirt for the first time in her life. Her bloody dress was the last evidence that she'd killed anyone; she yanked it out and returned to the stream. The woods were thick; she shoved her dress underwater until the stream soaked through, then let it go. The strong current quickly washed the last evidence downstream, into parts overgrown, hopefully out of sight of human eyes forever.

Forcing the reluctant horses to drive over the stone bridge, a plan formed in her mind. If she could find a sizable city, then she could abandon the wagon and disappear. She might have to sell her father's tools for a pittance, but better poverty than jail ... or a short drop off a gallows.

Her wagon creaking, she rode along, realizing her breaths were starting to calm. Yet fears grew as her alarm lessened. She was unaccustomed to having to fight for her life. She felt as if a noose were loosening around her throat.

She dared not return to the scene of her crime.

It hadn't been a crime ...! she told herself. *He would've violated her ...!*

Yet judges didn't consider testimony by a woman equal to words spoken by a man.

Going back would gain her only two last nights in her rented room, and then she'd be broke.

She'd starve ...!

Bread and apples; she hadn't eaten in a day. Although disgusted, she reached into the bag and grabbed an apple; it wasn't firm, yet she devoured it ravenously. Then she ate the rest of them.

Her dresses back home weren't worth her life. She could buy new combs and brushes. For that matter, with her father's tools, she could make combs. Glancing back, she wondered if she could build whatever she needed ... or sell the lumber ... and the cart itself ... and the horses ... *she could live for months off of the sale of the horses!* Yet someone might recognize them ... and the punishment of horse-thieves was no different than the doom of murderers ...

She heard a noise and glanced behind. Another wagon was rapidly approaching. Adella shook her reins, urging her horses faster.

If they caught up ...!

A tall hill rose before them. Her horses strained to pull the heavy wagon. Behind her, a whip cracked; she spied a carriage whip on the floorboard, yet she'd never used one. She kept shaking her reins, hoping it would be enough.

As they topped the hill, the noises and sight startled her.

She'd taken the wrong turn ...!

Marleigh Manor was huge. Atop the next hill, Marleigh Manor shined, wide, three stories tall, with multiple wings branching off its main structure, built of squared masonry and painted beams. It was the grandest building she'd ever seen, surrounded by manicured gardens and paved walkways.

Off to one side worked a vast construction crew, at least fifty men. Familiar hammerings echoed; when she was young, her father and she had often camped at sites like this ... but never at a project so big.

The beauty of Marleigh Manor was amazing, yet desperate thoughts chilled her. She'd chosen the wrong fork, and arrived at the one place she'd likely get caught. Someone would recognize the wagon, know she wasn't its driver, realize she was a woman, wonder why she was wearing a man's clothes, demand to know where she'd gotten them, ask if she'd stolen the wagon, and question where its real driver was ...

A hangman's noose awaited ...!

The other driver was right behind her; she'd be seen if she jumped off the wagon and ran for the woods. She couldn't escape a search; around here, there was nowhere to go for miles. She couldn't drive past the work site; the narrow, downhill road led only toward the manor.

Her only hope was that no one would notice her.

Horses pulled her loaded wagon over the hillcrest and down the long slope toward Marleigh Manor. The jarring of her creaky wagon, and her downhill speed, jostled her load and nerves.

She pulled her hood lower.

Two loaded wagons, with horses still rigged, stood nearby. One wagon was full of lumber, the other being unloaded by four men. Adella steered her horses beside the loaded wagon, and pulled their reins until they halted. Immediately a man walked toward her, so she dismounted on the other side, pausing only to grab her father's heavy tools. She also grabbed the bag with the half-loaf of bread and flask.

Keeping her head down, she walked as fast as she could. Her upbringing had accustomed her to busy worksites; she navigated with ease. No one spoke to or looked at her. She steered toward the back, seeking any escape. Yet the closest woods were far away, and several workmen stood near a privy-tent outside their half-built project; *she couldn't escape unnoticed.* She turned her steps onto a wooden ramp, and ascended into the new addition.

Inside, the hammering was deafening. The framing was finished, the roof overhead being shingled, and inner walls being completed. The floor was solid, ready to be planed, sanded, and waxed. Some rooms were already fully-walled, with doors fitted. At this rate, with this many carpenters, she estimated the whole project might be finished in two months.

The new wing was only one story, yet stretched long and wide, two parallel hallways with rooms against each outer wall, and pairs of inner rooms squeezed in the middle. Yet Adella couldn't explore; she found a finished room with a large closet; both the room and its closet had doors.

Although doorknobs had yet to be installed, she closed both doors and hid inside the closet.

Cowering in the dark, hours flowed like rivers of molasses. She nibbled on the dry, almost-stale bread, and sipped from the flask, which stung her tongue; her father had never allowed her hard liquor. Yet the burning liquid helped her swallow the dry bread. She hoped it would calm her.

Bangs! of hammers and *skrrrrtts!* of saws died, as

they always did at dusk, which meant suppertime.
Somewhere a cook was ladling gruel or stew into bowls
for hungry workers, who would eat no matter how it
tasted. Many times she'd stood in line, her father beside
her. Now she didn't dare.

In the middle of the night, silence fell. Adella
left her father's tools in the dark closet and crept around
the worksite. Windows were being framed. No glass
was yet installed, so she could hear nearby snores from
outside. Watchful for any guards that might've been set,
unlikely at a site this secluded, she snuck through the
half-constructed building, absently noticing evidence of
shoddy workmanship and shortcuts.

To escape, she'd have to get back to the fork in
North Road and take the other route. She didn't dare
return to town; she'd be recognized ... and no other
avenue existed. Yet traveling at night was difficult and
dangerous; evading a second attack seemed unlikely ...
and the idea of having to kill again twisted her stomach.

If she'd had another dress, then she could hide
in the woods by the road, and appear as if she'd walked
the whole way, and sell her father's tools. However, she
couldn't arrive wearing the dead driver's clothes ...

She couldn't hide on an empty, departing wagon,
or travel afoot, without food. Stealing a horse was
unthinkable. She was trapped ... until she found an
escape.

She peeked into a dark, inner room, lit only by
moonlight shining from the open doorway of the room

opposite it. This room was mostly-paneled, save the back wall. Through its bare wooden framework, she saw the back of a stone fireplace facing the room on its far side, with a closet on each side, but was mostly dead space. She wasn't surprised; all large buildings have dead spaces, this one to protect the wooden walls from the heat of the fireplace's stones. Yet she saw nothing helpful, so she continued.

The rest of the site was similar, with scattered bent nails and sawdust littering the floors. No one else was awake, so she wandered the length of both hallways. She peered out windows across the sleeping campsite on one side, and out the other side, into gardens behind the huge manor.

The cook's big pot was sitting by the low-burning fire in the center of camp. It held food, mostly being kept to mix with breakfast, the pot slid just far enough away from the fire to keep it from burning.

Adella pulled her hood low and walked outside, down the wooden ramp, out of the new wing. She knew construction sites; in the dark, if anyone saw her, dressed like a workman, they'd dismiss her as sleepless. Some carpenters slept under blankets around the fire; the poorest didn't have tents. They'd crawl under wagons when it rained. Their chorus of snores echoed, hiding her quiet footsteps.

She reached the table by the cook's wagon, snagged a bowl, and quietly lifted the thin metal lid off the huge pot. Inside was a ladle; she couldn't see what she was scooping into her bowl, yet she didn't care; food was food when you'd worked all day ... well, that's what her father had always said.

She couldn't see any clean spoons, and didn't dare search, so she hurried back as quickly as she could, found her little closet, and sat beside her father's toolbox. She tore some small hunks of dry bread from her diminishing loaf, and dipped them in what turned out to be oat gruel, which was barely warm, yet she ate with relish. She'd taken a large serving, more than she could finish, expecting to need it tomorrow. Every night she'd have to steal more ... until she found a way to escape ... or got caught.

The night seemed endless ...

The first hammer strike awoke her, yet she couldn't leave her closet. If anyone came in, she'd be caught, but the carpenter's priority would be to keep working on the roof, outer walls, and windows, until the new wing was secured from detrimental weather. The likelihood of someone searching mostly-completed closets was small ... yet, once the finishing began, then she'd have nowhere to hide.

All day she listened to gruff voices and familiar sounds of carpentry; nailing paneling, laying shingles, installing doors and windows ... and cursing, as she called it, blue fire. Yet no one discovered her. Later that afternoon, despite her fears, she fell asleep.

Silence awoke Adella, yet a quick glance outside her closet showed the sun still beaming its last rays over the horizon. She ate her final bites of gruel, wondering how she could wash out her bowl, when she heard deep voices. Two men were walking down the hallway outside her room.

"If you please, sir, the men are working hard," one man said. "This is the strongest roof I've seen in forty years, and these floors are ready to be sanded ..."

"How much longer?" barked a gruff, stern voice.

"A few months, not a day more ...," the first voice said.

"Hire more workers!"

"Begging your Lordship's pardon, there's not a carpenter within fifty miles who isn't here. Woodworking skills take training, and we've no one to spare. One novice could put us days behind ..."

"You have two months from today, not a minute longer."

"As you command, sir, but I don't know how we'll manage. If we do shoddy work, your Lordship will be even more displeased ..."

"I catch anyone doing shoddy work I'll flog them! Wake your cooks earlier, so the workers start at first light, and drive them until darkness. Focus on the exterior; when it's done, we'll provide lanterns so they can continue after dark ... all night, if needed."

"As you command, sir."

"We won't be giving this wing to the Berkeley-Marleighs; they can have our older rooms. Real Marleighs will be moving in here, which means this wing must be the finest. Any slipshod masonry or carpentry will be severely punished."

"I give you my word, sir."

"I expect ...!"

The two men wandered out of earshot, yet Adella had heard speeches like this before. Within days she'd have no place to hide ... and no hope of escape.

She considered hiding in the woods, yet she'd probably be caught there, and drenched when it rained. She considered just walking away, yet even if she reached the fork, it might be thirty miles to the next village; she'd starve. She couldn't leave carrying her father's tools, and even if she could sell them here, she'd have no place to stay; she'd end up sleeping in alleys ... and winter was coming.

No matter what she did, she'd be a beggar by spring.

Adella forced herself to remain calm. She had two months before the Marleigh family would be moving into this new wing, two months before the workmen would leave. Eventually she'd find a way to escape ...

She needed a better hiding place ...!

She needed ... *the room with the dead space ...!*

The next morning, as soon as the first hammer struck, Adella began pulling nails. She pried free three wide paneling sections on each side wall, closest to the dead space. Then she nailed the six removed panels to the back wall, covering the back wall, and blocking all view of the chimney from the doorway. Slipping into the dead space through the unfinished closet, she found more evidence of shoddy work; the framed wall was only held in place by two big nails at each end ... and it wasn't load-bearing. Working quickly, Adella freed the back wall, and scooted the whole wall three feet farther from the fireplace, widening the dead space. The wall slid to partially fill the gaps of the six side panels she'd removed. Then she nailed all four big nails into different beams, securing the back wall in its new location.

Unless they remeasured the room, no one would know she'd made it smaller!

She paused to admire her work, then opened the closet door, closed it behind her, and looked around.

She'd built a secret room. The dead space behind the stone fireplace, which had only been a one foot gap, was now four feet wide. It ran the length of both rooms from the closet of the room with the fireplace to the closet of the room she'd shortened.

She peered out of her secret room; thin cracks between the paneling allowed her to see into the rooms on either side.

No one would ever know she was there ...!

Working in the dark, by feel alone, she started shifting the framing of one closet to abut the moved closet door. Once she'd walled the closet, and built and installed a secret door, she could get in and out with ease. Her widened dead-space would be a perfect hideaway.

Adella smiled. Until she found a feasible method of escaping Marleigh Manor, Adella had built herself a secret, comfortable home.

Chapter 2

Late that night, on the far side of the wing, Adella removed a hung closet door, left it leaning against the wall, and stole both its hinges for her secret door. She collected all the bent nails she could find, then scavenged small wood scraps from the discard pile, and carried them into her hideaway.

Then she crept into the camp kitchen and stole more food.

When dawn came, amid the hammering of the roofing carpenters, she repeatedly scratched her sharpest chisel across thin, wooden panels, which easily broke free. She walled both closets, and in the closet of the room she'd shortened, under the lowest shelf support, she built a hinged door that lifted up. Unless someone entered the closet, climbed down onto their hands and knees, and looked up, they were unlikely to see the heads of the small nails she used to affix the lower half of her stolen hinges.

She built stout brackets for a thick wooden brace, so no one could accidentally push it open. She tested her secret door; she removed the brace, opened it, and several times climbed in and out. After shelves were installed, she could just reach up to twist the door handle, and then climb out.

Stealing more panels from other rooms, she walled both closets, so no one could enter except through her secret door.

That night, she slept safely ... finally.

Dawn slowly arrived. Safe in her hidden room, Adella ate most of her stolen oat gruel, and then stretched out to endure the day. Hammers thundered, saws rasped, and orders were angrily shouted. The noisy familiarity soothed her. For the first time since her father had died, Adella felt secure and comfortable.

She used the privy every night. When forced to use the privy during the day, Adella slipped on the concealing driver's hood, pulled it low, and walked right past the busy carpenters. Wearing a man's clothes, no one noticed her.

Late that night, before she snuck into camp to get more food, Adella emerged from her secret room to explore. She still had to find a way to escape across the countryside without being seen before the carpentry work was finished.

She doubted that the dead driver's body had been found. If so, every carpenter would've gossiped about it, and over the noises of the construction, all she heard was blue fire. She hoped the driver's body would never be found. She wished she'd paused long enough to cover his corpse with fallen branches, yet she could do nothing about it now.

Near the main manor, a short hallway joined the two long hallways of the new wing. The short hallway opened into a large room with no windows but a large fireplace; a common room. This room held the first painted wall she'd seen, and one finished door, but both looked weathered; Adella suspected this was originally an outer door of the main house. Now it was the entrance to the rest of the mansion. The door was locked; rich owners didn't want peasant workmen invading their private domains.

Adella snuck outside and slipped along the manicured, slate-paved garden behind Marleigh Manor. Beautiful flowers gleamed in the moonlight, although their dying blossoms were closed at night; summer had long ended. Those who lived here knew only luxury, yet the nights were cooler, the lit windows of Marleigh Manor tightly curtained.

She peeked inside where she could, seeing rooms of grand opulence and royal splendor; Adella had heard of the extravagances of the wealthy, yet never believed them. Room after room astounded her, with fine drapes, polished furniture, and thickly-woven carpets. She wondered what it would be like to live in such elegance.

She glanced in at a kitchen as large as a warehouse, filled with a fireplace, iron stove, and wide tables ... *a dozen cooks must work there!* Moonlight glowed on shelves of baskets, each filled with vegetables, and on one table sat a dozen loaves of freshly-baked bread. Adella had never seen this much food except at a marketplace; *these people eat like kings!*

Wandering onward, she spied illuminated rooms, and saw people walking past windows; she avoided lit rooms, ducking low and slipping past bright windows. She was taking more risks than she should, yet the enticements of seeing people who didn't work for a living, in their extravagant environment, made her yearn to see more.

Light flooded the window before her. Adella dropped to her knees to keep from being seen.

Crawling away, Adella fled back into the new wing. There she retrieved her empty bowl, peeked out a window to verify the camp of workmen was asleep, and then raided it for another bowl of what she was delighted to find wasn't gruel; the big pot held a watery stew. She ladled out as much solid food as she could from its unseen depths, and then returned to her secret room. There she discovered her bowl was filled with boiled carrots, cabbage, onions, and turnips ... all better than oat gruel. And it was still warm! She ate with delight, and sipped from her stolen flask.

True to the overheard discussion, lanterns were lit in the evenings, and finishers worked late. Adella peeked through the gaps in her panels and watched the carpenters hurry. Ceiling-painting began, a bright white. Then walls were stained and lacquered, which filled in the tiny gaps she looked through. Adella stayed hidden until after midnight; the workmen had taken only a brief break for supper. Then decorative, painted trim was nailed into place around every window, into which glass was carefully fitted. Chalk marks were made on high or rough places on the floors, where planing would be required, and then every floor would be sanded.

Five days later, mostly spent trapped in her hideaway, Adella listened as men on their knees sanded and waxed the room outside her closet, and she spent a nervous hour as someone sanded and waxed the floor of her closet. Every minute she feared they'd spot her secret door. When they finally departed, leaving a lit lantern, she felt relieved, yet she glimpsed the shoddy job they'd done, and scoffed scornfully.

She considered stealing their lantern, yet thought better of it; soft lights seeped in through cracks between panels, and dimly illuminated her hideaway. Any lights from inside her room would expose her.

Twice as many workmen labored inside the next day; Adella suspected the roof was mostly completed. Every hand was finishing. Orders were shouted in increasingly virulent tones. Lanterns glowed in the inner, windowless rooms, and late each night. Workmen labored with little rest.

As weeks passed, windows in the outer rooms were opened to let sawdust out, and brooms swept almost every hour. Men wore scarves around their faces to breathe through ... and still coughed wood-dust.

No one spied Adella, or noticed the one room was three feet shorter. However, she spent most of a month trapped in her dead space, unable to emerge until two or three in the morning, and then only to visit the privy outside and steal food and water; she'd emptied her flask, and then stolen a wooden pitcher of fresh water. While stealing food, she'd seen a man crawl out of his blanket, probably to go pee in the middle of the night. Before he'd come back, she was safely concealed in her hidden room ... with his blanket warming her shoulders.

However, as each day passed, the glass windows frosted over more. The morning when the carpenter's camp would depart approached ever closer ... which would leave Adella without food.

Hot-waxing floors was quieter than sanding ... yet doubly worrisome. *Construction would soon be complete.*

Inspections became a daily occurrence. Always the same voice, bluff and angry, shouted harshly and belittlingly to the carpenters, who were working day and night. Several times Adella had been unable to escape to get food or water; she learned to conserve what she stole. Also, the nights got chilly, and when she went outside to the privy, without her blanket, she suffered unwelcomed shivering as autumn deepened into early winter. The hard ground wasn't frosted, yet she felt certain snow was coming.

One morning, laughing young voices surprised Adella: children. They ran through all the hallways and rooms, then departed. An hour later, men's voices came, talking softly and lumbering down the halls, peeking into every room.

That night, shortly after dark, the noises ended. Adella snuck out of her room and hurried to a window overlooking the campsite.

The construction crew had left. Wagons, tents, and carpenters were gone.

All that remained was the sagging, stained privy tent, standing alone in the back, near the woods.

The camp kitchen was gone.
Adella had eaten the last of her food.
She'd found no means of escape.
The rich family was moving in ...!

She walked away from the window, out the door, and down the silent, finished hall. Moonlight showed fancy trim nailed around windows and gleaming, newly-waxed floors; the carpenters had completed their tasks. She passed by the largest room, on the very end, and stopped; a carpet lay on its floor. Glancing inside, she saw a couch, a low table, and two chairs, before a cold

fireplace set into the back wall. End-tables stood
between the chairs, glowing from the tiny flame of an oil
lamp, looking normal, where all other furniture and
boxes were stacked haphazardly. Paintings of unknown
people lay on the floor, leaning against walls, waiting to
be hung.

*The newly-painted door to the main manor hung
open ...!*

This door had never been unlocked before.
Adella stared; *she needed food.* She tip-toed into the
common room ... and peeked through the open door.

A wide hallway opened into a vast room with
many windows; a gallery of sorts, with several musical
instruments. She didn't see or hear anyone, so she crept
through its open doorway, for the first time entering the
heart of Marleigh Manor.

The gallery was amazingly elegant. One whole
wall was immense windows facing the front of the
manor, showing a clear view of the only road
approaching it. Potted plants filled the room, and a
magnificent harp stood silent in one corner, a tall stool
beside it, with a piano behind. A low marble table rested
in its center, surrounded by four couches, and another
couch faced a wide stone fireplace in which dull, red
coals burned. It seemed to be a gathering room where
the family rested.

Wandering further, she found other rooms of
equal magnificence. Fortunately, their doors were open
or ajar; she didn't dare risk surprising someone. She saw

only one person, and him only by the back of his bald head. Puffing a pipe, he sat with his back to the door, through which Adella peeked. He was resting in a thickly-padded chair, feet propped on a table, facing a small, yet cheery, crackling fireplace. Down the hall from his small room towered the main entrance to Marleigh Manor; Adella suspected he was a servant, poised to be at hand if someone arrived in the middle of the night.

She explored most of the first floor, yet didn't climb either of the two wide staircases. Old or poorly-built staircases creaked, and she didn't want anyone hearing her and investigating. Her exploration ended when she discovered the kitchen, which she startled to recall, from her brief glance inside its windows, held more food than she could eat in a month.

The baskets of vegetables she'd spied through the windows were just the beginning. Barrels of grain and bags of flour filled a huge pantry. Pots simmered on a still-warm cast-iron stove, and hung on hooks over dying coals in the fireplace. The kitchen smelled amazing, and Adella regretted she hadn't brought her bowl.

Jars of spices and bottles of wine lay in ordered rows. Hoping their absence wouldn't be noticed, Adella grabbed a whole loaf of bread, a half-empty bottle of wine, and fled back to her hideaway.

No one had seen her!
She'd found food ...!

Did she need to escape ....?

The next day, loud bumps and heavy footfalls awoke her; more furniture was being carried into the new wing. Workmen cursed blue fire, yet Adella was used to that. Their labors continued all day, long after laughing children again came running through the new halls.

As the day passed, Adella listened to the workers and kids, and twice a group of men inspected and yelled at whoever was moving the furniture, especially when they found one of them visiting the privy tent still in the back. One voice was the gruff shouter she'd heard yell at the carpenters, whom she suspected was the head of the family and absolute ruler of Marleigh Manor. He sounded big and imposing, and more than anything, Adella feared him finding her.

She ate her stolen bread in relative comfort. Sharp, tart wine was a pleasant change from water stolen from the camp. Yet nights grew increasingly colder, and Adella rested with her blanket tight around her and the leather half-cloak under her, wishing someone would start a fire in the fireplace whose back she faced.

The door of her entry-room was open, so the glow of sunlight from the window-filled room across the hall beamed into it. The lacquer which had been applied to the walls had sealed most of the cracks between the panels, yet enough light filtered into her hideaway to illuminate everything in a soft, dim glow. The room with the fireplace had the same cracks, but the gruff voice had shouted at the children for playing in it, ordered them out, and then closed its door, shutting off all light from that side.

Adella still wore the driver's clothes. Needing the privy, she waited until the movers left to fetch another load, then sprinted outside to the little privy tent, which the carpenters had left behind, although she didn't know why. She checked carefully before she returned; wearing a man's hood, she might be mistaken for a mover, yet this disguise wouldn't last much longer.

She needed a dress!

That night, Adella explored the new wing. The larger outer rooms, those with windows, held bedroom furniture, while the inner rooms remained mostly empty. Several colorful quilts looked warm and comfortable, yet they were sure to be missed. The room outside her hideaway held only two wide tables and two rocking chairs. The room with the fireplace that she shared hosted a small couch against one wall, empty bookshelves on the other, a massive desk, and four large, padded chairs facing the fireplace.

In the middle of the night, Adella repeated her venture to the kitchen, this time bringing her bowl. She filled it with a rich, hearty venison stew. She also took a sweet pastry tart as big as her fist, and a full bottle of wine.

More furniture moved in the next day, as did the playful, laughing kids, who seemed to be running down the newly-waxed halls until they could slide the rest of the way. She heard the gruff voice shout at the laborers most of the day, and other voices joined them, including one shrill, exasperated man who shouted blue fire to match any carpenter. Several women's voices added to the mix, including one who screeched like a peacock.

Adella slept as best she could, determined to explore more of Marleigh Manor when everyone went to sleep.

However, that night, Adella was trapped. To her horror, the only room into which she could emerge became a nursery. The two babies in it cried all night, and a servant spent the night sitting in a rocking chair, comforting both babies as best she could. She vanished only briefly, and then returned with a wetnurse to satisfy the children.

Adella cursed; she should've stolen another set of hinges. Then she could've made a second secret door into the closet of the study with the fireplace.

Furious at her short-sightedness, and certain she'd never find another set of hinges now that the carpenters were gone, Adella used a sharp chisel from her father's toolbox to clear a tiny section of lacquer from the gap between the panels ... just enough that she could clearly glimpse the movements of the servant and wetnurse holding both babies.

Hungry, but slaking her thirst on her bottle of wine, Adella examined the backside of the closet to the room with the fireplace, yet it was too dark to see anything. *Could she make another secret door ...?* She needed to examine it closely from the other side ... in real light.

The next day in the new wing was an exact repeat. Adella had to risk using the privy when the family went to breakfast, yet she couldn't get more food.

Both babies slept the next night, and Adella exited her hideaway without awakening either ... despite stumbling into a rocking chair in the dark. Checking to make sure the hallway was empty, she hurried around to the study with the fireplace, to inspect its closet, on the other side of which she slept. One of its shelves was already laden with a dozen bottles of liquor. The bottom shelf was lower than the one in the nursery, yet still high enough to crawl under.

The room was definitely a study ... or perhaps a smoking room or office. The wide desk had been moved near its only entrance, and many books had been placed on its built-in shelves. There wasn't enough light from the hallway to read the titles of the books, yet she didn't care. She was starving and thirsty, and headed straight to the kitchen.

To her surprise, the kitchen wasn't empty. Peering from the doorway, she spied two older boys gathering cookies from a ceramic jar she hadn't investigated. They fled laughing. She dropped down behind a sofa as they ran past, too intent on their success to notice a dark, crouching figure.

As they noisily vanished, hissing for each other to be quiet, Adella waited to make sure no one else had heard them, then duplicated their thievery. She stole three large cookies and filled her bowl with a steamy white, creamy food; leftovers from the family dinner. She also stole another full loaf and a bottle of wine, wishing she'd brought her pitcher to fill with water. However, she crept back to her hideaway undetected, and then ate half of her delicious dinner, which turned out to be warm potatoes and vegetables in a rich, cheesy sauce. Her cookies were coated with strawberry jam and currents, and she slowly ate one, saving the others for later.

Another day brought more footfalls heavy with the weight of additional furniture, and that afternoon, the children were loudly ordered into one room to play with the door closed. Adella wondered what was happening, then both babies started to cry, and someone entered the nursery.

She glanced at them through the tiny crack in the panels she'd cleared, which allowed her to hear as well as see better. Two women hurried in, one older nursemaid and one young servant. Each cleaned and diapered a baby while they talked.

"Master Mitchell yelled at me again," the younger servant said.

"He's yelling at every Prescott," the older nursemaid said.

"I almost wept."

"Don't do that. Master Mitchell hates tears."

Adella wondered who Master Mitchell was ... was

he the gruff voice? She was essentially living inside Marleigh Manor, albeit only until she could get away safely. It wouldn't hurt her to know who else lived here.

The young servant girl sighed heavily, a mighty huff of frustration.

"Master Mitchell takes after his father, more's the pity," the older nursemaid said. "Lester Hale Marleigh ... oh, I remember him too well. He terrorized the servants, especially the Prescotts. When he was a teenager, only the oldest crones dared approach him ... he couldn't keep his hands off young maids."

"Worse than my father ...?" the young servant asked.

"No one is worse than your father," the older nursemaid scowled. "Lester was only seventeen when he married Stella Theodosia Berkeley, bless her heart. Everyone hoped she'd calm him, as his mother had influenced his father, but Lester Hale was no equal to old Morley. Stella was the first Berkeley-Marleigh; she kept her family name as her father was governor of the whole district back then; a man of high repute. After Lester died in a drunken duel, Stella fled back to her father's family, swearing she'd never return."

"But ... she's moving in ...?" the young servant asked.

"Master Mitchell is behind that, I'm certain," the older nursemaid said. "Lester was the eldest brother, rightful Lord of Marleigh Manor, so that title should have fallen on his only son, yet Mitchell was too young, so old Morley took it back. Many were glad, yet old Morley had promised his dear wife, Vertiline, he'd give up being Lord of Marleigh Manor, and that sweet old man could refuse her nothing. When Lester died, Master Mitchell was only eight, so Morley passed leadership of the clan to his second son, Lord Middleton.

"Even when Morley lay on his deathbed, Master Mitchell refused to forgive that insult, so old Morley died leaving the house divided. Now Lord Middleton is deathly ill, and he and Letitia have only daughters. Master Mitchell will soon be Lord of Marleigh Manor ... if he has anything to say about it. I suspect he summoned the Berkeley-Marleighs to support his challenge to lead the clan."

"What about Lord Middleton's brothers ... and their sons ...?" the young servant asked.

"That's why they're arguing," the older nursemaid said. "Succession of Lordship will tear this house apart."

The two women sat down in the rocking chairs, each with a freshly-diapered baby. The younger wetnurse exposed both breasts and a baby was set atop each.

"After they eat, Mrs. Natalie wants them brought to her," the older nursemaid said.

"She's always happy to see her babies," the younger servant said.

"In this family, I don't know if twins are a

blessing or a curse," the older nursemaid said. "If they take after old Morley, then it's a blessing, but if they become twin Mitchells, I don't know how we'll survive. Imagine if Lordship was passed to one of them; how do you choose between twins?"

"Heaven forbid," the younger servant said. "Twins should be friends, not rivals."

"They're not in direct line, but in this house, who knows?" the older nursemaid asked.

Through the crack, Adella listened, noting all the names. She had no doubt Master Mitchell was the gruff voice ... he always sounded angry. Apparently his mother, Stella, was moving back in, with others of her family, to support his power struggle. Adella had heard that men of rich families always fought each other, yet she'd never known anyone wealthy enough to confirm it.

By mid-evening, Adella had eaten too much and needed to use the privy. Yet the family had come back from dinner, so she had to wait until late, so she set the remainder of her food and wine aside, determined to hold out.

As early as she dared, Adella checked to see only the sleeping twins were in the nursery. Then she emerged, peeked into the hallway, and found it empty. Stepping out, she sprinted lightly toward the far end, and the door to outside. A key was in the lock; she softly turned it until it clicked. She stepped outside into the wintry chill ...

It was raining lightly.

The privy tent was gone ...!

Adella froze. It must've vanished with the last of the workmen. She looked at the rain. She should've brought her oiled half-cloak, but her need was too urgent. Cursing blue fire, Adella ran into the downpour, headed for the distant woods.

Finished, she returned wet, shoes caked with mud ... which she couldn't track inside; *the family would follow muddy footprints to her hideaway.*

In the cold rain, Adella used fingers to scrape mud from her shoes, then wiped her hands off as best she could on the wooden rail. She tried to wash her hands in the thin rain-water, and ended up smearing the excess on the wet stone steps that had replaced the wooden ramp.

Peering in through a window, and seeing the common room empty, she opened the door and stepped inside, shivering on the small carpet, letting it soak off some of her drippings. She didn't dare leave a wet trail; they might have her arrested ... she'd certainly be cast out.

If they caught her, she'd never be allowed to go back for her father's tools ... or even her stolen blanket. She'd have nothing.

Soaked and half-frozen; she couldn't get sick. If she got the sneezes, then someone would hear her, even through walls.

She needed dry clothes ...

She peered down both hallways, each of which

were lit by two tiny oil lamps in wall-sconces. She couldn't keep wearing a man's clothes, especially not a dirty, ragged, dead driver's clothes, in a house of rich strangers.

Inside the family room, facing the fireplace, the first door to her left was slightly ajar. Adella peered into it to see a ratty carpet with a few toys scattered upon it. Doubtless this was where they sent the littlest kids to keep them out of the hallways, yet close enough to keep an eye on them. A similar room stood on the right side of the family room, but it was empty ... not even a carpet on its floor, although it held a small iron stove. Creeping up the right hallway, a pair of doors almost faced each other. She put an ear to the right door and heard snoring: a bedroom. She ignored it.

Checking the closed door opposite the bedroom, she heard nothing. Clenching teeth to keep them from chattering, she turned its latch. A tiny oil lamp burned inside, yet she'd never seen the like; five curtained closets faced her, and on a table by the door rested two basins of soapy water. She peeked behind the curtains to see ... *an indoor privy!* Each was a flat wooden seat with a wide hole cut into it, into which was set a deep metal bowl, one of which had already been used. On the floor beside them was a basin with a vinegar sponge with a wooden handle, for washing their backsides, and towels hung on drying racks over the table by the soapy basins.

She was soaking wet from having used the cold,

rainy woods for a privy ... *and she could've come in here!*

In the soapy water, she washed her dirty hands, then pulled down a towel. After drying her hands, she rubbed her wet hair, then blotted off as much of her shirt and trousers as she could. She even dried her shoes, so she wasn't leaving wet footprints, which could save her from being caught.

Seeing the towel smeared with mud, she feared to leave it, and thought to take it with her. Thinking better, she dipped the dirty towel into the soapy water, scrubbed it clean, wrung it out, and hung it back where she'd found it. Then she stole the clean, dry towel, and wrapped it around her neck, under her damp hair.

The next door down the hallway was on her left. She listened at it, heard nothing, and opened it; another empty room. Next were a pair of doors; to her left was the study, which held the cold fireplace she slept beside. The room opposite it was one of the larger rooms she'd explored when these walls were only half-paneled. She suspected someone important slept there, so she passed it by without bothering to listen at it. The next inner room, beside the study, was also silent, so she risked opening the door; empty. The next door on the right was another big outer room, so she ignored it and moved to the next inner door. She heard no snoring, so she risked opening it. A carpet was on its floor and a bureau was visible ...

"Hello ...?" asked a young man's voice. "Who's

there ...?"

Adella pulled the door closed and ran for her life. She dashed back the way she'd come, knowing the route behind her was clear, circled through the family room, found the other hallway empty, and ran for the nursery. One of the twins was awake, yet she ignored him and opened the nursery closet, crawled under the lowest shelf, pushed open her secret door, wriggled into her hideaway, and closed and braced her secret door.

The baby began to softly cry, and soon the other twin joined in.

Minutes later, a pretty girl came into the nursery. Adella put her eye to the crack and stared at this new girl; beautiful, she wore a lovely, lacy nightdress under a silk robe, and had thick blonde hair. She picked up one of the babies, then the other, and tried to comfort both, walking back and forth in the small room while bouncing them in her arms.

The door opened again and another girl, black-haired, entered wearing a gray servant's dress.

"Oh, Miss Grace, you needn't be awake," she said. "I can do that."

"I couldn't sleep," Grace said. "I've never had a room with a window. I was just lying on my bed, listening to the rain."

"They might be hungry," the servant said. "I could wake Rowena ..."

"We may have to," Grace said. "We don't want them waking Winnifred ..."

"She's surely awake by now," the servant said. "Poor thing can barely leave her bed, so she gets more rest than she needs. If she could, she'd be here herself."

"Maybe we ought to take the twins to visit her every day ...?"

"That's a kind thought, Miss Grace."

Nothing would quiet either twin, so Grace held both while the young servant went to fetch the wetnurse. Damp, Adella was shivering, so she ceased watching long enough to strip off her damp, dirty clothes, dry herself with the towel, and wrap up in her blanket. Her hideaway was exceedingly chilly, yet she could do nothing about it.

The door opened again, another dark-haired young woman Adella had never seen entered.

"Grace ...?" she asked.

"Sorry, mom," Grace said. "We were hoping not to wake you."

"We ...?"

"Lydia was here. She went to fetch Rowena."

"I'm their mother; I'll feed them."

When Lydia returned with Rowena, both women were rocking in the chairs with the twins attached to their mother.

"Mrs. Natalie ...!" Lydia exclaimed.

"It's all right," Natalie said.

"I can do that ...," Rowena offered.

"I was awake," Natalie said. "Good mothers can't sleep while their babies cry ... unlike fathers ...!"

Grace laughed, and Lydia and Rowena grinned.

"Is there anything we can do for you?" Lydia asked. "Blankets, something from the kitchen ...?"

"Hot tea would be nice," Grace said. "Why did they put the nursery in here? There're two inner rooms with fireplaces ..."

"Mitchell chose the rooms," Natalie said as if that explained it.

"There's a big fireplace in his study, just on the other side of that wall," Lydia said. "No one's lit it yet because Mitchell's still using the big study, but once the Berkeley-Marleighs move in, I'm sure it'll be lit every night. Anyway, smoke and too much heat isn't good for babies. I'll get your tea. Come, Rowena ..."

Both young maids departed, Rowena looking like she was still half-asleep.

"Poor Rowena," Natalie said. "I'll never understand ..."

"What ...?" Grace asked.

"The Prescotts," Natalie said. "I married into the Marleighs ... but they're all related, Marleighs and Prescotts. Middleton is Rowena's father ...!"

"She's more than half a Marleigh, yet her mother was a chambermaid, so she's illegitimate," Grace said. "No Marleigh will recognize a Prescott relative ... no matter how close they are."

"In the Parthena family, blood is blood," Natalie said proudly.

"We're Darbys," Grace said. "Yet, without

Charity, we'd be the same as Prescotts; allowed to live here only as servants."

Adella made little sense of this; too many names, too many unexplained references. She stored it away, determined to remember. If she was spotted, attempts at passing herself off as belonging would be far greater if she knew every name.

Natalie and Grace surprised her; both talked more like sisters than mother and daughter. The twins must be Grace's much-younger brothers. Natalie must have had Grace when she was little more than a child herself, more than a dozen years before the twins were born ... or did Natalie have other kids she hadn't heard about? Was Natalie remarried, having borne the twins from her new husband ...? This was a strange household, where generations of servants and masters lived under one roof.

Adella hadn't visited the kitchen tonight, yet she hadn't finished her last two cookies, most of her loaf, and a few mouthfuls of wine remained. Anyway, she had no dry clothes. The rough stones of the fireplace finally proved useful; she laid her wet shirt, trousers, and socks against the rough stones, where they clung and would hopefully dry.

Wrapped tightly in her dry blanket, she set her wet shoes aside, and laid her head down. With nothing else to do, and since the women in the nursery seemed to have ceased their conversation, she closed her eyes to sleep.

Adella awoke alarmed; something was wrong. She smelled smoke, looked up, and saw her clothes still hanging on the fireplace stones ... *but the air wasn't cold ...! It was hot ...!*

Adella jumped up and pinched her scorched clothes, yanking them off the fireplace stones and dropping them to the floor. Smoke rose even as she pulled off her last dry, hot sock.

Someone had lit the fireplace ...!

Naked in the heat, Adella knelt and examined her only clothes. Blackened, charred fabric broke apart at her lightest touch.

She had no clothes ...!

Chapter 3

She sat on her blanket before the ashes of her burned clothes ... now barely rags. She still had her oiled half-cloak, her blanket, and the bag she'd taken from the dead driver. She'd needed a new dress since before she'd arrived at Marleigh Manor, and now she had nothing. She had no choice; *like it or not, she had to steal a dress.*

All day she sat fretting, eating and drinking as little as possible, so she wouldn't need the privy. *How was she to find a dress ...?* She couldn't explore far in nothing but God's clothes. She had to slip into one of the rooms where a woman was sleeping, and hope she could locate a dress that wouldn't be missed ... without awakening anyone.

Her comfortable plan was falling apart.

After all sounds silenced, she waited an hour, then peered through the crack. The door to the nursery was ajar, as usual. The lamplight from the hallway barely illuminated the nursery and left her hideaway in total darkness. Her hooded half-cloak rustled loudly, so she had to leave it behind. Wrapped only in her blanket, she climbed out of the closet. The twins lay asleep, so she checked the hallway and emerged into the light.

She desperately needed something to wear. It was before midnight, yet she had to risk a bedroom, but she didn't know in which room a woman slept ...

If she made a single sound and woke anyone ... while naked ...!

She knew the old woman directly across the hall from the nursery seldom slept, so she didn't dare attempt to steal from her room.

Adella crept up the hall toward the main house. On the wall facing the small hall hung a sconce holding an oil lamp. She reached for the lamp. If she put out the light in the hall, which might awaken a sleeper, then no light would shine into a room when she opened its door.

She heard a soft sound. She hesitated, then snuck down the short hall to the entry room which held the door to the rest of Marleigh Manor. A carpet lay on its floor, small tables, couches, and chairs filled the room, and paintings hung on its walls. Its fireplace was crackling and the young, black-haired girl sat knitting before the fire ... *Lydia.*

Adella silently withdrew. Lydia was probably stationed close in case the babies cried out. She'd surely notice if someone extinguished the light in the hall.

With her there, how would Adella get to the kitchen?

She needed clothes!

Adella glanced down the long hall at all the doors. She had to risk a room ...

Tip-toeing to the other end of the hall, near the door to outside, Adella paused. Another oil lamp glowed on the wall ... but this far away, Lydia wouldn't see it unless she came out of the entry room. Quietly Adella blew out its tiny flame, then held her breath, hoping no one had noticed.

When no sounds signaled a reaction, Adella crept to the closest closed door and slowly turned its latch. The door swung open silently at her slightest touch, revealing moonlight shining through a window. Adella peered inside and saw a sleeping child, a girl no older than nine, buried under blankets with one arm hanging over the edge of her bed.

Adella glanced around to see a tiny table on which were scattered papers, an inkwell, and a quill, and a doll sat in the chair before it. Numerous other dolls were scattered about the room ... and a child-sized dress and chemise lay on the foot of her bed. A small wardrobe leaned against one wall, yet Adella doubted if it held any clothes she could wear. Adella stepped out and pulled the child's door closed.

Opposite it lay the door of an inside room; it must back up against the privy on the other side. It wouldn't have a window, so it'd be pitch dark unless someone lit a lamp inside it, and she couldn't afford either. She needed to find a woman sleeping in a room with windows.

Soft voices spoke from the other end of the hall. A shadow moved, and Adella ran back into the family room; she was too far from the nursery door to reach it before she was seen. Soft footsteps came down the hall; she glanced at the children's play room, yet she couldn't cross the hallway without being seen.

Glancing in the other direction, she hurried to the empty room opposite it. Its door was still ajar, as if no one had gone inside it since last night. It was still empty, except for the small iron stove. She closed its door as much as she dared, leaving only a crack wide enough for her to see through. She heard doors opening, then closing only minutes later.

A boy, about twelve, wheeled a cart half-loaded with firewood into the family room. He stopped before the wide fireplace and lifted three heavy, sawn logs from his cart onto the empty iron rack. Then he took the metal fireplace poker from its rack and pushed together the glowing coals inside the fireplace. When done, he returned the poker and added a small log atop the coals. Taking out a candle, he lit it at the fireplace, then went back to relight the oil lamp she'd extinguished. Finally, he blew out his candle, put it back in a pocket, and resumed his circuit, pulling his cart onwards.

About fifteen minutes later, the boy returned. No more firewood lay on his cart; it held ... *the deep metal bowls from the privy ...?* As she watched, he pulled his cart to the door to outside, turned its key, opened it, lifted a bowl and a vinegar sponge on a stick, and carried both outside ...

He was cleaning the privy bowls ...!

Adella sighed. He probably did this every night; she'd just never emerged this early. It made sense, but it would also make sneaking around the manor riskier if some servants performed their duties in the middle of the night.

The boy made one trip outside for each privy bowl, then wheeled them back to their room. She peeked out the door and watched as he emerged from the privy with his cart empty, and then he headed back to the main manor entrance where Lydia sat knitting.

Adella breathed easy. Being caught would be bad enough, but being caught wearing nothing but a blanket ...!

She needed clothes ...!

After the boy vanished, Adella emerged into the hallway. She blew out the oil lamp on the privy side, then crept past it and listened at the first door on the window side, hearing the same snoring. Taking a worried breath, she turned its latched and opened it.

Moonlight shined through the only window upon an empty floor ... not even a small fireplace. The loud snoring she'd heard was coming through the wall from the large room next door.

Adella passed by the empty room to her left and listened at the large room across from the study, from which the loud snores were coming. Opening its door, she peered at a room lit by a dying fire's glow and starlight pouring in through tall windows.

Fabulous furniture filled this room. A thick carpet covered its floor, a wide fireplace glowed red, and a huge bed lay against the far wall. Wardrobes stood on each side of the bed, and snores came from its rumpled blankets.

She crossed the room just enough to see the snorer. He was large, perhaps twenty years old, with black hair, deep asleep. A shirt and trousers lay on the carpet by his bed. Over his headboard hung a rifle, two pistols, and a matched pairs of crossed swords.

No woman slept beside him ...

Adella tiptoed back into the hall; *she had no need of a man's clothes.*

The next occupied room was equally large. Twin sets of snores came from a huge bed in a room as decorated as the last. She approached the couple; a man and a woman, both of excessive girth, lay on the bed in white nightshirts, covers mostly pushed aside. Adella frowned; any dress that fit this woman would wrap thrice around her; her clothes would be no disguise. Yet a silk chemise lay draped over the back of a chair, and Adella could stand being naked no longer. With a trembling hand, she reached out, snatched the silky chemise, and then backed out of the room, closing the door behind her.

An instant later, she was wearing the silk chemise.

As she entered the hallway, the soft whine of an infant reached her ears. She fled back into the empty room beside the family room, from where she'd watched the boy tend the fire. The voluminous chemise was too big, but not too long; if she found an over-dress, she could wear this underneath. She folded her blanket and wrapped it over her shoulders; with this, held around her, she'd look like a sleeper just out of bed, perhaps headed to the privy.

She was wearing a dress ... for the first time since she'd killed the wagon driver ...!

She peeked down the far hall; the door to the nursery was wide open and illuminated; someone had taken a candle inside it. She suspected Lydia, and was unsurprised to see a shadow move upon its wall, then vanish, then reappear. Lydia was walking at least one of the twins back and forth.

Adella circled around, past the study, to the entry room, where Lydia's knitting lay abandoned on a table. With no one watching, Adella passed through the door into the main manor, and headed for the kitchen.

She'd forgotten to bring her bowl ...!

Taking no chances, Adella grabbed a huge loaf, a handful of cookies, and a mostly-full bottle of wine. She found a half-eaten chicken in a pot, tore off a leg and thigh, and ate it standing. Then she hurried back ... yet only made it halfway before she heard approaching footsteps. She ducked low and hid in the gathering room, behind a wide couch, near the harp, and soon Lydia and Rowena walked past, headed for the nursery. She gave them plenty of time, then followed.

The entry room looked unchanged, Lydia's knitting abandoned on the table, and Adella snuck back down the other hall to the empty room where she could hear the snoring. Since both Lydia and Rowena would be in the nursery, she closed the door, sat down by the cold iron stove, and drank some wine and ate a cookie.

What would happen if she couldn't get back into her hideaway before everyone woke up? Adella fretted, but considered her options. She'd found nothing to suggest she'd be able to get far from Marleigh Manor safely and unnoticed before winter ended.

Like it or not, this was her new home ... living like a rat under the floorboards.

She wasn't worried that they'd notice the missing food; with boys stealing from the kitchen at night, the cook was probably used to it. However, sooner or later someone would see her ... or she'd suffer a nightmare and scream out in her sleep. The large woman was sure to miss her silk chemise when she awoke, and someday she'd need to use a privy in the middle of the day.

If she found an unwatched chamberpot, or even a bucket, she'd steal it.

What would they do if they caught her? Months had passed since she'd murdered the driver. Even if his body had been found, surely the constables had stopped looking for his killer by now. No evidence existed ... *unless they'd found her bloody dress!* They could've shown it around town. The smith might've recognized her dress and described her plainly.

Every constable in the county could be looking for her ...!

No; she was being silly. She had no reason to suspect her dress hadn't snagged on some thorny branches hanging in the stream. In the water, eventually his blood would rot, shredding her dress to rags. Besides, she'd overheard no one discussing an unsolved murder ... which was always ripe gossip.

If she could make it through the winter, then she could leave when weather permitted. Constables would no longer be searching. She'd be right back where she started ... only this time she'd be wearing a proper dress and be carrying a bag of food to last her to the next village. She'd still have to carry her father's tools, yet she could sell them openly, and perhaps find honest work ... or a kind, respectable husband.

If she did get caught, they might beat her and drive her off, yet they wouldn't murder her. She wasn't worth ransom, and had no relatives alive to pay. If arrested as a squatter, she'd spend a few weeks in jail, yet she'd done nothing terrible they knew of. Imprisonment would be uncomfortable, yet she'd be little worse off than now ... trapped in a small room until circumstances allowed her to leave.

She tried to get back into the nursery, only to hear Lydia and Rowena rocking side-by-side, so Adella carried her food and wine into the empty room beside the nursery. She'd never heard anyone enter there, so she was as safe there as anywhere. She sat behind the closed the door; if anyone opened it and merely glanced inside, they might not see her.

She should've made another secret door to her hideaway. She still could. It wouldn't be hard; she'd just have to do it quietly. Yet she didn't have another set of hinges ...

Multiple footsteps warned when morning came. Natalie arrived to hold her babies, and sat with them long after Lydia and Rowena, both yawning, begged permission to retire. Grace came to visit with Natalie, yet soon she left for breakfast. At her suggestion, Natalie took the twins to see Winnifred, the old lady across the hall who couldn't leave her room.

The new wing grew quiet. Adella listened intently, hearing only soft laughter in the old lady's room, and suspected most had gone to breakfast. She quietly opened the door, saw no one, slipped into the hallway, and hurried into the nursery with her food and blanket. Seconds later, she was safely hidden inside her hideaway, with food, drink, and clothes befitting a woman.

That night, after fully appreciating the warm, indoor privy, Adella spied Lydia clicking away with her needles right where she'd sat the night before, blocking the door to the main manor.

Adella returned to the nursery, and softly whispered to one of the sleeping twins, tickling him until he yawned and awoke. Innocent eyes opened and looked at her. The tiny face grinned; Adella loved children, and tickled him some more, and then she left the nursery, circling around through the family room, and approaching the entry room from the other hall.

As if on cue, the cry of the baby reached her ears.

Moments later, Lydia was walking toward her charges ... and Adella slipped through the entry room unseen.

Laughter; someone was in the gathering room ... even though only dim moonlight shined. Adella froze, and started to retreat through the door back into the new wing. Then she heard youthful whispers. Laughter followed; sniggering voices.

Adella could flee, yet she needed to get to the kitchen. She stood in shadow, too dark to see clearly. Noisily shaking the door latch, Adella took a deep breath, then cleared her throat as deeply and loudly as she could.

Youthful laughter instantly ceased, followed by

soft, padded footsteps running away.

Adella smiled, and waited until their sounds faded; she didn't know whose boys were sneaking around the manor in the middle of the night, yet she was certain they didn't want to get caught.

Amused, Adella hurried to the kitchen, filled her pitcher with water, found some sauce-covered venison to fill her bowl, and took four large cookies which were of a different texture but hard to see; little moonlight showed through rain clouds ... or would it finally snow?

Adella returned to find Lydia hadn't gone for Rowena, but had managed to quiet the baby without awakening its twin; she was still walking him back and forth in the nursery.

Stashing her food and water behind the door in the empty room beside the nursery, Adella returned to the main manor and began exploring. The bald head was in the exact same place, in the small room near the main entrance, only now he was snoring softly, asleep in his big chair. Adella almost passed him by, yet she spied his smoking pipe fallen onto the carpet, ashes spilled out.

She might not belong in Marleigh Manor, yet Adella doubted if she could hide successfully if the house caught fire. Quietly she stepped close, picked up the fallen pipe, and brushed the spilled ashes off the carpet to make sure they weren't glowing coals. Satisfied, she set his pipe in its stand on the table beside the sleeping old man, between two other ornate pipes, and departed to explore more.

The grand foyer to Marleigh Manor was amazing, with a ceiling taller than any she'd ever seen. A huge chandelier hung from a rope that crossed the ceiling and descended behind some drapes. Glancing behind the drapes, she found the rope tied to a brace on the wall with long coils; probably so they could lower it for cleaning and refilling the oil lamps.

Whoever designed Marleigh Manor had certainly known their business.

The polished foyer was roughly circular with a wide, curving staircase going up one wall. Open doorways led to adjacent rooms. No carpet graced it, yet its worn wooden floor gleamed of new wax. The walls were painted soft blue, the high ceiling white, and dark-framed paintings covered every wall space not hidden by tall, narrow, rain-splattered windows. Two curtains hung over each window, a sheer, snowy, lacy inner curtain, with blood-red heavier curtains overtop, the thick reds held back by gold-colored sashes. Ornate fringe hung everywhere, and glints of the chandelier's tiny oil lamps reflected off countless polished surfaces.

Adella had never seen a more-beautiful room.

Forcing her eyes away, Adella explored the adjacent rooms, unlit yet visible in the light of the chandelier. Each was a parlor, one with pink lace and white curtains, the other mostly brown with tall bookshelves. Both rooms were magnificent, one evoking gaiety, and the other solemn austerity, yet equally impressive. The whole first floor seemed to be rooms existing only to entertain, as if the Marleigh family business was throwing parties.

On the far side of the kitchen, she found a room with a long dining table with twelve chairs on each side. Although mostly hidden in shadow, she stared dumbfounded at the table and wondered how many people lived in Marleigh Manor. The family that had moved into the new wing couldn't fill half of that table. There had to be more ...

Seeing the size of the dining room, Adella felt a foreboding chill. She didn't know how many lived here, or even how big Marleigh Manor was. Looking out a window on the far side of the dining room, she spied another wing she hadn't known existed, and a barn beyond it, and from her only exploration outside, while construction was still occurring, she'd seen an entirely different wing hiding in back.

Most villages weren't as big as Marleigh Manor.

Struggling to carry more food, a pitcher, and a new bottle of wine, Adella headed back to her hideaway. Lydia wasn't in the entry room, yet she wasn't in the nursery either. Adella fetched her scavenged supper and stashed everything inside her hideaway, which required two trips.

Carrying her pitcher of water last, one of the babies made a noise as she passed by. She smiled, set her pitcher on the lowest shelf inside the closet, and came back to take one last look at the baby. She felt guilty for having disturbed him to lure Lydia away, and delighted when the baby reached out to her. She held out a finger and let the baby grasp it, and then she couldn't resist; she picked the baby up and cradled him in her arms.

The baby laughed, a sweet, high-pitched giggle that warmed her soul. She paced back and forth, bouncing it gently, enjoying the feel of a human touch.

Footsteps alarmed her. She glanced at the crib, but the door moved ...

Holding the baby, Adella jumped inside the closet, pressed against the shelves, and pulled its door mostly closed, tightly squeezed ... with the baby still in her arms.

The footsteps stopped abruptly. A silent moment passed, and then the footsteps retreated back into the hallway.

"Natalie ...?" Lydia's voice whispered urgently. *"Grace ...?"*

A knock on a different door; *Lydia was in the hall.* Adella didn't dare put the baby back; she opened the door just enough to carry the child with her into her hideaway. She reached up, drug down her pitcher of water, and pulled the closet door closed just as multiple pairs of running feet burst into the nursery.

"Where ...?" Natalie's voice asked.

"I don't know ... I thought maybe Grace ...!" Lydia said.

Both ran back out into the hallway, not bothering

to walk softly. Adella quietly braced her secret door.

The baby burbled in the dark.

Adella hugged it tightly. *If the baby started to cry, they'd tear open the wall ...!*

Doors slammed. More feet ran into the nursery, yet Adella didn't dare rise to look through the crack. A woman screamed, and several men shouted in alarm. Then a crowd poured into the nursery.

"He was here!" Lydia cried, nearly hysterical. *"I left them both here and went to the privy ...!"*

"Where'd he go ...?" a man demanded.

"Babies don't 'go' ... somebody took him!" a woman said.

"Who ...?" several demanded.

"Search the house!" a man ordered.

Utter chaos erupted. Loud footfalls and banging doors echoed, followed by more cries of alarm, and shouts from frantic voices.

In the dark, Adella held the infant tightly and berated herself. Her success at fooling the boys, by clearing her throat, had rewarded her with a false sense of assuredness. Now she was likely to spoil her entire plan.

"Nowhere ...!" a voice shouted.

"Nobody saw or heard anyone!" another voice said.

"Where can he be?"

"The outside door is locked ...!"

"Search the house!"

"It has to be one of the Prescotts!"

"Find him ... at any cost!"

"Awaken everyone!"

"Where's my baby ...?!?"

Her closet door was opened, empty shelves examined, and then closed again. Footsteps ran in and out of the nursery, and then down every hall. The whole house was being awakened, every room ransacked.

The baby giggled. Soon he would want breast milk and begin to cry.

Adella couldn't keep him quiet for long ...!

Voices became muffled, as if they'd moved to another part of the wing.

She'd have to risk it ...!

Removing the brace, Adella held the baby tightly, yet managed incredible speed. She lifted her secret door, reached up and twisted the knob, pushed open the closet door, climbed out, and deposited the baby back into his crib. Someone had taken the other twin for safekeeping. Then she dove back into her hideaway, pulled her closet door closed, and braced her secret door.

In the dark, still on her hands and knees, Adella realized she was gasping. If she didn't quiet her breathing then someone might hear. She stood up and peeked through the crack.

The baby lay in his crib as distant shouts and bangings echoed.

Several minutes later, a large, older lady, the

woman whose chemise she'd stolen while she slept, walked into the nursery. She looked into the crib ...

"*EEeeeekkkk ...!!!*"

Her deafening scream startled Adella. Instantly running feet approached.

The large woman lifted the baby and ran out into the hall.

"*I found him!*" the woman screeched. "*I found him ...!*"

Utter confusion reigned. A dozen people thundered into the nursery, all in night clothes, and demanded answers as the heavy woman babbled the same speech and pointed at the crib.

"*He was here ... just laying there, looking at me!*" she cried, but no one believed her.

"*He was gone ... I saw it!*"

"*Impossible!*"

Almost in tears, Natalie arrived, seized her baby, and hugged him desperately. Out in the hallway, Adella could see Lydia and Grace looking dumbfounded.

"It wasn't any of us ... and no one else has been here!"

"No one could've snuck in without us seeing them!"

"To take the baby, yes, but not to return it! We were all watching ...!"

"Maybe it was ... a ghost!"

Adella couldn't tell who'd said that. but it was a man's voice. She looked to see a bald man standing in the doorway beside Grace and Lydia; *the old man who sat near the foyer!*

"I nodded off, and someone moved my pipe!" he said. "I didn't put it back, but someone did!"

"Nonsense!" another man said.

"One of my silk chemises vanished yesterday," the fat woman suddenly announced. "I woke up ... and it was gone! Spirited away! It must be a ghost!"

"One of the boys ... playing tricks ...!"

"How could a boy get the baby back here?" the gruff voice demanded. "Gather the boys ... and the girls ... in the east parlor. I'll question them!"

"Shouldn't we wait until morning?" a woman asked.

"I won't give them time to invent excuses!" the gruff voice demanded. "Gather the children ... now!"

"Yes, Master Mitchell," Lydia said.

So, Adella mused, *the gruff voice was Mitchell.* She'd seen him before, the large young man asleep in the bed with guns and swords over his headboard. She'd suspected correctly ...

"The baby seems fine, no harm done," said a man.

"No harm ...?" a woman shrilly asked. "My heart's pounding! This night has scared the devils out of me."

"We've all had a fright ... I daresay we could use some rest."

"God help those kids if I find the one

77

responsible!" Mitchell snarled.

"Yes, well, if you don't ... we'll figure this out in the morning," a fat man said. "A little daylight always makes things clearer."

"Tell Winnifred the baby was found. I'm going to bed."

"I still say it was a ghost!" the older, heavy woman said.

They all shuffled out, taking both babies and leaving the door open.

Adella breathed a deep sigh, then sank down onto her blanket. *She'd almost been discovered!* She never should've picked up the baby. Even the pipe she'd picked up off the floor had been noticed. And her stolen silk chemise ...!

If anyone slept that night, Adella wondered how. Shouts filled the hours before dawn, interspaced by muted conversations, stomping footsteps, and banging doors. Needing to soothe her nerves, she opened her bottle and drank the flavorful wine. She wasn't hungry, yet she picked up a cookie and nibbled at it; it tasted of figs. She pulled the corners of her blanket up and covered herself as best she could; it was cold again; she wished someone would light the fireplace in the study. She needed more sleep, yet the noises of the house continued.

A ghost ...!
They thought she was a ghost ...!
Despite herself, Adella smiled. A ghost was a

good excuse. Perhaps all her mistakes might be blamed on the ghost.

The wine went straight to her head; Adella set it aside and drank water ... straight from her pitcher. She could steal a cup ... yet that was another unneeded risk ...

Maybe the ghost could steal a cup for her ...!

Amid hot air, Adella awoke to the slamming of a door; the fireplace had been lit.

"Was it you ...?" Mitchell's deep voice demanded, booming from the study.

"No, I didn't ...!" a younger voice replied.

"Don't lie to me!" Mitchell shouted.

Adella rose and pressed an ear against the warm wooden wall beside the lit fireplace.

"I swear, master, I ...!"

"Who else ...?" Mitchell demanded.

"I don't know, but it wasn't me. Where's profit in stealing a baby?"

"That's what I'd like to know," Mitchell growled. "A Darby baby ...!"

"I'd never do anything that crazy ... unless the reward was big," the youthful voice said. "Gold ... or jewels!"

"You may get that chance," Mitchell said. "I've a job for you. It pays in silver."

"Silver's good ...!"

"I'll let you know when," Mitchell said. "Until then, stay out of sight. Hide in here for a while ... until breakfast."

"In here ...? What am I going to do in here?"

"Read a book!" Mitchell snapped. "Unless you want to be an idiot your entire life ...!"

The door slammed again.

A long moment passed.

"You'll be the idiot when I get enough silver!" the youthful voice scowled.

Adella listened a while longer, yet all she heard from the study was an occasional pop from burning logs. Other sounds echoed from the rest of the wing; eventually she sat back down. She began eating her venison slices, wishing she had a fork. Finally she reached into her father's toolbox and drew out an iron awl with a wooden handle. After wiping it as clean as she could with her fingers and her towel, she speared her meat onto it and ate well enough.

The heat from the fireplace was comforting ...

An hour later, Adella was baking. She'd always known dead spaces existed around fireplaces because of excessive heat, yet she'd never imagined how hot the back of a fireplace could be. Sweating, she took off her silk chemise, not wanting to ruin it with stains, as it was all she had. Naked, she sat on her blanket, enduring the heat, glad she had water.

Much later, voices floated in through the nursery from the hall.

"Grace, they're here!" came a man's voice.

"Who ...?" Grace asked.

"Mitchell's mother, Stella, and the Berkeley-Marleighs," the man answered.

"Oh, great ...," Grace scowled. "Here we go ..."

"Best you come now," the man's voice said. "Unless you want to be introduced individually ..."

"She's our aunt ... and they're our cousins ...," Grace sighed.

"If we're not careful, we could all end up Berkeley-Marleighs," the man said.

"Heaven forbid," Grace said, and footfalls carried her from the nursery.

For a brief while silence reigned; everyone was at the presentation. Adella pulled her chemise on, climbed out of her hideaway, and checked the hallway. It was empty, so she headed for the privy; she should be back before anyone returned. Yet, from the open doorway opposite the nursery, an aged woman's voice called out.

"Hello ...? Who's there ...?"

Adella didn't stop, but kept her face from the door and hurried on. That must be Winnifred, the convalescent old woman she'd heard of. Her room, if it matched Mitchell's room, was long and narrow, reaching to the wall she shared with the nine year old girl. From the angle of her bed, she'd only be seen if she was walking the other direction, from the nursery directly to the entry room. Yet she seldom went that way. She kept her footsteps light, finished her business, and crept back into the nursery as quietly as she could.

A noisy tour soon arrived. They paraded down the hall, where the amazing story of the vanishing and reappearing baby was repeated, and then they were ushered into Winnifred's room, and names were introduced.

Amid jostling, footsteps, and soft murmurs, Adella couldn't make out specifics, yet greetings and welcomes were voiced to and from everyone. Well wishes rose from deep men's voices, often accompanied by common pleasantries.

Twenty minutes later, the parade clomped and stomped out of Winnifred's room and toured the rest of the new wing. She heard the door to the study open, yet no footsteps entered. Then the new arrivals were led back to the entry room, and footfalls paraded back into the main manor.

Adella ate some more, then removed her chemise again, as it was so hot. She stretched out, needing sleep ...

When Adella awoke, the house was silent. However, when she pressed her eye to the crack in the paneling, she saw Lydia rocking gently in a chair by the crib, her knitting in her lap, working in the dim light of the oil lamp in the hall with the door wide open.

No more leaving the twins unwatched ... *in case the ghost should return!*

Adella almost smiled, yet this complicated everything. With Lydia there, and everyone worried about the twins, chances of escaping her hideaway were decreased. She glanced at her father's toolbox.

She needed another secret door!

Fortunately, she still had food, water, and wine, and she'd recently used the privy. She stayed still, as amid the silence, Lydia was sure to hear any sound louder than the clicks of her needles. She ate a cookie and drank some wine, planning her new project as night passed into morning.

The next day was noisy; distant bumps and shouts. She assumed it was the furniture of the Berkeley-Marleighs, being unloaded and carried to distant rooms. However, from the hallway, she heard several snide comments.

"The Berkeley-Marleighs are certainly making themselves at home."

"Their manners are common."

"They're intruders, all of them."

Yet each comment was followed by a whispered warning.

"Don't let Mitchell hear that!"

Chapter 4

Adella devised a plan, yet it would require some tricky woodwork. The frame of the closet to the study had one beam that would have to be removed, to make it wide enough for her to crawl through, yet she could cut wood relatively quietly. What she couldn't do easily was hammer nails, yet she planned a clever twist. Her only challenge was that some of her work, the last cutting of the paneling inside the closet, had to be done from inside the study.

When everyone was awake, with soft noises coming from every direction, Adella started her project. She measured the length she needed three times to insure her cut would be accurate; otherwise this would take even longer. She started with a chisel. She couldn't hammer, so she pounded it repeatedly with the palm of her hand.

A vertical beam ran straight up the middle of the space where she wanted to make her new door, yet it was unneeded; when she was done, that wall section would be only half as strong, but it wouldn't collapse, and no one would bother to test it. Working with sharp tools in the dark was dangerous, yet she went slowly, always cutting away from her fingers, and never with great force.

Soon her palm grew sore from hammering against the butt of the chisel, yet she'd made a horizontal groove she could easily feel with her fingernails. She just had to keep running the blade of her chisel across it.

Hours she worked ... making little progress. The task grew wearisome; this process might take weeks. She'd starve to death inside her hideaway. Yet the bumping of new furniture and noisiness of the house were as much cover as she was likely to get.

Quietly she took tools, one at a time, out of her father's box, and set them aside. In the bottom, she found a thin, narrow rasp, one side tapered to almost as sharp as a saw. Carefully she slid it into her groove, and taking a deep breath, she pushed the metal serrations against the wood.

The noise was louder than expected; softer than using a saw, yet not quiet enough. Then she remembered an old carpenter's trick. She had some venison left, mostly the fat and gristle from which she'd bitten the good meat. With her fingers, she took some of the fat, pinched it between her fingers, and smeared it onto the narrow edge of the rasp. Then she scraped her rasp again over the wooden beam ... it made considerably less noise. Yet it could still be heard.

She checked both adjacent rooms. The nursery was empty. Natalie had taken the twins and vanished, leaving the door wide open. Worried, Adella opened her secret door and crawled out into the nursery just long enough to check the hallway, and she shut the nursery door ... to keep Winnifred from hearing. Then she returned to work.

She had to go slowly, and not apply too much pressure, but a half-hour later, the beam came free. She tested her beam sideways and it fit perfectly.

Then she looked at the back of the other panels and sighed. She needed a second beam, and since she couldn't steal spare wood anymore, she'd have to cut one from an inside wall.

After using the first beam to mark her cut exactly, she risked the saw. Its blade was rougher than the rasp, yet thinner, and cut faster. She used the same greasy trick, and several times stopped to regrease her serrated blade, and cut almost as quietly.

Several nails held her second beam to the bottom board, and one to the thin panel, yet a little effort with a small pry bar loosened them. She pulled the second beam free. It fit just like the first, which meant her preliminary cutting was done. She took out her drill and started cranking it, which was easy as drilling was almost silent.

At different angles, she drilled downward holes in the closet frame where her first brace would go. Then she held the first brace in place with loose nails as she drilled a hole into the other end. When finished, she slid more nails into the new holes. Her first beam hung flush against the back of the paneling ... exactly as she'd wanted.

She repeated these steps with her second brace, and marked the locations of both beams on the back of the paneling.

How proud her father would be to see the quality woodwork she was doing!

She piled the tools she'd need beside her soon-to-exist second secret door; a hammer, four short nails, and extra nails in case some bent, both braces, and the driver's oiled-leather hooded half-cloak.

That night, after she'd heard the boy finish his nightly chores, she watched Lydia intently. Hours passed, and finally Lydia stood and walked out, leaving the sleeping twins unwatched.

Bringing a knife, Adella stole out of her closet and checked the door. She didn't know where Lydia had gone, yet she suspected she was safe; she hurried around to the study, and finding it empty, she stepped inside and closed its door. Laying on the floor in the reflected light of the fire, Adella attacked the inside of its closet. She pressed her sharp knife's blade against the panel just under its lowest shelf, and cut.

Repeatedly she dragged her knife against the thin panel, scratching a narrow groove, until the thin paneling broke free. Then she pushed her knife through the new opening into her hideaway; she needed it no more.

Taking the rest of her things, she checked the hallway, and finding it empty, hurried to the back door. Unlocking it and going outside, she carried her tools in her arms, glad she wore the leather half-cloak over her thin dress. The night air was freezing; no snow had fallen, yet the muddy ground was hard and crusty.

In the woods, behind a large tree, amid tall bushes which she'd once used as a privy, she carefully aligned her braces to her marks on the back of the panel. Holding both against the tree, she nailed them together. Her hammer-strikes were loud, yet she struck true, and drove all four nails straight.

Shaking the result to assure herself it was firmly affixed, she paused and stared at Marleigh Manor, wary for any sign that her hammering had been heard. In the frozen, starry night, she waited. Fortunately, no doors opened or faces appeared at windows.

Freezing, she hurried back.

Shivering, she headed directly to the study. Opening its closet, she angled her affixed braces and panel so they slid into her hideaway, slipped her hammer and extra nails inside, and then she crawled through. She'd successfully built a second secret exit; all she needed was to affix its door.

Worried she might've failed, she slid her project into place. Holding in place the two beams nailed to the panel, she slid four long nails into her drilled holes; they pegged her project to the wall. A few minutes with the drill repaired her only misalignment. At last, she slipped the last nail into its hole, and it fit. She pushed against the beams and panel, testing its strength.

It held.

She had two secret doors!

Adella smiled.

She was more than a carpenter! She was her father's daughter!

Using the burned rags of the driver's clothes, she cleaned the greasy fat off her rasp and saw before returning her tools to her father's box. Her carpentry skills equaled any man's ... and better than many who'd built this new wing.

If she was a man ...!

... then she wouldn't be squatting in a dead space, or stealing food from a kitchen in someone else's house.

On a notion, Adella took a chisel and repeated her clearing of a crack between the panels until she could peer into the study as well as she could see into the nursery.

She glanced at the narrow wall sections behind both closets. If she widened cracks into them, then she could look into those empty side rooms. Yet she'd taken enough risks for one night ... and not even visited the kitchen or privy.

Only a few hours before dawn, Adella could wait no longer. Moving as quietly as possible, to keep Lydia from hearing, she removed the nail-pegs in her new secret door, and crawled out of the study closet. The one drawback of her new design was that it didn't have hinges; she couldn't pull the panel closed enough to fully hide its new purpose; if anyone opened the closet door while she was out, then they'd instantly notice her entrance.

Yet she had to eat ...

Only Lydia seemed awake, holding the twins in the nursery. Adella stole enough food and wine for two days and nights, as she couldn't predict when she'd be trapped again ... even with her second secret door. Returning, she first ate half of her bowl, as it was filled with vegetables in a rich, still-warm mushroom sauce. The rest she set aside for later.

Right before dawn, she slipped out again, creeping from the study into the privy. However, as she sat down, she heard the unmistakable sound of someone peeing ... *in the curtained privy right next to her ...!* She sat frozen, unable to do what she needed until after they'd finished, washed, and departed ... hopefully back to bed.

Adella climbed inside her new secret door, secured it, and only then started to breathe easier. *What she was doing was insane!* If she got caught, investigation of her hideaway would reveal her collection of empty wine bottles; proof she'd stolen from Marleigh Manor.

She'd have to clear out her bottles soon, leave them someplace where they wouldn't point to her.

Perhaps they'd be blamed on the ghost!

Adella slept long that day. When she awoke, she feasted on fresh bread and cookies. She was bored, but better boredom than freezing and starving on a lonely, snowy road.

Lydia again camped in the nursery. She fell asleep with her knitting needles in her hands, and the twins didn't awaken her until morning.

The next day was exceptionally cold. Several voices announced it had snowed. Excited kids ran up and down the halls laughing. Adella reached out and touched the stones of her fireplace; the cold of the snowy roof was flowing down the stones. Her tiny hideaway was exceedingly chilly, so she pulled her blanket tight around her, then pulled the half-cloak over that. She slowly drifted off.

Adella awoke to warm air and crackles. The study fireplace was lit, and angry voices filtered through the wall.

Adella jumped up and glanced through the crack she'd widened. Mitchell was stomping back and forth in his study before a young man with sandy hair.

"Middleton can't disgrace the Marleigh family by putting Rayden in charge!" Mitchell snarled. "Besides, that would make his idiot son, Laurence, next in line, and that would be the death of the Marleigh line. Reed's

Middleton's bastard; he's not a Marleigh ...!"

"Reed says Middleton could recognize him," the young man said.

"No Fulton can rule Marleigh Manor," Mitchell said. "Middleton fathered a dozen bastards. His only legitimate heirs are girls, and he should never have been made head of house; I was the rightful heir!"

"There're too many heirs to keep track," the young man shook his head.

"Focus, Harrington!" Mitchell said. "Our grandmother, Vertiline, convinced old grandpa Morley to surrender Lordship of Marleigh Manor to my father, your Uncle Lester. When he got himself shot, Morley should've made me Lord of Marleigh, despite that I was a child. Illegally, he appointed Middleton, who's never had a serious thought in his life, has a dozen bastards, and his wife bore only daughters. Middleton should return the Lordship to me, but he's fond of Reed, who isn't legitimate. Below him, next in line, is your father, Enfield, which would make your brother Hayden the next Lord. Will you ever bow to Hayden?"

"I'll spit on him first," Harrington said.

"Exactly, and if Hayden doesn't inherit, then your second brother, Harlow ...!"

Harrington scowled deeply.

"So, I'll never get to be Lord ...?" Harrington asked.

"If I get named Lord of Marleigh, I can appoint you as my successor," Mitchell said. "However,

Middleton and your dad have never gotten along. He could skip your father and give it to Rayden, who'd eventually bestow it upon Laurence."

"Laurence is an idiot!" Harrington snapped. "He can barely count over twenty!"

"Exactly," Mitchell said. "There're only two real choices: you and I. If I become Lord, I'll name you my heir. If you become Lord, you'll do the same for me. Between us, we'll rule Marleigh Manor."

"The treasury will be ours!" Harrington exclaimed.

Aghast, Adella stared at the two. Mitchell was huge, but looked barely twenty. Harrington was only a boy, not even fifteen, scrawny, with sandy hair and a sneering voice. He looked too immature to be anything. Adella doubted if Mitchell would honor any promise made to Harrington ... assuming he didn't have him killed.

"Yes, but you must perform one task to insure we get the family gold," Mitchell said. "I can't do it; they're watching me, but you can ...!"

"What ...?" Harrington asked.

"To prevent your brothers from becoming Lords over us, we need to insure that your father doesn't get chosen," Mitchell said. "Tomorrow he'll conclude a very profitable sale ..."

"Someone bought one of his paintings?" Harrington asked.

"No one's ever bought that trash he calls art,"

Mitchell said. "No, this sale is of land ... which will raise him in family esteem. We need to prevent that ... in a way that profits you!"

"*Me ...?*" Harrington asked.

"Three hundred silver coins," Mitchell said. "You steal it ... you keep it."

"How ...?" Harrington asked.

Mitchell held up a key.

"Your father stores all his valuables in his trunk at the foot of his bed," Mitchell said. "This is a duplicate key to his trunk; he doesn't know I have it. Take nothing but the three hundred silver coins ... and you can keep all of them!"

"*Thank you ...!*" Harrington effused, and he took the offered key.

"There's one stipulation," Mitchell warned. "You mustn't get caught! If you do, then I'll have to pretend I know nothing and condemn you ... or it'll ruin both our chances. Don't leave this key behind. Hide the coins somewhere only you can find them ... not in your room, my room, or this study. Don't let anyone, not even me, know where you have the coins hidden. Do you understand?"

"I'm on my own," Harrington said. "Once I steal it ... I get to keep it ...?"

"Every coin, and if I become Lord, I'll appoint you overseer of our whole treasury," Mitchell said.

"Wow!" Harrington smiled greedily.

"We'll both be rich," Mitchell said. "Now, I'll

check to make sure the hallway's clear. Give me a minute, then hide that key in your room. Tomorrow night, you become wealthy, and I become patriarch!"

Mitchell and Harrington shook hands, then Mitchell slipped out of the study, looked both ways, and closed the door.

Alone, Harrington held up the key and snorted.

"Three hundred silver coins ... and Overseer of Marleigh's treasury ...!" Harrington boasted to himself. "Who cares about Lordship? Once I steal that fortune, they'll never see me again!"

With a childish giggle, Harrington exited.

Adella stared into the empty study, watching the bright firelight flicker off the wide desk, closed door, and numerous books.

She shouldn't get involved. Marleigh family politics weren't her problem. She couldn't risk her safety for anyone.

She sat back down on her blanket, overheated by the fire. Yet she couldn't stop thinking about it. Not being able to talk to anyone for months was frustrating, more wearing upon her than anything else. Knowing secrets she couldn't tell was doubly so.

She could write a note, but who would she give it to?

She didn't know these people ...

She wasn't part of this family ...

Ghosts don't write notes ...!

Any action could reveal her. If she wanted to

leave a note, then she could do so in springtime, when she abandoned Marleigh Manor and its politics to rejoin the rest of the world. Until then, she had to stay silent ... and uninvolved.

She drank some water, yet it didn't help. She tried to uncork a bottle of wine; the cork broke. Frustrated, she quietly sorted through her father's tools until she found his awl, which she used to try and pull out the remaining cork, yet her efforts only shredded it into small fragments. Finally she scraped out all the fragments and used a thin chisel to push the remainder of the cork down into the bottle, where it harmlessly floated.

The wine calmed her nerves ... and she drank faster than she should.

The room was too hot. Sweating, she stripped off her chemise. She could do nothing else, so she ate, emptying her bowl.

That night, the twins awoke crying before the boy had accomplished his rounds. Lydia fetched Rowena, and they sat together in the nursery.

"I hear your sister, Ettie, wants to get married," Lydia said.

"Who's been talking?" Rowena asked.

"Hortence," Lydia answered.

"Hortence talks too much," Rowena asked.

"Is it true ...?" Lydia asked.

"Ettie's sweet on a boy from the village," Rowena said. "She's free to do as she wants; her mother's dead and Middleton never recognized her, but his parents don't approve."

"Too poor ...?" Lydia asked.

"Parents want their children to marry well, to support them in their decline," Rowena said. "Ettie has nothing but her spotless complexion."

"Who is he ...?" Lydia asked.

"I'm no Hortence," Rowena said.

"You do like secrets," Lydia said.

"Some fathers do more harm than good," Rowena said. "My son, Paxton, is better off never knowing who his father is."

"Your half-brother wouldn't say that," Lydia said.

"Reed may not be Middleton's oldest boy ... just the oldest we know of," Rowena reminded.

"Why else would Middleton let him manage the stable?" Lydia asked.

"Manage the stable ... never allowed inside Marleigh Manor," Rowena scowled. "He's forbidden to even enter the Prescott wing; Middleton didn't do him much of a favor."

"His mother died ...!" Lydia argued.

"A lot of mothers die in this district," Rowena said.

"What do you mean by that ...?" Lydia asked.

"I'm not saying anything," Rowena shook her head. "Paxton needs a live mother."

Adella gasped and covered her mouth with her hand to quiet her reaction. *What kind of household had*

she hidden inside? Yet the two girls rocked quietly in
their chairs, Rowena holding both twins to her breasts.
Finally each girl took one twin and patted them until they
burped. When they laid them side-by-side in their crib,
Rowena yawned.

"Before I head off ... I heard the doctor visited
again ...?" Rowena asked.

"Now who's been talking?" Lydia asked.

"Secrets die quickly in Marleigh," Rowena said.

"We're not supposed to talk about it," Lydia
said.

"How's Middleton?" Rowena asked.

"Better, but still coughing blood," Lydia said.

"How long ...?" Rowena asked.

"Let's just say ... if he's going to recognize Reed
... or you, he needs to do it soon," Lydia said.

With a glare, Rowena departed, and Lydia
picked up her knitting.

Adella snuck out through the study and visited
the privy, but she had no need to visit the kitchen, so she
hurried back. The fire in the study was red coals; she
used the tongs to break them apart, then crawled inside
her hideaway to sleep.

A child's shriek awoke Adella, yet from the
shouts of adults, Adella realized the children had been
playing, and one of them had fallen. The screams of the
child quieted quickly, followed by shouts for the children
to behave themselves.

Adella yawned, stretched, and accidentally knocked over an empty bottle. The glass didn't break, but rang loudly.

"What was that ...?" asked Grace's voice.

Adella froze and grabbed the bottle to keep it from rolling.

"Mitchell," Lydia said. "His study is on the other side of that wall. He makes a lot of noise. Sometimes I wonder what he's doing in the middle of the night."

"Don't poke the serpent," Natalie warned. "You've been up all night. Get some food and go to bed."

"Yes, Mrs. Natalie," Lydia said.

Setting the empty bottle aside as quietly as she could, Adella stood and peered through the crack. Natalie was nursing the twins. Grace was standing by the open door, yet she closed it and approached the wall, looking closely. Adella dropped down to keep from being seen.

"What do you suppose Mitchell is doing over there ...?" Grace asked.

"You shouldn't poke serpents, either," Natalie said. "Tensions are bad enough."

"You should take greater interest in your family," Grace said.

"My family is right here," Natalie said. "Sometimes I wish Acton had moved in with my family, rather than move me in here."

"Your parents let you marry him because he

lived here," Grace said.

"My babies would be safer elsewhere," Natalie said.

"They're Darbys ...!" Grace laughed.

"So are you, step-sister," Natalie said. "When you've had your own, you'll do anything to protect them."

"I'm not in line ... and neither are you," Grace said.

"When an heir to a rich family is about to be named, everyone's an ally or a threat," Natalie said.

"I can't marry a first cousin," Grace said. "Mitchell, Hayden, Harlow, or Harrington."

"Or Reed ... or Laurence ...?" Natalie added.

"I'm safe from all of them ... thank goodness," Grace said.

"Three eligible Berkeley-Marleighs just moved into the manor," Natalie said.

"They're all third or fourth cousins," Grace said. "One is too old ..."

"Marriage to a Berkeley-Marleigh would strengthen Mitchell's claim to Lordship of Marleigh ... and weaken others," Natalie said pointedly.

"That's why I'm protectively single," Grace said.

"If you were smart, you'd marry out from under this roof ... while you still have a dowry," Natalie said.

"Lady Winnifred likes me," Grace said.

"She holds a lot of power, but so do others," Natalie said. "Like it or not, your future is their pawn."

"If a pawn can stay out of trouble and keep advancing, it could become a queen," Grace said.

"Being queen doesn't mean you can't lose the game," Natalie said.

Twins fed, the girls rose and walked out, each with a baby over one shoulder. Adella breathed easier. She'd been heard ... not for the first time ... yet no one had noticed she'd widened the dead space, or they'd have investigated her clumsiness.

Mitchell and Harrington, Lydia and Rowena, Natalie and Grace; *how many secret conversations could one family have ...?*

Her towel around her neck, Adella took her bowl and pitcher and left them in the study. After using the privy, she washed her dirty towel as best she could, wrung it out, and swapped it for a clean towel. Then she fetched her things and hurried to the kitchen, yet the bald man who watched the front door stood there, talking to a portly old woman.

"How long are the Prescotts going to put up with this ...?" the old woman demanded.

"Mrs. Stella, there's nothing we'd like more, but your son ...? He hates us!" the old man said.

"If every Prescott supports him ...," Stella said.

"Gratitude is a trait your son has never shown," the old man said.

"I'll be grateful," Stella said.

"Promises are easy ...," the old man said.

"Camden Hadley Prescott!" Stella exclaimed.

"Are you questioning me ...?"

"Servants don't question those who could throw them into the street," Camden said. "I'll think about it. I'll talk to others. But you did your son no favor, letting him be raised alone in this house. He's worse than Lester ...!"

"My new husband doesn't like mention of my former marriage," Stella said.

"I won't ... in his presence," Camden said. "But you remember Lester, especially when he'd had too much to drink. He sent away six Prescotts before he got himself killed, and if not for Mitchell, you'd be cooking Middleton's meals ..."

"My son may be contemptible, but what alternative do you have? Enfield ...? Rayden ...?"

"This may not be a good time for any Prescott to voice an opinion," Camden said. "If only it were spring ...!"

"Middleton won't last until spring ... according to Mitchell," Stella said. "He's getting worse every day."

"He gets up every morning as cheerful as ever," Camden said. "He comes to breakfast ... and sometimes keeps eating until supper is cleared away."

"He knows he's dying," Stella said.

"Master Enfield wants to be patriarch," Camden said.

"When he's not painting or sculpting or writing nonsense poetry ...?" Stella asked. "That man's never performed a day's work in his life."

"He's no Plato either," Camden said. "Yet, he's been kinder to Prescotts than Lester ..."

"You may find Berkeley-Marleighs better tempered," Stella said.

"Prescotts would welcome any of your other sons ...," Camden said.

"I'd consider it a personal favor if you'd voice that opinion to Middleton," Stella said. "My younger sons have far better dispositions than my eldest."

"I'll consider it, Mrs. Stella," Camden said.

The two departed with respectful bows, and each left the kitchen through a different door. Adella was about to step out from the door she was hiding behind, when she heard two soft whispers.

"Are they gone ...?"

"I think so ..."

From behind a row of barrels topped with stacked white bags, three small heads poked ... all girls younger than twelve. Warily one ran to each door, peering to make sure Mitchell's mother and Camden had departed.

The three girls skipped to a water-cooled chest and opened it.

"Strawberries!" one girl hissed excitedly.

"Custard!" another girl whispered.

"Quiet!" the eldest girl whispered. "Weren't you listening? Don't you know what they meant?"

"No," both younger girls said.

"Do you ...?" one girl asked.

"The Berkeley-Marleighs want to take over Marleigh Manor!" the eldest whispered. "They said father's not getting better!"

"Mother says he'll be fine!" one girl whispered.

"Best we keep this secret!" the eldest said.

"Not tell mother ...?" one asked.

"Never!" the eldest said. "I'm not making tea for Prescotts!"

At a run, the three young girls dashed past the door Adella was hiding behind, each carrying a favorite desert. Yet they turned toward the entryway, and their footfalls padded up the curved staircase.

When their footfalls vanished, Adella executed her own raid.

Carrying back enough food and wine for two days, Adella smiled; she wasn't the only one eavesdropping, and Marleighs weren't the only ones plotting. She doubted if the three girls would remain quiet for long; little girls were as notoriously bad at keeping secrets as boys were at remembering them.

She had to stay out of family politics!

However, as she crept past the gathering room, on her way back, she heard footsteps, and dropped to hide behind the wide couch by the harp.

Furtive steps crossed the music room.

Fearing she'd been seen, Adella peeked.

Harrington reached the farthest corner, where she'd never explored, and there he set down a large bag that clinked loudly ... *three hundred stolen silver coins!*

He moved a heavy chair and opened a panel in the wall, slid the bag inside, and then replaced everything, so no trace remained.

Ducking, Adella heard Harrington tip-toe back past the couch, and reenter the new wing; he was headed toward his room. Yet she didn't know which bedroom was his and ... besides ... it was none of her business.

Yet trouble would come of this ... even for her. They'd tear up the manor looking for those silver coins ... *and possibly find her hideaway ...!*

She checked the hall, then hurried to move the heavy chair. The panel behind it was an old coal chute, filled with cobwebs, so filthy Adella doubted if it had been used in decades.

She couldn't take the money ...!

If it wasn't found soon, a search would begin ...!

She opened the bag of immense wealth. She'd seldom held a single silver coin in her hands, yet she pulled out two fistfuls and left the rest. Closing the panel and pushing the heavy chair back into place, she placed one coin onto the floor below the chute door, and one by the back leg of the chair. Then she dropped other coins, in a long line running along the wall, around shelves, tables, and chairs.

Her line of coins would be easily seen in daylight, yet was almost invisible in shadow.

When she got to her last coin, she held it enviously, then kept it as she slipped behind the couch to retrieve her ill-gotten gains from the kitchen.

Someone would clearly see that line of coins by morning ... and one silver coin was precious small reward, when she was returning two hundred and ninety-nine.

Chapter 5

All day Adella slept deeply, and awoke refreshed. Feeling useful made everything brighter, even while hiding inside her widened dead-space. She'd accomplished something real ... and she had a valuable silver coin as reward. She wasn't just a thief and squatter, or stowaway, which is what they'd call her on a ship.

Hot, she realized; *the fireplace stones were wafting heat.*

Adella wondered what had awoken her, then heard voices from the study, and rose to peer into it.

"I didn't leave a trail of coins ...!" Harrington insisted.

"Obviously ...," Mitchell snapped angrily.

"Who did ...?" Harrington asked.

"An enemy," Mitchell said, his voice almost a

growl. "Someone opposed to both you and me."

"Those are my coins ...!" Harrington demanded.

"If you announce that, the family will know who the thief was ... and you'll be punished," Mitchell said. "Someone must've been watching ...!"

"The ghost ...!" Harrington exclaimed.

"Can ghosts steal coins ... or lay them out to be found ...?" Mitchell said. "A spirit would've known who stole them ... and left a trail leading to your bedroom ... or mine. Why didn't they ...? Why expose a theft, but not the thief ...?"

"I'm not a thief if I didn't get any coins ...!" Harrington argued.

"Keep your voice down," Mitchell ordered.

"It's those kids ...!" Harrington insisted. "Those damn Berkeley-Marleighs ...!"

"Why didn't they keep all the coins?" Mitchell asked.

"I hid them well!" Harrington said.

"Impressive hiding space," Mitchell admitted. "I was born here, and I'd never found that coal chute. Yet someone had a reason ... a reason worth more than three hundred silver coins ...!"

"Four coins were missing!" Harrington said.

"The kids who found the coins probably took those," Mitchell said. "Yet someone had a motivation I don't know ... and it wasn't a ghost."

"Everyone's blaming the ghost," Harrington said. "It stole a baby ... and then returned it."

"That's the biggest mystery," Mitchell said. "Anyone could've watched you hide those coins, and left that trail, but babies can't disappear and re-appear ..."

"Ghosts can," Harrington said.

"Even ghosts act for a purpose," Mitchell said. "Before Middleton chooses his successor, I will discover that purpose!"

"How ...?" Harrington asked.

"We're going to set a trap ... for the ghost!" Mitchell said.

"How can you ...?" Harrington began.

"This ghost reports thefts," Mitchell said. "You're going to steal something ... from me. I'll spy ... and then unmask the ghost!"

Adella almost burst out laughing; *this was one theft she wouldn't reveal!*

Mitchell sent Harrington away, then sat musing in his study. Unfortunately, Mitchell didn't speak to himself like Harrington did, so Adella had no way of knowing what he was thinking. She watched for a while; Mitchell sat at his desk, poured himself a brandy, opened a notebook, and reached for a quill. He seemed to be drawing something, a plan or diagram, yet she couldn't see it.

Finally Mitchell exited, after carefully glancing in both directions. She frowned; he didn't like being seen, and that meant he was accustomed to actions he wanted kept hidden.

In her darkness, Adella stepped from the study

wall to the nursery wall, surprised to find Natalie and Grace holding the twins and talking in whispers.

"How can a new wing be haunted ...?" Grace asked softly.

"Maybe it's someone who died here, on the ground beneath us, and we built our new wing over their grave," Natalie said.

"The music parlor's in the main house," Grace argued. "It's never been haunted before."

"It's never had a fortune in silver hidden in it, either," Natalie said. "The ghost must've wanted us to know about that chute."

"Why ...?" Grace asked.

"That silver was locked in Enfield's chest," Natalie said. "He and Edwina were sleeping with the chest at the foot of their bed. Somehow the ghost unlocked their chest and stole the bag of silver ... then left a line of coins to its hiding place."

"It makes no sense," Grace said. "Why steal and reveal ...?"

"Maybe ... the ghost never meant to steal anything," Natalie said. "Maybe there's something about that coal chute that the ghost wanted us to know."

"Enfield and Rayden examined every inch of that chute," Grace said. "When they were kids, some peasant tried to break into the manor through there. It was nailed shut on the outside decades ago ... and those nails are rusty. No one's opened that chute in years."

"No one but the ghost," Natalie said.

Adella bit back laughter. She'd succeeded; no one was going to search inside the manor for stolen silver ... or a ghost!

Suddenly she heard a youthful cry:

"The ghost ...!"

High-pitched screams and laughter followed ... accompanied with running feet. Seven children ran past the nursery door, screaming in mock-terror, an older child chasing them. As Grace and Natalie watched them run past, Adella relaxed ... and one of the twins laughed.

Adella ate some food while Grace and Natalie continued gossiping, their suspicions of the ghost's methods and motives growing ever wilder. Grace suggested the ghost was the thief who'd tried to sneak in through the chute, but Natalie suggested it could be old Morley himself ... or Captain Marston.

"Who's Captain Marston ...?" Grace asked.

"That depends on who you ask," Natalie said. "Captain Marston Ramsay Marleigh is the recognized founder of the Marleigh fortune. By all accounts outside of the Marleigh family, he was a murderous rogue and scoundrel, who delighted in bullying. He'd murdered his pirate captain, and stolen his wealth ... according to the Prescotts. After that, he became a pirate, plunderer, and slave-merchant, who specialized in young girls. However, the Marleigh family honors him as a wise and stalwart young naval officer, who commandeered an enemy ship and, being gifted with it by his commanding officer, went on to build a financial empire through wise and cunning business transactions. Then he was wounded fighting pirates, and forced to retire from the sea."

"Captain Marston built Marleigh Manor ...?" Grace asked.

"No, he renamed it," Natalie said. "Originally this was New Prescott Manor."

Grace gasped.

"The Prescotts had two manors," Natalie said. "However he earned his fortune, Captain Marston offered to purchase this house, but instead he gambled his fortune against the head of the Prescotts, Morley Langdon Prescott ... and won it. The Prescotts were forced to move back into their old manor. Yet they still needed money. Within a year, Captain Marston Ramsay Marleigh married Sarah Ann Prescott, in a marriage arranged by her father, Morley the Elder, and for a few years, both families lived side-by-side. However, after bearing her only child, a son she named after her father, Sarah Ann Prescott/Marleigh died unexpectedly of an unknown sickness; many suspected she was poisoned."

"Captain Marston murdered his wife ...?" Grace whispered.

"No one ever proved it," Natalie said. "The Prescotts lived in their old manor, Captain Marston in this one, yet no more support was offered. Captain Marston refused to aid the Prescotts, unless he gained full ownership of their lands, which they wouldn't give. Then, less than a year after Sarah's death, in the middle of winter, a terrible fire consumed the entire Old Prescott mansion ... along with half of their family, including Morley Langdon Prescott: Morley the Elder. Over thirty Prescotts moved into Marleigh Manor that night. Yet Captain Marston hated them all."

"Why'd he let them move in?" Grace asked.

"Each Prescott was assigned 'chores' to earn their keep," Natalie said. "Those who stayed became his servants, the most notable of which were Quinton Hayley Prescott and his wife Orpha Parthena Prescott, who spent the rest of their lives serving the master of the home which had once been theirs. All of the Prescotts in Marleigh Manor are their descendants.

"Captain Marston Ramsay Marleigh never married again. He lived a long life of bullying servants, and died drunk. Only a handful attended his funeral. Sarah's son, Morley the Younger, was full grown by then, and became Lord of Marleigh Manor.

"Morley Hornsby Prescott Marleigh started as a bully equal to his father. At his father's command, he married young to an older, wealthy widow. His father sold all she owned, which greatly increased our family's wealth. Then she suddenly died, shortly after the marriage ... just like Sarah had. However, young Morley and his father never spoke another kind word to each other after her funeral; many suspected his father had murdered Morley's elderly wife. Morley then infuriated his father by marrying a poor village girl, who was unquestionably beautiful."

"Vertiline Charity Eastaughffe," Grace said. "Half the paintings in the east parlor are of her."

"Vertiline made a new man of Morley. He became respectable, kind, and doted on her day and night. She bore him three daughters and four sons, Uncle Lester, Aunt Winnifred, Master Middleton, Uncle Enfield, Uncle Rayden, Aunt Everleigh, and my mother, Charity. Morley died only three months after Vertiline. Both swore they lived long, happy lives due to the deep love they shared."

"But Uncle Lester got shot in a duel, leaving Mitchell as his only son," Grace said. "I never heard of Aunt Everleigh."

"I'm not surprised," Natalie said. "Aunt Everleigh drowned herself in the well when she was only eleven. She left a note, but no one knows what it said ... or at least, no one will say."

"How do you know all this?" Grace asked.

"Everyone outside Marleigh Manor knows this," Natalie said. "All the Prescotts know this. When I married your father, I was shocked to discover how little the descendants of Captain Marston Ramsay knew."

"All I was ever told was that the Marleighs are a long and noble line descended from an Admiral in the Royal Navy," Grace said.

"Captain Marston always claimed his father was an Admiral, and friends with all the British nobility, but no record proves this," Natalie said.

"I'm ... descended from a pirate ...?" Grace

asked.

"I don't know," Natalie said. "But if you ask anyone in the village ... yes."

Natalie fell silent while Grace sat thinking, and eventually a bell rang to summon them to supper. As the twins were still awake, they took them, leaving the nursery empty.

Soon the new wing seemed vacated. An older serving woman, probably a Prescott, brought Winnifred a tray, and sat with her while she ate, telling her loudly about the ghost.

No one was in the study, either, so Adella hurried to the privy and back, since she had plenty of food. Before she crawled back inside, she used Mitchell's tongs to break apart the fire baking her hideaway.

Adella pondered the mysteries of the Marleigh line. Thanks to her, Enfield hadn't been blamed for the loss of silver, which meant she'd foiled Mitchell's plan to remove him from consideration. She wasn't a thief or intruder; she was helping their clan, protecting them from sinister plots. Of course, she didn't know if Enfield was any better than Mitchell, yet she'd prevented a deception, saved a man from a false accusation, and felt that more than made up for any food, silk chemise, or silver coin she'd stolen.

The next day, a loud knock rapped on the door to the study. Adella's eye reached the crack just in time to see Mitchell open his door.

"We need to talk," said a formal, breathy voice.

"Come in," Mitchell said, and he set his drink upon his desk.

Three men entered, all well-dressed and considerably older than Mitchell, who closed his study door behind them. The older men looked a proud and pompous lot, two with graying hair, and one obviously a little younger, at least in appearance. Their features bore the striking resemblance of close relations. Adella recognized all of them from the nursery after the baby had vanished. The eldest, who was also the fattest, had been sleeping in the bed beside his wife when she'd stolen her chemise.

"As Lord of Marleigh, I'm deeply concerned," the oldest man said in with his breathy voice, and he gestured to the men beside him. "Enfield and Rayden share my concern."

"Middleton speaks for us," Enfield said.

"It's this 'ghost' business," Middleton said. "We're baffled as to how this phantom operates ..."

"Surely you don't believe in ghosts ...!" Mitchell said.

"It doesn't matter if we believe in ghosts," Enfield said. "Anything that steals Marleigh silver from a locked chest is a threat to all of us."

"The servants aren't doing their chores ... not well, when they do them at all," Rayden said.

"All they talk about is the ghost," Middleton said.

"We must do something."

"It has to be a Prescott," Enfield said.

"Not all the servants are Prescotts," Rayden said. "All we know is it wasn't a Berkeley-Marleigh; they hadn't moved in yet, so when this nonsense began, there was only one Berkeley-Marleigh in residence."

All four men stiffened at this remark.

"I'm not a Berkeley-Marleigh," Mitchell said slowly but emphatically, his youthful face flushing. "I was born in this manor ... the first son ... of your eldest brother."

"We're not here to argue succession," Middleton said. "We need to uncover the secret of this 'ghost' ...!"

A brief silence fell as a war of angry glares raged. Finally, Enfield broke the pause.

"Mitchell, you're closer in age to our sons ...," Enfield said.

"... and our daughters," Middleton said. "I wouldn't put this past any of my girls ..."

"We need you to ... discover who's perpetrating this ... false haunting," Middleton said.

"If you can," Rayden added.

"I, too, have been pondering the 'ghost'," Mitchell said. "I'm trying to discover who it really is."

"How ...?" Middleton asked.

"I intend to stage a theft," Mitchell said. "A false theft ... to draw it out ..."

"Excellent idea," Middleton said, and then suddenly he began coughing, loud and harshly, such that his whole body shook. His white handkerchief, before he hid it in his hand, showed stains of red spots.

"You should be in bed," Rayden said, taking his brother's arm and supporting him.

"Nonsense," Middleton said. "Mitchell, when shall we expect your 'theft'?"

"I hope to orchestrate it tonight," Mitchell said. "Only, this time, I'll be watching."

"Excellent," Middleton said. "We'll return tomorrow for your ... unveiling."

Middleton, Enfield, and Rayden exited, and Mitchell closed the door behind them. He went back to his desk, drew out his ledger, and began writing, pausing only to sip brandy.

Adella drew back from the tiny crack between panels, then decided to check the nursery, yet saw only the back of Natalie's head as she sat in a rocker; Adella assumed she had a baby at each breast. Like Mitchell, Natalie didn't talk to herself, so Adella quit watching.

Her hideaway was stiflingly hot again, yet there was nothing she could do about it. Starting to sweat, she took off her silk chemise and laid it on her blanket, then sat beside it. She drank a few sips of wine.

She needed to visit the kitchen again ... but how could she ... when a trap for the ghost was being laid?

Most of the family departed for the midday meal, but other than to use the privy, Adella could go nowhere. However, when they returned, Harrington followed Mitchell into his study.

"In the music room, behind the harp, there's a small table with a drawer in it," Mitchell said to Harrington. "Tonight, I want you to steal a bag with a single silver coin in it and place it in that drawer."

"Can I keep the coin?" Harrington asked.

"Obviously not ...," Mitchell sighed. "The whole point of this is to catch the 'ghost'."

"I want the coin!" Harrington insisted.

"You can have the coin after we catch the ghost," Mitchell said. "I'll be hidden on the other side of the room, watching. After you deposit the bag in the drawer, I'll see who comes for it."

"I don't want no part of meeting a ghost!" Harrington said.

"I'll manage the ghost," Mitchell said. "The bag with the coin will be right here, on my desk. Come in, get the bag, and deposit it in the drawer. Can you do that?"

"Of course ...," Harrington said.

"Don't tell anyone," Mitchell said. "Harrington, if this succeeds, you'll be credited for revealing the thief, which will look very good when I recommend you to be Lord of Marleigh Manor. You'll be rewarded far more than a single silver coin."

"How much ...?" Harrington asked.

"Get out," Mitchell snapped. "Fetch the coin exactly at midnight."

Adella plotted all day and evening. She

considered stealing the bag after Mitchell went to hide in the music room, and then returning it after Harrington went to report the bag wasn't there. However, she'd drawn attention to the nursery already; she didn't want more attention pointing to any room adjacent to her hideaway. Besides, she had a better idea.

Two hours before midnight, in the nursery, Lydia was clicking her knitting needles as she rocked, the twins sleeping in their crib. In his study, Mitchell left the cloth bag on his desk, and closed his door behind him, all but a crack. At exactly midnight, Harrington entered the study, grabbed the bag, looked inside it, and then departed.

Moments later, Adella opened her secret door. She quietly set each of her empty wine bottles into the study closet, then crawled past them. One bottle in each hand, she checked the hallway to insure it was empty, then carried the first two across the hall into Mitchell's room. She set both bottles in a line, on the carpet just inside his room, then went to fetch the others. After all her empty wine bottles were laid out in a row, just inside his door, she hurried to his bed, pulled off his blankets and sheets, and draped them about his room, one over each wardrobe, one over a chair, and the rest spread wide upon the floor. Then she hurried back to her hideaway and sealed herself inside.

She'd never make it to the kitchen tonight with Mitchell hiding in the music room, watching for any movement. All she had left was a little bread, water, and a few sips of wine, yet it would have to suffice. She'd be starving tomorrow night, but ... today would be a celebration.

Near dawn, she heard footsteps, unusually loud for such an early hour, and then she heard a door open amid the usual pre-dawn silence. She held her breath, then nearly burst out laughing as the sound of breaking glass exploded. Her empty bottles, set in a line just inside Mitchell's room, had been walked into ...!

"Cursed ghost ...!" Mitchell's voice shouted.

Adella rolled on her blanket, choking back laughter. She couldn't afford to be heard.

Voices rose in alarm. Footsteps filled the new wing, all rushing toward Mitchell's room. Exclamations and cries arose over shouted questions.

"I just walked in here ...!" Mitchell scowled. "Someone ... invaded my room ... and did this!"

"The ghost ...!" several voices cried.

No one returned to their bed. Lydia was summoned and severely questioned, and Mitchell loudly pointed out that she was the only servant in the new wing when the 'ghost' had visited.

"I'm here every night ...!" Lydia defended herself. "I never left the nursery, and if I'd seen a ghost, they'd hear my scream in the village!"

Adella ate the last of her bread, sipping at the last of her wine to delay her running out. When she wasn't sleeping, everything she heard was about the ghost.

"This whole manor is haunted!"

"It must be old Morley, bless his soul!"

"Where'd it find all those empty bottles?"

"It must've known Mitchell was watching ..."

"Never try to deceive a spirit."

Adella spied Grace with a group of six young women, all teenagers whom she'd never seen before, wander past the open nursery door. All were frowning and walked past with worried looks, without speaking a word.

That afternoon, a name she'd only heard spoken appeared in the nursery.

"Laurence, would you like to hold a baby?" Natalie asked.

She rose and peeked into the nursery. A young man she'd never seen was holding one of the twins as if afraid of breaking it.

"He's very soft," Laurence said in a monotone voice.

"Yes, babies are soft ... and delicate," Natalie said as Rowena giggled. "You must be careful with him."

Laurence appeared to be nearly seventeen; Adella wondered why he needed to be told this.

"This is my cousin," Laurence said.

"That's right," Natalie said. "Your Aunt Charity is his grandmother."

"Aunt Charity is Acton's mother," Laurence said.

"Yes, and Acton is my husband, which makes Aunt Charity my mother-in-law," Natalie said.

"I'm done now," Laurence announced.

"I'll take him," Rowena said, and she lifted the infant from his hands.

"You can go work on your collection, if you want," Natalie said.

"No, Cousin Grace is playing piano this afternoon," Laurence said.

"Then you can go listen," Natalie said.

"Is there really a ghost?" Laurence asked.

"I haven't seen it, but that's what everyone says," Natalie said.

Without another word, Laurence departed. With knowing expressions, Natalie and Rowena glanced at each other and sighed.

"What do you really think?" Rowena asked.

"I never believed in ghosts before, but I'm starting to," Natalie said.

"Nobody but Marleighs and Lydia were in the wing," Rowena said.

"Lydia's trustworthy, and I don't believe any Marleigh would leave a trail of silver coins," Natalie said.

"The Prescotts are scared," Rowena said. "Even if it's a ghost, someone alive will be blamed."

"Middleton knows he's your father; you're safe," Natalie said.

"The ghost is giving anyone who wants to make a false accusation the perfect excuse," Rowena said.

"Winnifred wouldn't allow it," Natalie said.

"If you say so," Rowena said.

"You don't have to talk carefully to me," Natalie

said, lowering her voice. "Mitchell doesn't like Darbys any better than Prescotts."

"Then you should be as worried as I am," Rowena said. "We both have babies that need warm roofs."

"No one's being cast out," Natalie said.

"Marleighs have done it before," Rowena said.

"That was Lester," Natalie said.

"Every new Lord of Marleigh changes how the Prescotts live," Rowena said. "Captain Marston married a Prescott, then treated us like garbage. Morley was awful at first, then kind and generous, but wouldn't free us. Lester weeded out Prescotts he didn't like. Middleton ignores us."

"You're worried about the succession," Natalie said.

"Every Prescott is," Rowena said.

"Perhaps I should worry more," Natalie said.

"Charity protects you," Rowena said.

"I'm a Darby," Natalie said.

"I'm a Prescott," Rowena said.

An aged woman's voice called; Adella couldn't make out the words. Yet Natalie and Rowena both rose at once and, carrying the babies, walked out of the nursery and into Winnifred's door.

Naked and sweating, Adella checked the study, to find it still empty, then sat back down. The fire crackled loudly on the far side of the stones, and she wondered at their wastefulness of firewood; these people seemed to enjoy no lack of extravagance. Yet their family politics seemed no gentler than rivaling factions of bloodthirsty pirates in the stories of sailors ... only Marleigh cruelty was hidden behind false veneers of gentility.

Adella had never known family other than her parents. She'd never met a single aunt or uncle, if any existed. She wondered who her grandparents had been ... if they were still alive. She'd never known what city her parents had come from. She didn't know why they'd never talked about their parents.

Had her mother and father both fled from family politics this vile ...?

Perhaps her grandparents had refused to let her parents wed ... and they'd fled, unable to endure life without each other. *Perhaps they'd been rich ... !*

Romantic fantasies swirled, each more unlikely than the next. Yet it didn't matter. Her parents had kissed first thing every morning and last thing every night. Each had always tried to help the other, caring for their comfort and wants. Their few cross words had always ended with long hugs and promises of fidelity.

Adella wanted a marriage like that.

Hungry and baking, she sat all evening, unmoving except after the family marched away to the bell-summons for supper, when she slipped out to visit the privy. Their dinners always lasted longer than she could account for. Afterwards, she tried to sleep, but her empty stomach complained, and she couldn't risk someone hearing her tummy rumble through a wall.

That evening, Mitchell's voice rose from Winnifred's room. He sounded angry, yet she couldn't hear Winnifred's voice, whom she knew spoke softly. Both were too far away. She only made out a few words of Mitchell's: 'bloodline', 'rightful', and 'ghost'.

After firewood had been piled by every fireplace, and the privies scrubbed, the new wing fell silent. Lydia sat beside the twins, but to Adella's astonishment, tonight Lydia was reading a book by candlelight ... and she kept the nursery door closed.

Being extra quiet, Adella snuck out through the study. On the wide desk lay the book Mitchell constantly wrote in. Curious, she opened it.

To her surprise, only one out of every three pages held written notes. The rest were drawings of incredible detail; Mitchell was a masterful artist. Many birds, but also a sunset over trees, three horses in a pen, and several interior rooms. A few pages held detailed drawings of plans of complex devices. One drawing was a floor plan of the new wing with every room identified.

Mitchell had skills she'd never guessed. Yet she couldn't waste time admiring his work. The little writing was terse notes, each preceded by dates ... nothing incriminating. She closed his book.

Adella was starving. The hall was clear, so she slipped out of the new wing into the short hall that opened on one side into the music room. She glanced behind the harp, but clouds hid the moonlight. She

couldn't see the tiny table with the drawer where
Harrington had stashed the 'stolen' bag containing a
single silver coin. She also wondered where Mitchell
had been hiding ... waiting for the 'ghost' to appear.

The kitchen was empty of people, yet full of
everything else. She found three plates of roasted
chickens, mostly uneaten, tore off another leg and thigh,
and devoured the meat off its bones. A bowl of potatoes
rested under a cover; she filled her bowl, and used a
knife to slice breast-meat off the bones of two chickens,
which she piled atop her potatoes. She filled her pitcher
with water and snagged a bottle of wine, then carefully
balanced her bounty all the way back.

Yet, as she stepped into the long hallway toward
the study, footsteps arose in the other hallway coming
around the corner. Already exposed, she hurried
onward, certain she'd be seen. She didn't dare stop to
open the study door.

"Hello ...?" Lydia called behind her.

She quickened her pace, rounding the corner of
the family room, yet the footsteps behind her also
quickened. She spied the locked door to outside, in
which the key rested, but she'd never make it through in
time. She saw the kid's toy room, yet she'd easily be
seen in there, so she passed it by. She didn't dare
attempt to run the length of a long hall again; she was
sure to be caught.

The door to her left hid a sleeping nine year old
girl. She'd never explored the first door to her right.

She could stumble upon someone sleeping, yet she was going to be caught anyway ...

Adella pushed inside; it was a laundry room. Lines strung with clothes blocked her view of the back wall; she quietly pushed the door closed behind her.

Several moments she stood in the dark, pressed against the wall behind the door.

"Hello ...?" called Lydia's voice.

She heard a door open and close ... the door across the hall to the little girl's room. Then the door beside her opened. She froze, terrified. Yet the door didn't open fully, and Lydia didn't look behind it. Seeing only dresses and sheets hanging on lines, Lydia withdrew and closed the door.

Trembling, Adella struggled to remain calm; she'd almost been caught! If she'd pushed through the clothes, if Lydia had looked inside and seen them moving, then she would've been revealed. Yet she'd escaped detection again ... for the moment.

She'd been seen ... but only the back of her head and stolen chemise ...!

Unable to resist, she ate some more chicken while she waited; if she was going to be thrown out into the frozen night, she might as well have a full stomach. Yet eventually she quietly opened the door a crack and peeked out.

The hallway looked empty, and she didn't dare wait.

She fled through the family room back to the

study, through its closet, and into her hideaway.

Terrified of making a sound, she quietly slid her secret door back into place and slipped in its nail-pegs, sealing herself inside. Lydia wasn't in the nursery, yet she didn't move again until the family started to awaken and their footsteps and voices masked any noises she might make.

Famished, she finished off one chicken breast before she tried the potatoes. Yet, after a few mouthfuls, she was full. Her nerves were still afire so she opened and drank from her bottle, and after a few gulps, she laid down to rest ... yet sleep wouldn't come.

She'd been seen ...!

Yet another thought thrilled her; *the laundry room!* When spring came, when she would finally be able to escape from Marleigh Manor, she'd easily be able to grab a dress or two to take with her.

She could leave her silver coin behind to pay for the dresses ...!

Troubled dreams tormented and awoke her several times. Yet she detected no cause for alarm. Children's voices laughed in the halls. Rowena nursed the twins in the morning, Natalie in the afternoon, and Mitchell sat in his study most of the day reading and then drawing in his journal. She tried to force herself to sleep, yet that never worked. The fireplace grew so hot she again disrobed.

She silently cursed. *She'd been seen ...!*

That night she slipped out through the study to use the privy. She was cold; outside of her sweltering hideaway, the rest of the house was chilly. She wanted something warm to wear, but the more more she stole, the more likely the family would notice. Rubbing her arms for warmth, she quietly checked the halls; Lydia had returned to the entry room, again knitting before the hot fire, this time with an open book in her lap.

With no one else awake, Adella opened the laundry room door wide, letting the light from the lit sconce shine in. Sheets and clothes hung; pushing through them, Adella found three half-barrels of soapy water on a low table. Some of the clothes were still damp. Several of these dresses would fit her. Yet she left them untouched; she'd be instantly noticed wearing a dress everyone recognized. She'd hoped to find a gray servants' dress, such as Lydia and Rowena wore; it would look less conspicuous. Yet the servants' laundry was probably in the Prescott wing, and she'd never explored that far.

She considered venturing to the far wings, but a shiver ran up her spine; she dared not explore any farther than necessary.

She checked the hallway, and stepped out of the laundry, determined to head straight back to her hideaway, when a soft noise wafted down the hall, barely audible. It caught her attention; *a pained moan.*

Adella crept up the hall. The anguished cry came from Winnifred's room ... as if the old lady was hurt. She knew she shouldn't, yet the cry was too soft for Lydia to hear, several rooms away and sitting before a crackling fire. She snuck up to Winnifred's door and peeked inside.

The moonlight through the windows was dim, leaving most of the room shadowy. Soft moans floated from the floor in the far corner; *the old woman had fallen out of bed.*

Feebly-waving arms gestured helplessly from the floor. She wondered what she should do; if she called for Lydia, then she could sneak back inside her hideaway while Lydia was helping the old woman. Yet others might hear, too.

The room was dark; no one could see clearly. Unable to abandon a helpless woman to suffer, Adella stepped inside, and hurried to grab her waving arms. With her youthful carpenter's strength, she easily lifted the thin, elderly woman and set her back onto her bed.

"Thank you ...!" the old woman spoke softly.

Adella turned to flee ...

Suddenly a hand gripped her arm tightly and a glowing lantern was uncovered. Adella tried to pull free, but the old woman's nails dug into her flesh.

"Stand still, ghost, or I'll scream ...!" the old woman hissed.

Chapter 6

Terrified, Adella looked down into piercing, aged eyes.

"So ... you're the ghost," she whispered. "I'm Winnifred, eldest daughter of Marleigh Manor. I scream and every relative I have comes charging in here ...!"

"P-p-p-please ... please don't ...!" Adella stammered.

"Quiet!" Winnifred hissed. "Go close my door, then come back. We need to talk ... and we can't afford to be caught again, can we ...?"

The sharp fingernails released her arm.

"Don't try to run," Winnifred whispered. "I

know you're real ... there's nowhere you can hide now."

Adella didn't know what to do. *Her whole plan was ruined!*

Trembling, she walked to Winnifred's door. She considered running, but where could she go? *One scream would bring everyone ...!*

With a sigh, Adella closed the door and returned to the old woman's bedside.

"What's your name, child?" Winnifred asked, now sitting up in her bed.

"A ... Adella," she answered.

"Where are you hiding?" Winnifred asked. "Don't lie ...!"

"In ... inside a wall," Adella said.

"How did you get here?" Winnifred asked.

Staring at the carpet, her arms limp at her sides, Adella told her story, leaving out only the killing of the lecherous driver. She claimed to have walked here, hoping to sell her father's tools, but no carpenter would offer her a decent price. She explained how she'd grown up around carpentry, and with nowhere to sleep, she'd hidden inside the half-finished wing during the first night, and then built a secret door to her dead space ... no point in confessing she'd moved a wall.

"So, you've been living inside our house all this time," Winnifred shook her head. "My brothers aren't the brightest. I'd have spied on the kitchen right away; ghosts don't steal silver ... and everyone else needs to eat."

"I didn't steal your silver ...!" Adella argued.

"I know," Winnifred said. "That was quite ingenious. You saved my brother from a costly embarrassment. But ... *why ...?"*

Adella shrugged.

"It ... seemed right," Adella said.

"You could've stolen a fortune ...," Winnifred said.

"And gone where ...?" Adella asked.

"So, you're a thinking girl," Winnifred said. "That's good. I assume your 'secret door' is in the nursery?"

"Yes," Adella said.

"That explains the reappearing baby ...," Winnifred said.

"I was trying to comfort him," Adella said. "Lydia came ... I didn't have time ..."

"I assumed that," Winnifred said. "You returned the baby, you exposed the hiding place of the silver, and you redecorated Mitchell's room while he was attempting to catch you ...?"

"Yes, 'mam," Adella said.

"Interesting," Winnifred said. "You've lived in this wing for how long ...?"

"Close to three months," Adella said.

"Without getting caught ...?" Winnifred asked.

"Yes, 'mam," Adella said.

"Stealing food from our kitchen ...?" Winnifred asked.

"Only since the workmen left," Adella said. "Before that, I ate with ... from the carpenter's camp."

"Are you aware what will happen if I summon my brothers ...?" Winnifred asked, and her brows knit with seriousness.

"I ... think so," Adella said.

"Do you want me to summon them ...?" Winnifred asked.

"I'd ... rather you didn't," Adella said.

"If I were to keep your secret, would you be ... grateful?" Winnifred asked.

"Very ...," Adella said.

"Who stole the silver?" Winnifred demanded suddenly.

"Harrington ...," Adella said reluctantly. "He was ... put up to it."

"By whom?" Winnifred asked.

"Mitchell ...," Adella said. "I overheard them ... in Mitchell's study."

Winnifred smiled wickedly.

"I've been thinking a lot about you," Winnifred said. "I'm trapped in this bedroom ... while my brothers and nephews ruin our family. I need eyes that can see, and ears that can listen, in places I can't. You could be exactly what I need ..."

"I ... I just need shelter ... for the winter," Adella said. "In spring, I'll vanish and never bother you again ... I promise!"

"You'll not leave until I give you permission,"

Winnifred ordered. "If needed, I'll have the countryside scoured ..."

"Yes, 'mam," Adella sighed.

"Excellent," Winnifred said. "Adella, I think we're going to be very good for each other. Is there anything you need? Do you have enough food?"

"Yes, 'mam," Adella said.

"I don't want you sneaking to the kitchen again," Winnifred said. "I'll have them bring extra food to me. Come to me each night and I'll give you plenty."

"Thank you, 'mam," Adella said.

"I'll decide your actions from now on," Winnifred said. "Continue to listen and report to me."

"Yes, 'mam," Adella said.

"My name is Mistress Winnifred."

"Yes, 'mam ... Mistress Winnifred," Adella said.

"Marvelous," Winnifred said, and she leaned back against her headboard. "Now, I need to know everything about you ... and about every conversation you've heard. Begin ..."

With no small amount of prompting, Adella described her whole past, from her childhood memories of her mother to the day her father died. Then Winnifred demanded to hear every conversation she'd eavesdropped upon ... from Mitchell, Grace, Stella, Camden, Stella, Harrington, Lydia, and Rowena ... asking many questions ... and Adella told her everything.

"That's enough for now," Winnifred said. "Pour me some water, then go back to your dead space. Wait;

is that Letitia's chemise?"

"It's Master Middleton's wife's chemise," Adella said. "I never knew her name."

"Letitia, and she's as worthless as my brother," Winnifred said. "Leave it with me."

"I have no other clothes," Adella confessed.

"Open that wardrobe," Winnifred ordered. "My clothes ... from when I was younger."

Adella saw amazing gowns on the right. She drew out a red one that glittered with tiny gems.

"Not that," Winnifred said. "You need something discreet ... dark and quiet."

Adella examined the magnificent gowns, and chose one of black velvet, and she chose a dark green chemise to go under it. At Winnifred's instruction, she changed clothes and left the silk chemise behind.

"Set the chemise on that chair ... as if someone sitting there was wearing it," Winnifred said. "These fools think you're a ghost; we're going to continue that pretense."

"Why ...?" Adella began.

"So they don't start looking for you," Winnifred said. "Now, how long will it take you to get back inside your dead space?"

"A minute," Adella said.

"Go now, and then stay quiet," Winnifred said. "I'll give you time to get safely hidden before I wake everyone up. Tomorrow night, come here, to me, as soon as you can. Do you understand?"

"Yes, Mistress Winnifred," Adella said.

"Obey me, Adella, and I'll keep you safe," Winnifred said. "Disobey me ... and you'll regret it."

Swallowing hard, Adella nodded silently, then she bowed and walked to the door. Checking to see the hallway empty, Adella glanced back once at Winnifred, then slipped out, leaving her door open. She hurried around to the study, crawled inside her hideaway, and sat silently, her every nerve afire.

She'd been caught ...!

She was being blackmailed ...!

She was wearing the nicest dress she'd ever worn ...!

Suddenly a horrible scream made her jump. Other voices cried out in the night. Doors slammed open and stomping footsteps pounded.

"I saw it!" Winnifred's scream filtered through the wall. *"I saw ... the ghost!"*

Pandemonium erupted and voices shouted over aghast cries.

Adella jumped up and pressed her eye against the crack to the nursery. The doorway to Winnifred's room was blocked by people, all peering inside. Voices shouted for quiet, and then Middleton's sleepy voice demanded an explanation.

"A noise awakened me ... a soft moaning," Winnifred said loudly. "It floated in here ... wearing that nightgown ...!"

"My chemise ...!" Letitia exclaimed.

"It came toward my bed, then sat down in that chair!" Winnifred said loudly. "Then it just vanished ... leaving only the nightgown ...!"

Winnifred's screechy voice wailed; Adella wondered if she was speaking loudly so that she could hear. However, the early tumult awoke the twins, and both started to cry. Lydia and Natalie came in and picked them up, trying to calm them; neither liked being awoken.

Adella couldn't hear the rest of the conversations over the cries of the babies, yet even infantile shrieks couldn't drown out shouts. Several Berkeley-Marleighs arrived, awakened by the screams, and horrified to hear proof they'd moved into a haunted house.

"Mitchell, is this true ...?" Adella heard Stella ask.

"Certainly not!" Mitchell shouted. "I'll reveal this ghost!"

An hour passed before Adella relaxed. She liked being properly dressed in a warm, fine gown, the like of which she'd never imagined. She wouldn't have to sneak into the kitchen anymore, just across the hall. Winnifred would help cover her tracks ... but only as long as she did what she was told.

Yet ... could she trust Winnifred ...?

She knew nothing about her ...!

Do I have any choice ...?

Adella considered fleeing out into the wintry cold. She wondered how far she'd get ... and if they'd find her frozen corpse.

Adella wasn't hungry, but she was too awake to sleep, so she ate the last of her chicken and some potatoes for lack of anything better to do. When everyone fell asleep, she'd have to face Winnifred ... whose steely eyes unnerved her.

Wine soothed her. She wasn't any worse off than she'd been before. If she did what the old woman asked, she should be safe ...

But what if the old woman asked her to do something horrible ...? Something illegal ...?

She never should've tried to help her back into bed ...!

Like it or not, she was trapped in the old woman's graces ...

In dread anticipation, Adella sat as the night deepened, listening to the Marleighs vanish into their bedrooms, watching as Natalie nursed her twins, and Lydia laid them down to sleep. Then Lydia vanished from the nursery. A long time later, the boy appeared, pulling his wagon. She listened as he placed dry wood beside every fireplace, then she heard the door to outside open and close repeatedly; he was washing out the privy bowls. Finally he wheeled his cart up the hallway, through the entry way, and back into the main house.

Adella could wait no longer. Reluctantly she rose, and using her secret door into the nursery, she slipped across the hall and entered Winnifred's room.

"I was afraid you'd forgotten," Winnifred said.

"The boy ...," Adella said.

"I understand," Winnifred said, and she gestured to a small table beside her bed which hadn't been there before, yet now stood laden with covered dishes and a bottle of wine. "This is for you."

"Thank you, Mistress Winnifred," Adella said.

"Close the door, then sit and eat," Winnifred said. "It's still warm."

"Yes, 'mam," Adella said, and she did as told. The food was delicious, hotter than anything she'd found in the kitchen, and she had a plate and cup and proper silverware.

"Did you hear any conversations today?" Winnifred asked.

"Only about the ghost, Mistress Winnifred," Adella said. "No one's talking about anything else."

"What about Mitchell?" Winnifred asked.

"I don't know where Mitchell went for most of the day," Adella said. "The only time he was in his study he was alone, and he doesn't talk while he's alone."

"That's a pity," Winnifred said. "You said young Harrington talks to himself?"

"Yes, 'mam ... often," Adella said.

"We must make that work for us," Winnifred said. "Tomorrow I'll summon him ... to discuss his future. I've seldom talked to Harrington. He's sure to tell Mitchell ... hopefully in his study. Listen closely ... and report everything they say."

"Yes, Mistress Winnifred," Adella said.

"You also said Harrington lusts for wealth ...?" Winnifred asked.

"It's all he talks about," Adella said.

"Marvelous," Winnifred said. "That'll make everything easier ..."

"Mistress Winnifred, may I ask a question?" Adella asked.

"Certainly," Winnifred said.

"You said that you ... wanted me to do things for you," Adella said. "Exactly ... what kind of things ...?"

"My father, rest his soul, was the last good Marleigh in this house, yet he was a terrible father," Winnifred said. "My brother Lester was abominable. Lester tormented us kids and teased my beautiful sister, Everleigh Esther Marleigh, until she killed herself."

"Drowned in the well," Adella said.

"Yes," Winnifred said. "I was never so pleased as the day I got Charity's letter telling me Lester had been shot dead. I'd left Marleigh Manor shortly after my sister killed herself; I couldn't stand living under his roof. I was young; I traveled the countryside, and married a man who managed a circus. Oh, he was a good man, a gentle man, and he loved the theater. We had four children, the youngest of which is Rufina, whose room is adjacent to mine."

Adella nodded; the room with the nine year old girl.

"Nibley Deighton Northcott was my husband,

and we shared many years together," Winnifred said. "My three eldest children grew up as circus performers, and shortly before Nibley died, shot by a thief, I learned my brother Lester had been killed. Well, my older children wanted to stay with the circus, and I couldn't blame them. So I took Rufina and came home."

"That must've been a big change," Adella said.

"For Rufina, yes; she was only seven," Winnifred said. "However, my parents, Morley and Vertiline, had died only a year before, so life was tolerable. Then everything fell to ruin because of Middleton's unbridled lusts. Middleton's never suffered a serious thought in his life, Enfield hated him, and Rayden was back in prison ..."

"Prison ...?" Adella asked.

"He'd gotten drunk in the village and assaulted an officer of Her Majesties' navy ... the fool," Winnifred said. "Spent a year in prison. He'd always been a troublemaker. When he was young, he got caught stealing and spent three months in prison. Then he came back and married that barmaid, Phoebe Polly Charleston, who had the lowest reputation in the district. That was the final straw, a disgrace upon our house, but ..."

Winnifred paused to shake her head.

"Phoebe hates to come in here, into this room," Winnifred said. "She knows what I think of her. She spends most of her days in her room, sleeping off endless hangovers. She gave Rayden one son, and she drank so much while pregnant, his brain was born as addled as hers, the poor thing."

"Laurence," Adella said.

"Exactly," Winnifred said. "Sweet boy, but can barely tie his shoes ..."

"What about Enfield?" Adella asked.

"Enfield cares only for his art," Winnifred said. "Enfield writes and paints, and only mixes in family politics when he's forced to."

"What about Rayden?" Adella asked.

"Never trust Rayden," Winnifred said. "He's smart, clever, and will murder you, if it suits his fancy. Rayden has a self-mastery none of his brothers equal ... and whatever his thoughts, his actions are cruel and swift. He believes he deserves to be the next Lord of Marleigh, since Mitchell's cruel and Enfield's an artist."

"Mitchell is cruel," Adella said.

"The day after he becomes Lord of Marleigh, there won't be a Prescott left in Marleigh Manor ... if he has his way," Winnifred said. "Everyone hates him."

"I hear him yelling," Adella said.

"It's his only tone of voice," Winnifred said. "He barely knew his father, Lester, but he's the spitting image of him ... just as vile and intemperate."

"What about Master Middleton?" Adella asked. "Is he really sick?"

"Consumption," Winnifred said. "The village doctor says he may last until summer, but he's never diagnosed anything right in his life."

"What happens ... if Middleton dies ... without naming a successor?" Adella asked.

"Mitchell is the legal successor," Winnifred said. "On his twentieth birthday, only five months from now, he'll go to the courts to enforce his claim. That will spark a bloodbath. When Lester died, his mother Stella could've gone to the courts, but after suffering multiple threats and an attempt on her life, she fled this house. There are those in this family who will circumvent the rule of law ... if they can."

"Too many ...," Adella said.

"Succession has torn many wealthy families apart," Winnifred said. "My goal is to keep this family together. If you help me, then I'll keep your ... squatting ... secret."

"I won't do anything illegal," Adella said.

"Squatting in our house without permission is illegal," Winnifred said. "If I were to summon the constabulary ...!"

"You leave me no choice," Adella said.

"I can't afford to," Winnifred said. "The last wealthy household that sundered during a succession suffered three murders, one suspect was hung, and two were imprisoned for life. Those left ended up in multiple courts, fighting for years. Their fortune was squandered. Half of their relations moved to distant lands."

"You fear that will happen ...?" Adella asked.

"My job is to keep this family alive ... in the hope

of a generation better than today," Winnifred said, her old woman's determination radiating from her aged face.

"That I can support," Adella said.

Chapter 7

Before morning, Adella returned to her hideaway with a new nightgown, a thick quilt, Winnifred's covered lantern, matches, and more than enough food to last the day. She slept comfortably until the fireplace was lit, and shortly afterwards she awoke bathed in sweat. Pushing back her warm new quilt, and stripping off her soft, damp nightgown, she heard voices coming from the nursery. Yawning, she rose to listen at the crack.

"They're cousins," Grace said. "I can't marry any of them."

"Fourth cousins at best, and none by blood," Natalie said. "Stella's second husband, Barton Marlowe

Quinton, has a younger brother who's moved in: Norton Oakes Quinton."

"Mom, he's twice my age," Grace said.

"He's unmarried," Natalie said. "Stella's second son is married, but her third ..."

"I've no interest in Harlan," Grace said.

"I never said you did, but he's your age ... and if Mitchell becomes ...!"

"No one chooses my husband but me!" Grace said defensively.

"Others have had husbands chosen for them ...," Natalie said. "Then there's ..."

"Dalton's too young," Grace said.

"Only by a few years," Natalie said.

"I've no interest in marriage," Grace said.

"Mine worked out," Natalie said.

"You married outside the family ... and settled here," Grace said. "I've two requirements for a husband: he must be from a wealthy family ... and want me to move into his house."

Both girls laughed.

"I hear Mitchell and Norton had words," Grace said.

Natalie pretended surprise, raising her voice. "Someone didn't get along with Mitchell ...?"

"Norton hates eating with the Marleighs," Grace said. "Mitchell wants them at dinner to support him, but Norton wants the Quintons to dine alone."

"Can Darbys eat with the Quintons?" Natalie

asked.

"No one but us would like that," Grace said.

The girls laughed again.

Adella envied their laughter. She wished she could join them, rather than spy upon them. Carpenters loved to talk, and her father wasn't the only one who'd drug his kids around. Adella had enjoyed countless short-term friends, losing each when their fathers went to work on different projects. She'd never known a friendship to last a whole year.

Once the twins were fed, Natalie and Grace took them to see Winnifred, leaving the nursery empty. Sweating, Adella sat back down, wishing she had a window to let out the heat.

When the bell rang, Marleighs and Darbys trooped out for lunch, then returned, and the afternoon drug on. Adella ate what little she had left, and drank some wine, bored, until she heard the door to the study burst open. Footsteps hurried inside and the door closed hard.

"What did she want ...?" Mitchell's gruff voice demanded.

"She ... asked questions ...," Harrington's voice said.

"What questions ...?"

Adella rose and pressed her eye to the crack.

"She asked what I ... what I liked," Harrington said. "What my goals were ..."

"Why ...?" Mitchell demanded.

"I don't know," Harrington said. "I've never spoken to her ... never entered her room before."

"Why now ...?" Mitchell asked. "Of all days, why today ...?"

"Ask her," Harrington said.

"I may ... curse her," Mitchell scowled.

Harrington looked surprised. Mitchell looked at him pitiably, then poured himself a brandy.

"Although a woman, Winnifred carries considerable weight, both in influence and wealth," Mitchell said. "Letitia, your mother, and Charity listen to her, and they're the mothers of most of the Marleighs and all the Darbys. Even the Prescotts support her; they consider her a friend."

"Who cares about Prescotts ...?" Harrington asked.

"They do, and Winnifred does, and with the new additions of Quintons, one Manley, and one Marston, they outnumber the Marleighs," Mitchell said.

"Cast them out," Harrington said.

"Without their support, neither of us will become Lord of Marleigh," Mitchell said. "Besides, without the Prescotts, who'll do the cooking and cleaning? We can't bankrupt ourselves hiring new help all at once."

"Couldn't we do something else?" Harrington asked.

"You could wash and sweep ...!" Mitchell snapped.

"I'm a Marleigh!" Harrington argued.

"So am I, but someone has to keep this house running," Mitchell said.

"Maybe the Quintons ...," Harrington said.

"Don't say that!" Mitchell shouted. "Don't even think it! The Quintons are here to support my succession. Without them, you and I are doomed! Do you think that thought hasn't crossed their minds? They'd storm out if I even suggested it!"

"What about afterwards ...?" Harrington asked. "Will they stay ...?"

"Best we don't dwell on that now," Mitchell said. "Some will ... not all."

"I can't stand Harlan," Harrington said.

"Neither can I," Mitchell said. "But we must tolerate him ... and the others ... until we've no use for them."

"Then we can get rid of them," Harrington said.

"Marleigh Manor has long needed a purging," Mitchell said. "There hasn't been a Marleigh-Prescott marriage in four generations. Some we'll send away on ships ... so far that they'll never return ... once you or I am Lord of Marleigh."

"Don't waste money on them," Harrington scoffed.

"We'll send them off slowly, a few at a time, as our profits allow," Mitchell said. "Replace them with younger, less lazy servants ... who don't have blood-ties."

"New servants," Harrington smiled. "Young,

pretty maids ...!"

"Yes," Mitchell smiled. "We'll need fewer servants once we've weeded out those we don't like. You'll have all you ever dreamed of ... if we can just hold on a little longer."

"What about Aunt Winnifred?" Harrington asked.

"Leave her to me," Mitchell said.

Mitchell tossed Harrington a silver coin, and Harrington's grin widened. With a respectful nod, Harrington left.

As soon as the door closed, Mitchell chuckled darkly, yet voiced no clue as to the cause of his mirth.

"That's quite interesting," Winnifred said to Adella in the middle of the night.

"Which part ...?" Adella asked.

"All except for Grace," Winnifred said. "So ... Grace wants to leave us. I can't blame her, but we can't let that happen."

"Who do you want her to marry?" Adella asked.

"Unhappy brides make terrible mothers," Winnifred said. "She's one of the few raised inside this house who hasn't been infected by the family curse."

"Curse ...?" Adella asked.

"Wealthy families are always cursed," Winnifred said. "In medieval times, families squired their sons. At the age of seven, boys were sent to serve another family ... to grow up where the status of their birth wouldn't cripple them."

"Rich kids grow spoiled," Adella agreed.

"Vertiline Charity Eastaughffe made a good man of Morley Hornsby Prescott Marleigh, but she couldn't make him a good father," Winnifred said. "Their kids ran wild, and the family turned horrible. We need girls like Grace to mother decent, disciplined kids."

"The Prescotts seem disciplined," Adella said.

"Their enslavement was the worst crime of Captain Marston Ramsay Marleigh ... even worse than murdering his wife," Winnifred said. "Prescotts and Marleighs are one family, but the break between us is written in four generations of cruelty."

"Why do they put up with it?" Adella asked.

"Money," Winnifred said. "Most left, but Old Merton Kinsley Prescott, the nephew of Sarah Ann Prescott, believed another Marleigh/Prescott marriage could seal the rift between the families. When his brothers and sisters left, Merton remained, determined to restore the Prescott family to its former glory."

"A pity it never happened," Adella said.

"Spoiled kids don't marry servants," Winnifred said. "To make matters worse, both Marleighs and Prescotts ruined Mitchell, tormenting him for not being made Lord of Marleigh ..."

"Kids can be cruel," Adella said.

"Every family makes their own worst enemy; that's what Mitchell is," Winnifred said.

"And he's legally the next Lord of Marleigh?"

Adella asked.

"The law is very clear," Winnifred said.

"So ... you're trapped," Adella said. "You can't fight the law ..."

"Wealthy folk use the law, they don't get abused by it," Winnifred said. "Half of this family has committed acts that would get them arrested, if the law knew ..."

"Poor folk go to jail ...," Adella scowled.

"Then you'd best do what I say," Winnifred said. "We need a way to prove Mitchell did something ..."

"If the next in line is just as bad, how will getting rid of Mitchell fix anything?" Adella asked.

"My brother Enfield is a moron," Winnifred said. "He paints terrible oils, writes awful poetry, and thinks he can sing, but our family can survive 'bad'. Mitchell will drive away the Prescotts and infuriate the Marleighs. Even the Quintons can't stand him."

Winnifred provided a picnic basket. Adella ate all she could and packed up the rest. Yet before she rose to leave ...

"Mitchell mentioned a Manley and a Marston ...?" Adella asked.

"Stella's niece and nephew," Winnifred said. "They arrived with the Quintons."

"Mitchell's taking no chances," Adella said.

"He's stacking every deck," Winnifred said. "He's got that fool Harrington believing he's in line for Lord of Marleigh ..."

"Harrington doesn't care about anything but money," Adella said.

"That's for the best," Winnifred said. "We can work with that."

Before dawn, Adella crawled back into her hideaway, pushing her picnic basket before her. Fortunately, it wasn't baking; Mitchell's fire must have burned out. Yawning, she changed into her nightgown and wrapped in her new, thick quilt.

Sweating, Adella awoke amid an unexpected silence, then checked the study and nursery. Finding both empty, she slipped out for a visit to the privy, then returned. Yet she was barely back in her hideaway when the family returned from lunch, talking loudly. The study remained empty, however Natalie entered the nursery, carrying both babies. She nursed them, burped them, and then laid them side-by-side in their crib. Both babies seemed already asleep, and she left at once.

That night, as Adella was about to sneak out through the nursery, her secret door accidentally slipped from her grip. It slammed down, and a second later one baby began crying, and then the other started. Lydia entered only a minute later and tried to quiet their wails. One baby over each shoulder, she walked them back and forth in the nursery, speaking soothingly but with little success.

Trapped, Adella peeked through the crack. The

nursery door was wide open. With Lydia there, even if she left through the study, she couldn't sneak into Winnifred's room without being seen.

Natalie stumbled into the nursery, looking half asleep. She didn't speak, just took one of the twins and began walking beside Lydia.

"I was hoping you wouldn't awaken," Lydia said.

Natalie shrugged.

Two hours later, after both women laid the sleeping babies in their crib and departed, Adella crawled out, careful not to make any noise. Dressed in her black dress and carrying the empty picnic basket, she snuck past the sleeping twins, and crept across the hall into Winnifred's room. Her windows were dark and no lanterns lit.

"*Winnifred ...?*" Adella whispered as she approached the bed.

"Oh!" Winnifred gasped, suddenly awakening. "I ... seem to have drifted off ..."

"The twins ...," Adella said.

"I heard them," Winnifred said, striking a match and lighting a candle. "This arrangement isn't working, is it?"

"It's worse," Adella said. "No one in the nursery had any conversations and no one came into the study all day ... although the boy relit his fire."

"We must try something else," Winnifred said. "Besides, eventually you'll get caught ... no matter how well we hide you."

"What can we do?" Adella asked.

"It's useful for me to hear what's being said in the nursery and study, but it still leaves me deaf to most of the house," Winnifred said. "I need you to spy for me all over Marleigh Manor."

"I'll be seen ...!" Adella argued.

"Yes, you will," Winnifred said. "That's my plan."

From a writing desk, Adella fetched papers and ink, and Winnifred scribed three letters.

* * * * * * * * * * * * * * * * * * *

Dear Mr. Reed Crawford Fulton, please drive into the village today and deliver these two letters, the first to Mr. Galstrom, the innkeeper, the second to Mr. Cotton, whose farm is near the outskirts of the village, before sunset. In two days, you'll return to the village, and from Mr. Galstrom, receive the granddaughter of a friend of mine, Miss Adella Hester Cumberbatch, who will be staying at the inn. Please bring her to me.

Thank you for your service,
Winnifred Eastaughffe Marleigh/Northcott

* * * * * * * * * * * * * * * * * * *

Dear Mr. Galstrom, I wish you to receive the granddaughter of a friend of mine, Miss Adella Hester Cumberbatch, who will require a private room at your inn. Due to unusual traveling circumstances, she will arrive at your door in the middle of the night. Please see she is provided with all she desires, and do not bother

her with questions. I will send Mr. Reed Crawford Fulton with our carriage to retrieve her as soon as possible. Present your bill to me personally and I will cover all expenses, and a handsome gratuity in exchange for your quiet discretion regarding this matter.

Thank you for your service,
Winnifred Eastaughffe Marleigh/Northcott

* * * * * * * * * * * * * * * * *

Dear Mr. Cotton, I am again in need of your discreet services. A personage whose name is unimportant will be awaiting you at the top of the hill overlooking Marleigh Manor tonight at the hour of midnight exactly. Please bring your wagon and transport this person away. There is no need for you to speak to this person. Deliver them safely to Mr. Galstrom's inn; he will be expecting them. Then, at an appropriate hour, come to Marleigh Manor and I will reward you generously for this errand. Speak to no one of this. Please don't fail me.

Thank you for your service,
Winnifred Eastaughffe Marleigh/Northcott

* * * * * * * * * * * * * * * * *

Adella read all three messages.

"The granddaughter of a friend of yours ...?" Adella asked.

"I had lots of friends when I was young, while Morley was still alive," Winnifred said. "No one will question your claim."

"B-b-but ...," Adella stammered.

"I'll see you get a room ... a real room of your own," Winnifred said. "You won't need to sneak around anymore. You can go anywhere and talk to anyone ..."

"Why ...?" Adella asked.

"As my friend, everyone will try to endear themselves to you, to try and figure out why you're here," Winnifred said.

"Why will I be here?" Adella asked.

"Let's say ... your mother is off to Paris and didn't want to leave you alone, so she sent you to visit your god-mother," Winnifred said.

"You're my god-mother ...?" Adella asked.

"Yes," Winnifred said. "You'll have access to the whole house ... and be part of the living again."

"Not a ghost ...?" Adella asked.

"We may yet need the ghost," Winnifred said. "Your hideaway will still allow you to spy on conversations ... and you can endear yourself as part of our household. I'll provide a cloak and luggage to make you look like a traveler. The one thing I won't provide is money. With money, you could flee across the countryside ... but I need you to return. I require your word, Adella; will you flee ... or come back?"

"Again, you leave me no choice," Adella frowned.

Winnifred grinned.

The next day passed slowly. Mitchell spent hours in his study, writing, drawing, and drinking brandy. No one visited him. Grace and Natalie gossiped in the nursery, but Adella couldn't pay attention; *tonight everything would change.*

As a precaution, Adella took the one silver coin she'd kept.

That evening, Adella said good-bye to her hideaway and snuck into Winnifred's room. She returned her picnic basket for the last time. The table was laden with food, covered platters of steaming dishes and delectable pastries. Adella ate with abandon.

"You'll need to sneak outside after eleven," Winnifred said. "It's snowing, and you won't want to suffer the cold any longer than necessary. If there's no old, bearded man waiting for you with a two-horse cart at the top of the hill, don't stay too long ... come right back. You'll never make it to the village on foot."

After Adella had eaten all she could, Winnifred had her dig through her wardrobes. She pulled on three sets of thick socks. Winnifred gave her a sturdy set of boots too big for her feet, yet the extra socks made them tight. She kept her black dress over her green chemise, and was given a thick hooded cloak, maroon on the outside, soft fur on the inside.

"Keep the hood up," Winnifred said. "Don't look directly at Mr. Cotton; it's best he doesn't see your face. When he drops you at the inn, knock loudly, and Mr. Galstrom will admit you. Tell him nothing. You'll have one day in town; walk about, be seen by as many townsfolk as you can, and tell anyone who asks that your grandmother arranged for you to stay with me. Always refer to me as Mistress Winnifred Eastaughffe Marleigh/Northcott. If people ask, tell them you've never seen me before ... and then ask what they know about me. Don't expect them to answer truthfully; they know who I am. Remember; you've never seen Marleigh Manor and don't know how far it is from the village."

"I'll remember," Adella promised.

"Forgive me if I'm anxious," Winnifred said. "We won't get another chance like this."

She pointed at a large gray carpet-bag suitcase strapped shut. "Take that with you. Don't bother to open it; it's nothing but towels ... in case someone offers to lift it for you, it must weigh like clothes. When you get back, I'll fill it with dresses, and you can carry them to your new bedroom."

"I won't fail you," Adella promised.

"You can leave by any door except the front," Winnifred said. "Camden Hadley Prescott sits by that door every night. In the morning, I'll summon Middleton and tell him of your imminent arrival; he won't be happy. I'll try to get you a nice room ... but I can't promise that."

Adella felt nervous. She'd spent the last three months trapped in this house. Now she was about to escape ... but only temporarily. She had one silver coin, not enough to buy food or shelter until spring. She could sell the dress and cloak she was wearing, but even their profits wouldn't last.

Unless a miracle happened, she'd have to come back.

At eleven-thirty, Adella and Winnifred exchanged a silent nod, and Adella left. The halls were empty. She exited through the family room into thick snow.

She ducked to pass under Mitchell's and Middleton's windows, in case someone looked outside. The moon wasn't out, yet enough starlight shined that she could see the distant hill from which she'd first seen Marleigh Manor. Yet she couldn't wait; the deep snow slowed her, and she had a long ways to walk.

After she reached the road, her path was slightly easier. Wagon tracks lay driven through the snow, yet were half the width of her boots, and the snow had partially melted and refrozen. Each step crunched loudly; she glanced back at all three floors of the huge manor, fearing she'd be heard, watching for faces in the few lighted windows. She had to high-step, and then drag each boot out of crusty whiteness. She was both sweating and freezing before she reached the base of the hill and started climbing.

She was halfway up when she heard the clatter of a rig; *Mr. Cotton had gotten Winnifred's letter.*

Before she neared the summit, two speckled horses came plowing through the snow and topped the rise. The driver started to stop his horses, spied her, and slowed his horses, yet let them continue. She moved to the side of the road as he approached. He stopped right before her.

He reached out; she took his hand, let him pull her aboard, and settled onto the driving board beside him. Without a word, he flicked his reins. His horses started off, heading toward Marleigh Manor, and he drove through its gates, then turned his horses around in the circle and drove out again.

Adella never looked at him, and he never spoke. His horses needed prompting at the base of the hill, then struggled their way through their former ruts. Despite winter-shod hooves, their horses slipped more than a few steps, yet finally topped the hill and descended out of sight of Marleigh Manor.

Other than loud crunches of snow, clip-clops of hooves, and creaks of the wagon, no sounds disturbed the night. Adella wanted to watch their route, yet a chill wind blasted her face, and she tilted her head to keep her hood as closed as possible. Riding in the wagon wasn't any warmer than walking; she could do nothing to warm up.

She stared downstream into darkness as they crossed a small stone bridge over a frozen creek ... where she'd washed off the blood of the driver and sent her incriminating dress into oblivion.

An hour later, the stars mostly blocked by clouds, she spied the village; had she been walking, she'd have frozen to death. It was a small village, barely two dozen buildings crowded together, divided by a single narrow road. Every building was buried in snow, and surrounded by pines laden with frozen white. No movement was visible, not even branches waving in the wind. Right before an icicle-hanging sign so frosted over it couldn't be read, Mr. Cotton drug his horses to a halt.

"This is the inn," Mr. Cotton said, speaking for the first time.

"Thank you," Adella said automatically, and he held out his hand as she lifted her carpet-bag. She took his hand to steady her, and stepped down off the wagon, crunching into the thick snow.

She stepped up to the door of the inn, then turned and waited. Mr. Cotton rode off, his long gray hair sticking out from a thick coat, hat, and muffler.

She waited as he rode away. When his horses drew his wagon out of sight, she hammered her fist upon the frosty door. It hurt; cold had numbed her fingers. Yet she heard movement inside and waited less than a minute for the door to open.

"Miss Cumberbatch ...?" a man's voice asked.

"Mr. Galstrom," Adella said, and she pushed inside.

He was a tall, thin man, younger than she'd expected. He had long brown hair, tied back, a short, scruffy beard, and was holding an ornate oil lantern in one hand; the only light in the room save a dimly-glowing fireplace.

He closed the door behind her, and she threw off her hood. She spied four small tables crowded together before the fireplace, where tiny flames flickered; she hurried to hold her hands before the flames.

"Chilly night for traveling," Mr. Galstrom said, lighting some candles from his lantern, and setting them about the room. "Would you like some hot tea before I show you to your room?"

"Please," Adella said, drinking in the heat.

The kettle was already hot; he poured and set her cup and saucer onto a table beside her, then held out the chair closest to the fireplace.

"Thank you, sir," Adella said.

Hot tea and the warm fire quickly restored her. She could've stayed there longer, but Mr. Galstrom stood near a narrow stair and seemed to be waiting on her. Rising, she thanked him for the tea.

"My pleasure," Mr. Galstrom said. "Your room is ready."

She allowed him to carry her carpet-bag and ascend the stair before her. He opened a door and set her bag beside a small bed buried in quilts. Adella was delighted to see a tiny stove with a grate, red glowing from inside it, sitting in the corner. Mr. Galstrom handed her a large brass key.

"If there's anything you need in the night, there's a bell on the hearth downstairs," Mr. Galstrom said. "Ring and wait; someone will attend you."

"Thank you for waiting up so late," Adella said.

Mr. Galstrom nodded politely, then stepped into the hallway and closed her door. Staring at the key in her hand, Adella locked her door, then cast off her cloak and huddled beside her stove, which was warm but not hot. A coal bucket sat beside it; Adella took the tongs, opened the grate, and lifted several large lumps onto the glowing coals. She smiled; she'd learned to use tongs watching smiths forge at construction sites, yet she'd never used tongs; carpenters threw coal onto fires with their hands.

Slowly the new coals brightened and the air grew warmer. Her room was tiny, yet had a reading table a little bigger than her combined handspans, and a stool, which she moved to sit before the warm stove. She had a window which was shuttered; she suspected it looked down upon the town's only road. Her room was only slightly larger than her hideaway in Marleigh Manor, and its smallness heated up quickly.

All she needed to do was wait for Reed.

Checking to insure her door was firmly locked, she removed her outer dress and crawled into the first bed she'd slept in since her father had died.

Its comfort felt luxurious.

Chapter 8

Adella awoke late. Daylight glowed yellow-white through frosted, snow-capped shutter slats, illuminating her room. She pulled tight her warm blankets; she didn't want to get up. The tiny room looked deliciously comfortable in real light. She appreciated having a window, and relished the soft mattress under her, so much more comfortable than the thin blanket she'd been sleeping on.

She unburied herself from soft quilts and dressed quickly in the cool air; the coal in her tiny fireplace had burned out, yet she'd no desire to stay hidden. Excitement filled her, free from the entrapment of her secret hideaway. She could go out, see things, make noise, and talk to people. Fearlessly, she laid her warm cloak over her arm, unlocked her door, and descended the narrow stair.

"Good morning, Miss Cumberbatch!" Mr. Galstrom said as she reached the bottom step.

She smiled at being properly addressed.

"Please, call me Adella," she said.

"Any guest of Mrs. Winnifred Northcott may have anything she likes," Mr. Galstrom said. "Would you care for some hot breakfast?"

"My mother told me to always call her Mistress Winnifred Eastaughffe Marleigh/Northcott," Adella said. "Actually, I've never met her; she and grandmother were friends. And yes, I am hungry."

"We'll take care of that," Mr. Galstrom said. "Take any seat."

Only one other table was occupied; two men sat at it. Before each sat a steaming bowl and wooden mug. They stared as she sat at the table closest to the fireplace, laying her cloak across the back of a chair. She paused to warm her hands before the fireplace, then Mr. Galstrom arrived from the kitchen with a steaming bowl, the handle of a spoon sticking out of it.

"Here's some hot porridge, and it'll be just a moment to toast your bread," Mr. Galstrom said. "We've got some sweet honey and berry jam, too. I could have Mrs. Galstrom fry some eggs and bacon, if you'd prefer."

"Perhaps later," Adella said. "I was told a driver

would be coming for me ..."

"That would be Mr. Reed," Mr. Galstrom said.
"He's the master of stables at Marleigh Manor. I'm
afraid I don't know when he'll arrive, but my orders are
to provide anything you might need."

Mr. Galstrom vanished into the kitchen again,
and emerged with a hot cup of tea and a jar of jam.
Minutes later, he reappeared with a plate of freshly-
toasted bread.

Adella reveled in the pleasure of eating hot food
in the company of others. She stole enough glances at
both men to notice them stealing frequent glances at her.
One was short and heavy, the other tall and lean. She
wondered how they fed themselves through the longest,
thickest mustaches she'd ever seen. Yet she had a
mission to accomplish.

"Gentlemen ...," she acknowledged their
presence.

"Our pleasure," the short man bowed as best he
could while sitting.

"So ... going to Marleigh Manor?" the tall man
asked.

"My mother was required in Paris, so I'm being
sent to stay with my grandmother's friend, Mistress
Winnifred Eastaughffe Marleigh/Northcott."

"She's a great lady," the short man said.

"Highly respected," the tall man added.

"I know nothing about her save that she and my
grandmother were friends," Adella said. "I'd love to hear

anything you know. Oh, I'm Miss Adella
Cumberbatch."

"Mr. Heap, at your service," the short man said.

"Mr. Murdstone, at yours and your family's," the
tall man said. "I'm afraid we only know Mrs. Winnifred
by reputation ..."

"Mistress Winnifred Eastaughffe
Marleigh/Northcott," Adella corrected him.

"Of course; please forgive me," Mr. Murdstone
said.

"Mistress Winnifred Eastaughffe
Marleigh/Northcott is of the wealthiest and most-noble
family in this district," Mr. Heap said. "I never met her
husband, God rest his soul, but she's been the jewel of
this village since she returned with her precious little
daughter."

"She has a daughter ...?" Adella asked.

"Rufina Northcott, a sweet child," Mr. Heap
said. "I believe she'll be ten soon."

"I'm afraid the news isn't all good," Mr.
Murdstone said. "Mistress Winnifred Eastaughffe
Marleigh/Northcott has suffered several illnesses since
she returned, after her saintly husband passed. All
report she's stricken to her bed."

"That's terrible," Adella said.

"It's a great sadness for anyone young to suffer
the invalidity of the aged," Mr. Heap said. "Yet I hear
her spirits have never dimmed; the fire of life burns hot
inside her."

174

"That's good to hear," Adella said. "How far away is Marleigh Manor?"

Both gave the answer she expected, and she kept the conversation loud enough for everyone to hear, even in the kitchen. She asked many questions; Mr. Murdstone managed a shipping company, which his new young wife had inherited. Mr. Heap was a humble lawyer who'd recently acquired a string of apartments in a district by the river from a widow he described as jolly and wealthy. Both knew each other from long acquaintance, and were intending to return to London soon ... after certain contracts had been signed by a notorious character named Mr. Quilp, whom neither held in high regard, yet had offered to buy Mr. Heap's apartment buildings.

Having long finished breakfast, Adella announced that a brisk walk was what she needed.

"I may be here at least two months, so I'd like to see the village," Adella said, and she stood and faced Mr. Galstrom. "I'm sure I won't be long ... this cold is beastly."

All three men stood when she did, and each bowed and wished her good health and happiness. Mr. Galstrom promised tea hot would be ready when she returned. With a polite nod, she drew on her thick cloak, and Mr. Heap held the door for her.

The brisk air was bright with morning light reflecting off the snow. She strode through the thick drifts, seeing a shop where a door opened just long enough for a woman to sweep the dust out onto its sheltered porch.

The shop was a feed store. She wasn't a farmer; Adella knew their wares only by name. However, she stared at their selection of carpentry tools; she was experienced with each. Yet she didn't remark; she was pretending to be a high-born young woman, and doubted if wealthy hands ever touched tools of hard work. Purposefully she fell into conversation with Mrs. Wickfield, the middle-aged wife of the shopkeeper.

Adella and Mrs. Wickfield held almost the same conversation she'd had with Mr. Heap and Mr. Murdstone. However, she treaded carefully; Mrs. Wickfield was smart, educated, and sturdy, fully down to Earth. She taught a tiny school for the few children of the village. She equaled any man on pleasantries, yet her questions included those no gentleman would ask.

"Have you come to Marleigh Manor seeking a husband?" Mrs. Wickfield asked.

Adella hated inventing excuses on the spot.

"I've not purposed to," Adella said.

"That would be a pity," Mrs. Wickfield said. "There're plenty of young, single men in Marleigh Manor who could only benefit from a woman's influence."

"I'm sure my mother would agree, but I've no desire to marry ... until I find a man I deem worthy," Adella said.

"That's wise ... yet another pity," Mrs. Wickfield

said. "Perfect husbands are few and hard to find.
Examine suitors without haste; in Marleigh Manor, first
appearances are often wrong."

"My mother would never leave me with people
unsuitable," Adella said.

"I meant no offense," Mrs. Wickfield said. "Mrs.
Winnifred is the cream of any society; that I know."

"Mistress Winnifred Eastaughffe
Marleigh/Northcott," Adella corrected.

Mrs. Wickfield's implied questions grew more
personal, yet Adella enjoyed talking to the woman,
whose intelligence was obvious. Several hours they
talked, and then Adella returned to the cold, trudging
through the snow, wondering what else there was to see.
Yet no other shops existed; she was forced to return to
the inn. Mr. Heap and Mr. Murdstone rode past her in
a buggy as she reached its door; both waved to her and
tipped their hats. She nodded to them, then re-entered
the inn.

Mr. Galstrom was busy, and an elderly woman
who could've been his mother served Adella hot tea.
Adella asked if the fire in her room had been stoked; the
old lady promised to attend to it, and then returned to
the kitchen. A ten year old boy then ran out and up the
stairs with a brass key. Adella warmed herself by the
fireplace and waited.

Finishing her tea, Adella arose and ascended to
her room. He'd stuffed her furnace with coal, which was
now blazing; heat was wafting off her stove, but not as

badly as off the fireplace in her hideaway. She sat on her bed, bored yet worried; she wouldn't have to hide inside Marleigh Manor anymore, yet she'd have to pass herself off as a stranger to people she already didn't trust.

She could run away, but where could she go? One silver coin wouldn't support her long in the heart of winter. She had no choice; her options were limited. Until the snows melted, she had to trust Winnifred.

No driver or other visitors arrived. Adella ate supper alone in the downstairs parlor and sat sipping tea. She peeked outside to see it was snowing, yet held no desire to endure its cold again. When she could drink no more tea, she visited their privy, which felt colder than outside, and then returned to her room.

The next day, shortly after breakfast, she heard a horse-drawn carriage drive past the inn. It turned around, and then pulled up right before its door. A large young man with black hair entered.

"Miss Cumberbatch, this is your driver, Mr. Reed Crawford Fulton," Mr. Galstrom said. "If your bag is ready, I'll bring it down ..."

"It is ... and my cloak is on my bed," Adella said, and Mr. Galstrom nodded. She turned to Reed. "Thank you for coming to collect me."

"My pleasure, Miss Cumberbatch," Reed bowed politely.

Reed was a handsome man, solidly built, yet Adella said no more. She couldn't reveal she knew about his illegitimacy ... or occupation ... or character.

Mr. Galstrom came back down and handed her bag to Reed and her cloak to her. She returned her key to him.

"Miss Cumberbatch, I personally thank you for staying at my humble inn," Mr. Galstrom said. "Please extend my warmest regards to Mistress Winnifred Eastaughffe Marleigh/Northcott, and if ever my services are needed, please consider me at your beck and call."

"Thank you, Mr. Galstrom," Adella said. "It has been a delightful stay."

With a nod, Reed opened and held the door.

Read's covered carriage was far more comfortable than Mr. Cotton's open wagon. He held the door open for her and assisted her inside, then set her bag beside her feet.

"There's a warming pan under that blanket, if you wish," Reed said.

Delighted, Adella pulled the warm blanket over her skirt and nodded her thanks. He closed her door, then climbed atop the driver's seat and began to shake his reins. Two horses pulled the carriage into motion, and Adella watched out the tiny windows as they started back to Marleigh Manor.

The coals in her metal warming pan were still burning. Their warmth soothed her nerves. She was trading hiding for pretending, yet her chances of getting caught seemed unchanged. She'd known what would happen to her if she'd been caught squatting. *What would happen if she was discovered as a fraud?*

Would Winnifred cast her out?

Her fears grew as they rode closer, yet there was no turning back.

They topped the hill and Marleigh Manor appeared, almost unseen in the snowfall.

Reed shouted at the horses as they struggled us down the hill; he didn't want them hurting themselves, and Adella couldn't blame them; their warm stable was in sight, and her warming pan no longer felt warm. Yet they creaked and crunched through the snow to the front of the manor.

Reed jumped down and opened her door; Adella was shocked to see his red, wind-burnt face.

"Oh, you're freezing!" Adella exclaimed as he helped her out. "Come inside ...!"

His smile failed.

"I can't ... but thank you," Reed said. "Got to get these horses inside and water them before they freeze."

Reed took her bag and led her to the door, pounded its huge knocker, and opened it. As Adella stepped inside, Camden came forward.

"Miss Cumberbatch, to see Mrs. Winnifred," Reed said.

"Welcome to Marleigh Manor, Miss Cumberbatch," Camden said, and he took her bag and nodded.

"Thank you, Mr. Reed ...," Adella said.

Reed nodded, yet quickly before Camden closed

the door, Reed looked her up and down. She wondered what he was thinking, and then the door fully closed.

"I am Mr. Camden Prescott, at your service," Camden said. "I was not informed Lady Winnifred was expecting a visitor."

"She's been long corresponding with my grandmother, and agreed to host me while my mother was away," Adella said. "Please take me to her at once."

Camden glared at her impertinence, yet Adella had to play the role of a noble-born daughter ... and she wouldn't feel safe until she was in Winnifred's room.

"As you wish," Camden said, and he led the way.

Adella glanced curiously about, pretending to be seeing the house for the first time. Its bright colors, which she'd only seen in shadows, stood out in the daylight. Several young boys hurried into the hallway, saw her, and suddenly stopped, staring. Adella didn't smile; she'd seen them sneaking into the kitchen at night, although they'd never seen her.

As they passed the music room, Stella was standing beside Grace with two men Adella didn't know, one old, another young. Camden didn't speak to them, yet their conversation stopped as they saw Adella. Their eyes followed as she paraded past.

Camden opened the door to the new wing and led her inside.

Lydia was sitting before the fire, knitting, and she looked up. Adella ignored her and followed Camden in silence, but then hard footsteps approached. Mitchell entered the entry room, headed for the main manor. He stopped and stared at Adella.

"Camden ...?" he asked.

"Miss Cumberbatch, here to see Mrs. Winnifred," Camden said.

Mitchell looked affronted. Eyes drilled into Adella as he stepped to block their passage.

"Master Mitchell Myerscough Marleigh, at your service," Mitchell said. "Welcome to Marleigh Manor."

"Adella Hester Cumberbatch," Adella replied. "Thank you for your welcome."

"Mrs. Winnifred didn't inform me of your coming," Mitchell said brusquely.

"Perhaps you should accompany me to her presence," Adella said.

Mitchell stared into her eyes, a silent challenge which Adella knew terrified the Prescotts. He stood inches away, as imposing close up as he'd seemed through the cracks in her hideaway.

"I'll ... allow you to get reacquainted first," Mitchell said, and he suddenly stormed past Adella, flung open the door to the main manor, and stomped through it.

Adella glanced at Lydia, whose young mouth hung open.

"Allow ...?" Adella asked irritatedly, yet then she gestured for Camden to continue, giving Lydia no chance to answer.

Moments later, they arrived at Winnifred's

room.

"Mrs. Winnifred, I present to you Miss Cumberbatch," Camden announced.

"Thank you, Master Camden," Winnifred's voice came from within. "Please show her in."

Camden stepped out of the doorway, and Adella stepped inside.

"Adella ...!" Winnifred called. "So lovely to finally meet you! Come, come closer, child. Take off that cloak and let me see you."

Adella walked to the foot of her bed and nodded, dropping her cloak onto the chair where she'd laid Letitia's chemise.

"You're the mirror image of your grandmother when she was your age," Winnifred smiled. "What a beauty she was! Thank you, Master Camden."

Both looked at him; with a slight bow, Camden set her carpetbag down and walked away.

Winnifred and Adella exchanged a glance.

"I was worried you wouldn't be back," Winnifred whispered.

"Where else did I have to go?" Adella asked.

"Young girls don't always choose wisely," Winnifred whispered.

"Now what ...?" Adella asked.

"We wait," Winnifred whispered. "It won't be long."

Shortly afterwards, a young girl entered carrying a tea tray with two cups.

"Hortence Jane Dryden, this is the granddaughter of a friend of mine, Miss Adella Hester Cumberbatch," Winnifred said to the girl.

"A pleasure to meet you, madam," Hortence said.

"The pleasure is mine," Adella said.

"Adella will be our guest until her mother returns," Winnifred said. "Please take her to the kitchen and see she gets something to eat ..."

"I'm not ...," Adella began, but Winnifred's eyes flashed. "I ... I mean, I'm not intending to be any bother ..."

"No bother at all," Winnifred said. "Hortence, leave the tea, escort her to the kitchen, and summon Master Mitchell for me ... I wish to see him right away."

"I will, madam," Hortence said, and she set the tea beside her bed, poured one cup, and bowed before leading the route Adella knew well.

Adella asked no questions as she was again paraded through the halls. The music room was practically crowded now, and all stared as Adella followed Hortence. More heads peeked out of doors and from around corners.

In the kitchen, which looked entirely different with sunlight shining through windows, two elderly cooks worked side-by-side.

"Gentlemen, this is Miss Adella Hester Cumberbatch, a guest of Mrs. Winnifred," Hortence said. "Miss Cumberbatch, this is Mr. Hallewell Ogden

Prescott and Mr. Hartford Ogden Prescott, our chief cooks."

Each paused and bowed respectfully. Both looked old and weary, yet had bright eyes.

"Brothers ...?" Adella asked.

"Only since Hartford was born," Hallewell said.

"Which was the best thing that ever happened to him," Hartford said. "Without me, he couldn't stir gravy."

Adella couldn't help but smile.

"Miss Cumberbatch just arrived, and Mrs. Winnifred asks that she be fed," Hortence said.

"I'm really not that hungry," Adella said.

Brothers exchanged glances.

"I'm sure Mrs. Winnifred wouldn't have asked if you didn't need something," Hallewell said. "Would you like to sit in the dining hall?"

"Oh, anywhere is fine," Adella said, not wanting to be alone at a huge banquet table.

"Here, sit by the window," Hartford said, setting down his rag and wiping his hands on an apron. He led her to a small table and pulled out a chair.

Before Adella could object, enough food for three meals was set before her, along with hot tea and scones.

Both Hallewell and Hartford looked heavily wrinkled, with thinning white-hair, identical mustaches, and the same paunches. Hallewell was shorter, his face slightly thinner, and Hartford bore a faded scar along one cheek. Both wore worn, white, short-sleeved shirts and matching aprons. They moved about the kitchen with obvious familiarity.

An elderly woman came in as Adella nibbled at her feast. She eyed Adella yet said nothing; she went to a pile of dirty dishes beside the sink and began washing.

Adella felt strange, sitting in plain view after having so often snuck in to steal food. Yet she was surprised at how accepting everyone seemed. She wasn't ignored as a child or a carpenter, which would've happened if they knew who she was.

Watching Prescotts work reminded her that, eighty years ago, they owned this house, and another just as big, before Captain Marston Ramsay Marleigh had married into their family, probably burned down their other house, and ruined their lives. This alone validated her choosiness; one bad marriage devastates a family for generations.

Finally Camden appeared in the kitchen, carrying her bag in one arm and her cloak in the other.

"When you're ready, Miss Cumberbatch, a room has been prepared," Camden said.

"I'm quite finished," Adella said. "My thanks to the cooks."

Hallewell and Hartford bowed appreciatively.

Adella followed Camden out into the main foyer and ascended the curved stairs. She'd never risked trespassing into this part of the manor, and was amazed at how many doors lined each hallway. Marleigh Manor was indeed larger than she'd suspected.

Camden led her into a side-wing, and then they descended another stair.

The woodwork here was old and worn. Paint peeled in corners. Walls looked warped by decades of moisture. She glanced disdainfully at the untended woodwork, then they turned to the right and entered yet another wing. The woodwork here wasn't new, but not as aged as the middle; this wing was built long after the last, yet was only halfway toward disrepair, not fresh and polished like the main section or new wing. It was also smaller.

Camden led her to the far end of the wing and opened the last door on the right.

"This room is yours," Camden said.

Adella glanced inside; its only furniture was an old bed that looked saggy despite its ragged quilt. No fireplace was visible.

"This is where you house guests ...?" Adella asked.

"Master Mitchell insisted on this room," Camden frowned as he said. "If this room isn't satisfactory, I suggest you describe it to Mrs. Winnifred as 'the old boarding room' in the previous Marleigh living quarters."

"Thank you, I will," Adella said.

"Do you require help unpacking?" Camden offered.

"Unpack onto what ...?" Adella asked.

"Miss Cumberbatch, I'm sorry if your room isn't

to your liking," Camden said. "If I may be so bold, there are better residences. I suggest you speak to Mrs. Winnifred ... but not until after lunch."

"How will I know ...?" Adella asked.

"A bell is rung in each wing for meals," Camden said. "If that is all ...?"

"Thank you, Mr. Camden," Adella said.

As he began the long walk back, she stared at her room. Cracks around the broken-shuttered window leaked cold air, causing a slight breeze. Her view through the frosted glass showed a barn, behind which stretched low, flat fields, with a small frozen pond and forested hills in the distance. Wide gaps yawned between peeling, warped wall panels. Faded white paint on the ceiling showed brownish stains of water damage. Flecks of ceiling paint spotted her gouged and splintery floor.

Her hideaway was a palace compared to this.

Adella had to tell Winnifred ... yet Camden had suggested she wait until after lunch. *Was he suggesting this for her benefit ... or his ...?*

Adella had no choice but to trust Winnifred; *she couldn't afford to trust anyone else.*

A few seemed trustworthy; Grace, Lydia, and Rowena had sounded honest ... at least in the conversations she'd eavesdropped upon. Yet she knew some couldn't be trusted, like Mitchell and Harrington.

Adella dropped her carpetbag onto the floor and sat on the bed ... a thin mattress over crossed ropes.

It sagged deeply.

Noises came; conversations wafted through thin walls and echoed down the hall. Adella stood and closed her door, noting to never speak loudly in here ... unless she wanted everyone to hear. Yet she had nothing to do but wait.

When the bell rang, Adella shoved her carpet bag under her miserable bed, draped her cloak over it, and then hurried to find her way back. She left her door closed; no point cooling off the whole wing. It took five minutes to arrive at the dining room table, where everyone else was already seated. All eyes stared at her.

The children were seated at a smaller table in an adjoining room, and a servant closed the door between the rooms to muffle their conversations.

"Please, join us," Mitchell said. "Everyone, this is Miss Adella Hester Cumberbatch, here to grace us for a short stay."

Several older men stood as Adella was seated. Adella nodded her thanks, then stared back at their curious eyes. True Marleighs sat at one end of the table, with Mitchell at their head. Berkeley-Marleighs crowded the other end, with Stella opposite Mitchell. Adella sat in the middle, closer to the Marleighs, with two empty chairs between her and the nearest Berkeley-Marleigh; Norton, Stella's brother-in-law.

Wealthy families even ate by politics!

A young man was asked to say grace, and afterwards, bowls and platters of food were placed on the table. Her wine glass was filled, and Adella drank.

Enfield, Winnifred's brother, began introductions as all started to eat. Names flew past far too quickly for her to catch. Some Adella already knew or had heard. Stella was the only Berkeley-Marleigh she knew; five were introduced as Quintons and two as Manleys. Everyone nodded or waved as they were named.

"Miss Cumberbatch's mother is on business in Paris, and Winnifred agreed to guest her daughter until she returns," Mitchell said. "By correspondence, of course."

"Welcome, my dear," Letitia said. "I hope your stay is pleasant."

Adella thanked her. Letitia was the large wife of Middleton, the sickly Master of Marleigh Manor. She appeared to be wearing her voluminous white silk chemise, stolen by the ghost, under a ghastly yellow dress with pink trim. Adella wondered if she'd be as cheerfully inviting if she knew Adella was the mysterious 'ghost'.

Adella was asked to tell a little about herself, and repeated the story Winnifred had invented.

"I was born in Castleford, on my grandfather's estate, north-east of Sheffield," Adella said. "I went with him on outings and business trips; I'm afraid I was never the music-and-needlepoint daughter my mother wanted. She did take me to every theater and ballet performance, which I enjoyed. Back home, I liked to ride my surrey over the countryside ... in spring and summer, of course. I detest heavy snows."

"As do I," Grace said, nodding. "Winter turns homes into prisons."

Conversation turned to the weather, and several men reminisced about skiing, snowball fights, and other wintry games. Adella listened intently, glad to let them speak, rather than be interrogated. Yet she tried not to look at Mitchell, who glared daggers at her.

After lunch, Letitia invited her to the music room.

"I'll be there presently, but first I must attend on Mrs. Winnifred; my mother insisted," Adella said.

"We'll await you there," Letitia said.

"The old boarding room ...?" Winnifred asked, frowning. "That's where we stored tools and firewood."

"A pity there's no tools now," Adella said. "I could begin repairs."

"Don't do carpentry!" Winnifred warned. "How bad is it?"

"Cold air gusts through the window's cracks, and its only furniture is a rotting bed," Adella said.

"What would it take to make it livable?" Winnifred asked.

"A match," Adella said, yet when Winnifred didn't smile, "Sealer on the window, glue or tar ..."

"I could get you a better room, but not a better location," Winnifred said. "Being on the far side will let you eavesdrop on conversations you'll never hear in this wing. Tools and maintenance supplies are in Reed's room, adjacent to the barn. If I were to get him out, could you fetch what you need?"

"I could claim I wanted to see your horses," Adella said. "Is his room locked?"

"There're few locks in Marleigh Manor," Winnifred said. "Most are rusted solid. It's said Captain Marston hated locks for anyone but himself. I'm afraid my brothers enjoy bursting in on others ... as long as no one can surprise them."

"My hideaway is more secure than your rooms," Adella whispered.

"Tomorrow, just after breakfast, I'll send a boy to fetch Reed to come and see me," Winnifred said. "His presence in the house is forbidden, but I can't go to him, so Mitchell will have to allow it. Every eye will be watching him; you'll have plenty of time."

"I'll manage," Adella said.

"Good," Winnifred said. "Now we must prepare for tonight. Your bag is still full of towels. Bring the towels back when all are sleeping. I'll give you several nice dresses; you must start wearing them tomorrow."

Winnifred directed her to her wardrobe, and again Adella rummaged through it. With Winnifred's approval, Adella selected four elegant dresses and stacked them in the corner.

"Now, go join the household in the music room," Winnifred said. "Listen carefully; I want to hear everything."

Chapter 9

Entering the music room, Adella noticed no one was playing any instrument. Afternoon sunlight was streaming through the windows, making the room warmer and brighter than ever. No children were playing, yet many adults stood watching ... obviously waiting for her.

"Miss Cumberbatch, please come in," Letitia called as Adella stepped into view.

"Adella," Adella said, approaching the circle of people near her, half of whom were seated.

"Adella," Letitia said. "What a lovely name!"

"It was my great-grandmother's name, I'm told," Adella said.

"What type of business is your mother engaged in?" Mitchell asked.

"Mitchell ...!" Letitia exclaimed. "She doesn't need to be reminded that she's been ...!"

"Abandoned," Adella finished her sentence. "My mother wanted me away from our family."

"Nothing terrible, I hope ...?" Letitia asked.

"Father favors a suitor mother and I find unsuitable," Adella said.

"Why didn't she take you to France...?" Letitia asked.

"This suitor lives in Florence," Adella explained.

"Nothing as unsuitable as a bad marriage," Charity said.

"How long will we have the pleasure of your company?" Edwina asked.

"I can't say," Adella said. "It could be a few weeks ... or until the snows melt."

"We'll make your stay as comfortable as we can," Charity said.

"Thank you," Adella said.

"What business is your father in?" Mitchell asked.

"Many kinds," Adella said. "He mostly buys old properties and has our people repair them, then he sells them. With him, I've visited many construction sites."

"What a strange place to take a young girl!" Edwina said.

"I excel both of my brothers at studies," Adella said. "Someone must be able to manage the family business."

"But, when you marry, your skills will go to your husband's family," Mitchell said.

"Which is why I've not yet chosen to marry," Adella said.

"Chosen ...?" Rayden asked.

"Rayden, I'm sure a young lady as pretty as Adella has had many proposals," Letitia said.

"I avoid suitors," Adella said. "When I'm ready, I'm sure they'll appear."

"Your mother sounds as wise as her daughter," Charity said.

"Nonsense," Letitia said. "It's never too early for the elite to produce heirs. You mustn't wait too long."

"I don't plan to," Adella said. "What business supports the Marleigh family?"

"Shipping, timber, and a fleet of workhouses," Mitchell said.

"*Workhouses ...?*" Adella gasped.

At their reactions to her outburst, Adella struggled to control herself. Workhouses were the basest of employments, little better than prisons. Workers couldn't quit, as the cost of their upkeep was always more than their pay, so they never escaped ever-mounting debts. Carpenters despised workhouses. Only those starving to death worked there.

"All this talk of business is upsetting me, too," Charity said. "Let's change the subject. Adella, do you like music?"

"I was never good at it," Adella said. "I'd love to

hear some."

At her prompting, Charity rose, went to the harp, and began strumming. Beautiful sounds flowed from her strings, and all conversations paused to listen.

While Adella stared in rapt amazement, she discretely glanced about. None of the Quintons or Manleys were there. Stella was sitting in the chair hiding the nailed-up coal chute, where Harrington had hidden the stolen silver coins, with a circle of others around her.

While Charity strummed her harp, Enfield slipped behind the piano and sat waiting. When her song ended, he began playing with no less mastery, and she matched his tune.

At the end of their duet, everyone applauded.

"Shall we ladies abscond with Adella, so we can talk in private?" Letitia asked.

"Actually, if you don't mind, it's been an exciting day ... with an early start," Adella said.

"Would you prefer to take a nap before dinner?" Letitia asked.

"If you wouldn't mind," Adella said.

"Can you find your way ...?" Rayden began.

"I'll escort her," Edwina said. "Can't let her get lost on her first day ...!"

Adella was quite sure she could find her way back, but to refuse might look suspicious. Edwina suffered a few dagger-stares as she gestured to Adella, yet both pretended not to notice. They walked back into the foyer, past Camden in his usual chair, puffing away at his pipe.

"What do you think of Marleigh Manor?" Edwina asked.

"I've never lived in a house this big," Adella said. "My family's home is grand, but not half as large."

"We're almost a city," Edwina said.

"I'm afraid I may not remember everyone's name," Adella said.

"We couldn't expect you to," Edwina said. "It took me months."

"You weren't raised here?" Adella asked.

"My husband was," Edwina asked. "I'm a Kimberly ... from York."

"How did you meet Enfield?" Adella asked.

"My father was a business associate of old Morely before he died," Edwina asked. "I met Enfield at our wedding."

"No courtship ...?" Adella asked.

"Not all girls are allowed to be choosy," Edwina said. "Did your mother ... or Winnifred ... speak to you about the Lordship of Marleigh Manor?"

"Lordship ...?" Adella asked. "No, not a word ..."

"It's nothing, just family politics," Edwina said. "We're delighted you've come, but this is a tumultuous time."

"Nothing serious, I hope ...?" Adella asked.

"Nothing women need to worry about," Edwina said. "You said you excelled your brothers at studies;

what subjects did you study?"

"My father hired me tutors for bookkeeping, mostly," Adella said. "Arithmetic, budgeting, ..."

"*Law ...?*" Edwina asked.

"*Law ...?*" Adella repeated. "Women can't be barristers ..."

"But smart women can learn anything," Edwina said.

"Only a little law, concerning taxes," Adella said. "If something happens to father, someone needs to be able so support the family, until my brothers can hire others to bookkeep for them. Father tried teaching them, but one of them are ... mathematicians."

"Inheritance is itself a complex set of laws ...," Edwina said.

"I suppose so," Adella said.

Adella purposefully took a wrong turn to change the subject. Edwina set her on the right path, and soon they walked down the hall to her room. Upon reaching her door, Adella faked a yawn and excused herself.

"Have a lovely rest," Edwina said before she closed the door.

Inheritance law; Edwina had been seeking to reveal her as a legal plant, an expert arrived to upset the passing of the family reins. How many others would pump her for information? All these people cared about was the mantle of leadership when Middleton's illness reached its inevitable end.

In some ways, Adella couldn't blame them. In

other ways, no Marleigh or Prescott deserved to live in wealthy splendor. She'd known better people; none had lived like this.

Adella didn't need rest; she just wanted to get away from their blatant conniving, which she found distasteful. Edwina seemed no different; her husband Enfield would be next in line if Mitchell was denied his claim.

Adella looked out her drafty window at the thick snow. *She wasn't trapped forever.* She and the snow would vanish from Marleigh Manor at the same instant.

Could she keep up this pretense until spring?

She wrapped her cloak around her, and her blanket overtop it, and still she could feel the slight breeze from the window. She stretched out atop her saggy bed, wishing she could sneak back into her warm hideaway.

As the dinner bell rang, Adella stepped out into the hallway to see a young girl ringing it at the far end of the hall. However, the child walked away before Adella got close enough to see her. She assumed the girl was a Prescott, and determined to ask Winnifred who she was.

At dinner, everyone sat in exactly the same places. Adella took the same chair and sat down while others were still arriving.

"Did you sleep well?" Letitia asked.

"Yes, thank you," Adella said.

Grace was said, and Adella began the biggest feast of her life. Ribs of roast mutton steamed in a thick, velvety gravy, and four kinds of vegetables, and black and brown bread, were shared. Hallewell and Hartford had outdone themselves; everything was plentiful and delicious.

Yet something was wrong; worried eyes swapped silent warnings, and no one spoke. Few attempts at conversation, forced and distracted, failed, rambling answers to banal questions. Adella pretended not to notice everyone's nervousness.

A knock at the front door dropped several forks from startled hands. Mitchell, Enfield, and Rayden practically jumped from their chairs and ran out of the dining hall. Stella hurried after them.

"What is it ...?" Adella asked.

No one rushed to answer. Finally Grace broke the silence.

"The doctor has arrived," Grace explained. "Master Middleton has taken a ... bad turn."

No one stayed to talk. Adella finished quickly and excused herself, rising and leaving the last few at the table. To no surprise, voices rose in argument as soon as Adella stepped from the room. Adella continued listening, stepping in place as if walking away.

"Mitchell will be Master of Marleigh before dawn," said a man's voice.

"We can't afford new servants!"

"No Marleigh serves ...!"

"No Darby, either," said Grace's voice.

"Mitchell has no love for any of his uncles ... or

their wives," another woman said.

"Hasn't anyone read ... or even seen the will ...?"

"Rayden has ..."

"Rayden wishes he had ... my husband would've told me ...!"

"Mitchell won't order a mass-exodus," a man said. "He'll spend a year getting rid of us, one by one. Trust me; he'll keep just enough servants to cook his meals, and empty the rest of the house."

"You can't know that ...!"

"I've known him since he was born ... *curse that day!*"

Scrapes warned of chairs being pushed back. Approaching footsteps urged Adella into a run. She quickly turned a corner, dashed passed the empty music room, entered the new wing, and heard voices to her left. She turned right. Lydia was standing in the door to the nursery, holding one of the twins and staring, her mouth hanging open.

Adella nodded to her, then swiftly darted inside Winnifred's room.

"What is it ...?" Winnifred asked. "Middleton ...?"

"A doctor arrived," Adella said.

"Ah, this could be it," Winnifred said. "I expected another month, at least."

"Is he ...?" Adella asked.

"No, not dead," Winnifred said. "Our family has a tradition; started by old Morley; when a Lord of

Marleigh Manor dies, his death is honored by a military salute. All the men go outside and shoot rifles and pistols into the air."

"Has this ever happened before?" Adella asked.

"More than a few times," Winnifred said. "My brother clings to life, yet each time his recovery is longer. He's been pitifully weak lately ..."

"He may pull through," Adella said, and then Adella lowered her voice. *"I heard them speaking in the dining room ..."*

"Quick, tell me everything," Winnifred whispered.

Adella repeated what had been said, yet Winnifred had heard it all before.

"Tell Lydia I wish to speak to her," Winnifred whispered. "Then enter your secret room and wait for Mitchell. It may be a while."

Adella nodded, then stepped into the hall and relayed Winnifred's request. As Lydia hurried to Winnifred's bedside, carrying both twins, the nursery was left empty; Adella slipped inside the closet, under the lowest shelf, and sealed her secret door behind her.

For the first time since she'd returned, Adella felt safe; the comfortable familiarity of her hideaway eased her nerves, letting her breathe freely. On the floor lay her blanket, warm quilt, nightgown, her father's tools, her closed lantern and matches, the cart driver's bag, her bowl, and two empty wine bottles. The fireplace was hot, the tiny room stifling. Adella peered through the crack into Mitchell's study; firelight illuminated it, although the room was unoccupied.

No doubt Mitchell was overseeing the death-throes of Middleton, his oldest uncle, if in fact he was dying. Middleton's passing would be his moment of triumph.

As the long minutes passed, Adella started to sweat. She'd never be able to explain sweat in the middle of winter, so she reluctantly undressed, hoping to spare her fancy gown. Laying it atop her old blanket, Adella stood by the fireplace and peered into the empty office for long minutes before she began to feel foolish. Middleton might not die tonight ... and even if he did, hours might pass before life left him.

Lifting her dress aside, she sat down on her blanket to wait.

Hours passed.

Lydia returned to the nursery, and soon Natalie arrived to feed her sons, shortly followed by Grace.

"Any news ...?" Grace asked.

"I heard Mitchell tell Harrington how it began," Natalie said. "Middleton started coughing, and blood flowed from his mouth like from an opened vein. Reed was sent to fetch the doctor, and Harrington was to wait in his room and make sure all his pistols were loaded."

"Who else knows?" Grace asked.

"Hayden and Harlow forced Harrington to tell them what Mitchell said," Natalie said. "Harrington tried to lie, but his brothers bent his arms until he confessed, then they drug him to his room and confiscated all his pistols."

"They want their father to inherit," Lydia said. "God, please make it so."

"Enfield's a poet, not a Lord," Grace said.

"Mitchell will throw me out," Lydia said.

"We'll be right behind you either way," Natalie said. "Mitchell hates us, and Enfield's not strong enough to master Marleigh Manor."

"Mitchell will sue for his inheritance," Grace said. "If he does get it, he'll purge us, and start the family anew. If he doesn't, we'll be awash in lawsuits. Should he lose, Enfield will have to kick him out, and Rayden will manage the family through Enfield ..."

"God keep them, Morley and Vertiline were good souls, but terrible parents," Natalie said.

"Please ...!" Lydia hissed. *"If Mitchell hears ...!"*

"They won't open that bedroom door until Middleton's fate is known," Natalie said.

"I pray he survives ... at least a while longer," Grace said. "No one should be cast out into snow."

Adella listened, yet no more was said. Each girl seemed consumed by fears, too terrified to repeat frightening beliefs.

Adella folded her dress to be her pillow, then laid down on her blanket, wondering how long Middleton could last. Consumption took some people in days, some in weeks, and some in months ... but none in years.

In the middle of the night, the door to Mitchell's study opened, and numerous footsteps entered. Adella jumped up to stare through the crack.

"Charity, this isn't ...!" Mitchell snarled as soon as the door closed.

"Middleton's her brother, too," Rayden said.

"We should examine the will," Mitchell said.

"No one's reading his will while he's alive ...!" Letitia snapped.

"The doctor said he may never awaken, my dear sister-in-law," Enfield said. "There may not be much we can do."

"Then we wait," Letitia insisted.

"We must respect my brother's wishes," Charity said. "Can we all agree on that?"

"It's only honorable to obey last wishes ...," Enfield said.

"Wishes bow to the law," Mitchell interrupted. "Last wishes may be sacred, but needs of the living remain paramount."

"Middleton's last wishes will be honored!" Rayden insisted.

"My husband isn't dead ...!" Letitia snapped.

"We all pray he'll recover," Enfield said to Letitia.

"There's no point arguing," Charity said. "Besides, if we're going to discuss this, we should include Winnifred."

"Winnifred can't leave her bedroom," Mitchell

said.

"Then we should talk there," Charity said.

"There's nothing to talk about," Rayden said. "Middleton breathes, and until that changes, nothing happens."

"I'm trying to avoid trouble," Mitchell said.

"Is that why you brought your mother and our cousins here in the middle of winter ...?" Enfield asked.

"Why is Adella here ...?" Mitchell asked.

"Only Winnifred knows," Rayden said. "She's no kin of ours."

"She's a nice girl," Letitia said. "Leave her alone."

"It's nice to have a guest who isn't playing politics," Enfield said.

"It would be nicer if we knew what she was playing ... or what game Winnifred has dreamed up for her ...," Mitchell sneered.

"Good luck getting Winnifred to talk," Rayden said.

"I think we're done here," Enfield said. "Middleton will sleep all night, at least. Abigail will alert us if there's any change."

"I don't like leaving that Prescott alone with my husband," Letitia said.

"She's the closest thing in the house to a healer," Enfield said. "You may sit with her, if you wish. Come, let's retire. If needed, we'll meet again in the morning."

"Might as well ... since I'm not going to get my

way," Mitchell growled.

The door opened, and all but Mitchell left; their meeting was over.

Adella glanced back into the nursery; Lydia sat alone, rocking and softly singing to the twins. Adella peeked back to find Mitchell alone in his study, writing in his journal, pausing only to sip brandy.

She was trapped in her hideaway ... again.

Adella was half-asleep when a soft knock came to Mitchell's door.

"Now ...?" Harrington asked.

"Get in here," Mitchell said.

"Is he going to die ...?" Harrington asked after he closed the door behind him.

"Eventually ... the question is when," Mitchell said.

Adella peered between the cracks; the light was dim, the fire burned to coals. Her hideaway wasn't hot anymore.

"Anything we can do to ... help speed ...?" Harrington asked.

"Don't say that ...!" Mitchell snapped. "Don't think it! The law is on our side; we must be patient."

"I hate waiting ...," Harrington said.

"Middleton's known he's dying for months," Mitchell said. "If he can endure the wait, so can we."

"I overhead a message," Harrington said. "Winnifred wants Reed to come to her room, to visit her, tomorrow after breakfast."

"Reed ...?" Mitchell asked. "What's Winnifred trying to do now?"

"He's not allowed in here," Harrington said. "Why let Winnifred talk to him?"

"Winnifred owns Vertiline's jewelry," Mitchell said.

"Who ...?" Harrington asked.

"Vertiline Charity Eastaughffe ... our grandmother," Mitchell said. "Vertiline married old Morley, and he gave her anything she desired, including a fortune in jewelry."

"Where is it?" Harrington asked.

"Only Winnifred knows," Mitchell said. "She inherited all of it, and then it vanished. She says her will tells where it's hidden ... yet she won't say who she's leaving it to."

"How much ...?" Harrington asked.

"Do you not know what a fortune means?" Mitchell asked. "Why aren't you armed?"

"Hayden and Harlow took my guns," Harrington said.

"When we're in charge, they'll never do that again," Mitchell said.

"I can't wait," Harrington said.

"Yes, you can," Mitchell said. "Do nothing unless I tell you to." Mitchell drew a pistol out of his desk and handed it to Harrington. "Hide this. Don't let your brothers know you've got it."

"Someday I want them to pay ...," Harrington

said.

"When they're begging on street corners while we ride past in a coach, then you can laugh at them," Mitchell said.

"I don't want Reed driving my coach," Harrington said.

"Reed will be starving to death beside them," Mitchell said. "We'll have the house, the land, the money, the workhouses, and Vertiline's jewels; we'll get rid of everyone else, and fill Marleigh manor with pretty whores."

"I like that," Harrington said.

"Go to bed," Mitchell said. "Our dreams are about to come true."

Harrington departed. Mitchell sat back down before his desk and began writing again.

When Lydia vanished, Adella snuck back out of her hideaway and found Winnifred napping, yet she woke up when Adella approached her bed.

Adella told Winnifred everything in whispers.

"I won't last a day if they get rid of the others," Winnifred said. "We may have to act soon ... sooner than I'd have liked."

"We ...?" Adella asked.

Winnifred stared at Adella.

"We need another Vertiline ...," Winnifred said.

Adella's eyes widened alarmingly.

"You're a strong, beautiful young woman," Winnifred said. "Do you think ... you could tame

Mitchell ...?"

Adella stepped back.

"Me ... marry ... Mitchell ...?" Adella gasped.

"You'd never have to worry about a roof over your head ...," Winnifred said.

"Only about poison in my tea ...!" Adella exclaimed.

"Marleigh Manor needs a strong woman," Winnifred said.

"I won't marry an evil man ...!" Adella said.

"Better than being cast out into the snow," Winnifred said.

"I prefer snow," Adella said.

"Who else is there?" Winnifred asked.

"Rowena ... or Lydia," Adella said.

"Mitchell will never marry a Prescott," Winnifred said.

"Lydia is a Brixton," Adella said.

"Her mother was born Sarah Elizabeth Prescott," Winnifred said.

"Is this why you didn't reveal me ...?" Adella asked. "You want me to ...?"

"The fall of Marleigh would affect many lives," Winnifred said. "Hundreds rely upon our businesses for their livelihood ..."

"I won't be forced to marry," Adella said.

"No one can force you," Winnifred said. "The final choice will be yours. Please, just consider it; you're my only hope. It could work; true love comes in strange ways."

Resolute, Adella stared into the old woman's desperate face.

"If there was any other way ...," Winnifred pleaded.

"I'll stay until spring," Adella promised. "I'll be your ears and eyes. I won't be your sacrifice."

"See how strong you are?" Winnifred asked. "Mitchell needs your strength ...!"

"I don't need Mitchell," Adella said.

Winnifred struggled to rise up off her pillows, failed, and reached out a hand to Adella.

"My dear, no woman needs Mitchell," Winnifred said. "All I ask is that you stay here ... get to know him. If things don't work out, I'll give you whatever you need to start a new life elsewhere ... if only you'll stay until spring."

"Whatever ...?" Adella asked.

"Money, clothes, even a carriage with a horse ... and signed deeds of ownership," Winnifred promised.

Reluctantly, hesitantly, Adella nodded.

"Excellent," Winnifred said. "Now, when Reed comes to see me after breakfast ..."

"I'll be ready," Adella said.

"Bless you, my dear," Winnifred said. "But don't forget what I said. Think about it. You could find ..."

"You can't find true love," Adella interrupted. "There's no such thing as true love. What does exist is true lovers; open, honest, devoted people, looking for one person, to whom they can dedicate their life, to pleasing, supporting, and protecting. Sadly, true lovers are rare. A pity; when true lovers find each other, it can be magical."

"Girls grow old waiting for magic," Winnifred warned.

"Then I'll grow old," Adella insisted.

Adella returned to her freezing room alone. She wished she could've brought her father's tools, but without a lock on her door, how could she explain hammers and saws? Yet her mind was foggy, lost in horrified thoughts.

Winnifred wanted her to marry Mitchell ...?!?

Chapter 10

Everything she'd done since her father's death had been specifically to avoid a cruel husband. If she'd just wanted to marry, not caring who, she could've wed the blacksmith in town ... or a dozen just like him. She'd known Winnifred had been using her ... yet she'd seemed to be just a nice old lady. Now Winnifred was a threat to her lifetime of freedom ... *possibly an enemy.*

Yet, despite her best efforts to force them out, unwanted thoughts floated from the back of her mind:

The Lady of Marleigh Manor.

Her Ladyship Adella.

Matriarch.

Mitchell was the rightful heir of Marleigh Manor. His wife would be a lady of great wealth, power, and position, and perhaps ... minor nobility. What peasant-born girl didn't dream of riches and titles ...? She could have wealth ... *dreams hovered within reach ...!*

Yet the price was a nightmare. Ambitious, jealous, vengeful, scheming; Mitchell couldn't be trusted. Life with such a man would be no woman's dream. He'd never treat her as her father had treated her mother.

She undressed to her chemise and crawled inside her blanket with her thick cloak atop her sagging bed.

Dreams were torturous.

The next morning, she dressed in a dark green gown with black ribbons over a pale chemise. She liked Winnifred's old clothes, which fit her well enough. She reached the end of the hall just as a young girl no more than eight appeared and began ringing a bell. Seeing her, the young girl bowed deeply. Adella nodded back.

"Good morning," Adella said to the girl. "What's your name?"

The little girl looked suddenly frightened. With childish swiftness, she turned and ran away ... as if scared. Adella watched her go, wondering what had startled the child.

What had the Marleighs done to inspire fear in children ...?

She didn't need an answer. To her knowledge, Marleigh Manor was a house without love.

Breakfast was quiche and scones, both of which tasted buttery. After grace, Mitchell offered a prayer for

Middleton ... which was humble and trite and rang with falseness. Glancing eyes told her everyone thought the same, yet Mitchell played his part ... setting up an alibi, and quietly presenting himself as the Lord of Marleigh Manor ... in preparation for his takeover.

Banal comments were made on the weather, prospects for a merchant ship scheduled to arrive soon, and other topics no one was really thinking about. Adella was asked how she slept, and she answered as demurely as she could.

Almost all the food was eaten, several plates pushed back, when Lydia came running into the dining room.

"*Masters, come quick!*" Lydia's voice was frantic. "*Middleton ...!*"

Whatever she meant to say was drown by chairs scraping backwards and hurried footsteps almost running to the new wing. Lydia pressed against the wall to give them room to pass by. Letitia went with them, her pallor pale.

"What's happened ...?" Stella asked Lydia after the stomps and clomps faded in the distance.

"Middleton ... Abigail just told me to get his brothers ...," Lydia said. "He's coughing in his sleep ... blood everywhere ..."

Eyes told volumes. Adella set down her fork; *she had to tell Winnifred ...!*

As Stella stood, all the Berkeley-Marleighs rose. Together they filed down the hallway toward the new wing.

The only family remaining seated were Edwina, Enfield's wife, their older sons Hayden and Harlow, Charity and her husband, Garrick, whom Adella had never spoken to, and their son, Acton, his wife Natalie, and their daughter Grace.

"Forgive me; this is a family matter," Adella said softly, and she rose.

Leaving the dining room by the closest door, she found herself in the smaller dining room where the kids ate. She recognized most of them; Harrington, his eyes ablaze, Rufina, Winnifred's youngest daughter, Vivian, Jennie, and Isabell, Middleton's three legitimate daughters, and Laurence, Rayden's only son. All looked up at her.

"Is Middleton ...?" Harrington asked excitedly.

Adella frowned at his impropriety before Middleton's young daughters.

"Remain here," Adella said. "You'll be summoned if needed."

Unwilling to return to the adult dining room, Adella crossed the kid's dining room and exited by another door. She found herself in a small hallway she'd never seen before, facing a tiny parlor, elegantly decorated, with only two chairs and a small table by a tall window, its thick drapes pulled shut. Yet she had to get back to her room; she had work to do. She began searching for a stairs.

Inside her room, she pulled her cloak on and

exited by the door at the end of the hall. The windy winter outside was blinding, sunny, reflecting off the snow. One set of footprints led from the barn to the outside door nearest her room; Reed had gone to see Winnifred. Stepping into his larger boot prints, Adella crossed the field to the door they'd come from, which opened into the low side of the barn.

She had to hurry. She pushed inside to find a tiny, rusty stove burning warmly. This warm room appeared to be a workshop, full of tools she knew well, a wide, rough-cut workbench, and tall shelves. Her father had always dreamed of having a workshop like this. One door was open to another small room, in which she spied a bed and an old wardrobe.

Adella hurried to the shelves and quickly found sealed jars of resin and glue. The lids of each were smeared with soft wax to keep their contents fresh, and she opened them and pressed a finger inside each to find both usable. She needed a brush or scraper, didn't see any, yet found a pile of thin wood scraps which would suffice. Selecting several, she hid her stolen treasures under her cloak, and opened the door to step out into the cold ...

Standing in the snow, Reed stopped abruptly, frozen as he stared.

"I'm sorry," Adella said. "I ... was trying to find the horses."

"This is my room," Reed said, although from his expression she suspected he doubted her tale. "They're this way."

Reed led her to the left, around the corner of the barn, and opened a narrow door. Adella followed obediently, one hand holding the front of her cloak closed, the other clutching her stolen jars and wood-scraps.

"Did you wish to go somewhere ...?" Reed asked.

"No ... I ... just wanted to find someplace out of the way," Adella said. "Family matters."

"I know," Reed said. "I was summoned to see Winnifred today, but Master Middleton's health seems to be ..."

"I'm sorry for all of you," Adella said. "That's why I sought to be elsewhere ... out of the way. And I do love horses ..."

"I care for them," Reed said. "Come, let me introduce you."

Reed led her to four wide stalls, each of which held a tall, powerful horse. One was white speckled with black, two brown, and one a deep shade of red. Reed introduced them by name, yet Adella wasn't listening, walking slowly to keep from dropping her hidden treasures.

Other stalls were crowded with cows, pigs, and goats. Clucks of chickens came from a large penned area, and several ran to the edge as if hopeful of food. Reed was still telling her about the horses, their breeds and lineages, and Adella pretended attentiveness. Yet

Reed seemed equally distracted, as if focused on something else.

"Is anything wrong ...?" Adella asked.

"Wrong ...?" Reed asked, as if coming out of a reverie. "No, but ... I understand Master Middleton is violently ill ..."

"Do you suspect ...?" Adella asked.

"This is a troubling day," Reed said. "I asked if I should run into town to fetch the doctor; I was told no."

"That's troubling," Adella said.

Reed nodded.

"I'm disturbing you ...?" Adella asked.

"No, not at ... it's a disturbing time," Reed seemed unable to continue.

"I'll go back to my room," Adella said. "I'm intruding ..."

"No, please ... forgive me," Reed said.

"I may not be a Marleigh, Prescott, or Darby, but I know what this day means," Adella said firmly. "Thank you for showing me your horses."

"Anytime ...," Reed said, and he bowed slightly.

Adella walked slowly back to the barn door, fumbled to open it without dropping the stolen jars and scrap wood strips, and slipped out into the snow. She stepped in his wide boot prints again, struggling to conceal her treasures.

When she reached the manor, she hurried inside her room and closed her door, then set both jars on the floor by the window. Moving aside the ragged curtains, she wiped each pane's leaky recesses with her finger to clean them, then dipped a thin wooden slat into the resin. Taking only a tiny amount, she carefully traced each pane's edges, angling the slat so the resin was forced into the tiny gap between wood and glass.

She spent half an hour tracing every pane twice, first sealing it, then applying a second bead of resin to hold the first in place. No carpenter could've done a better job, applying the resin thinly and evenly to hide her work.

Finishing the gaps around the glass, she turned her attention to its leaky wooden frame. Peeling and cracked white paint clung to the ancient wood, and resin would leave dark, telltale stains. Using a different slat, she scraped away as little paint as possible, then applied glue to every edge where she could feel cold air streaming in. She had to work around large cracks and peels of paint, lest her repairs become obvious. No one would ever open this window again, but she doubted if anyone would ever want to, if in fact it wasn't too warped to open, and she planned to be gone before summer anyway. As with the resin, she pushed the glue deep into the gaps, sealing the cold breeze outside. She held a thin ribbon of her dress before each repair, reapplying until the breeze moved it no more.

Finished, she stepped back to admire her work. *Her father would be proud!*

Resealing both jars so they wouldn't harden, she set them in a corner, then attacked her bed. Its aged rope was loose, so she threw off the thin mattress and wrenched on the thick, rough cord, tightening it through one hole at a time, until the ropes on her bedframe were as tight as violin strings. Then she tied off the excess and laid her mattress atop; her bed sagged no more. She laid down on it to test it; *far more comfortable!*

She had no way to return the jars, yet she wasn't worried; Reed wouldn't be searching his woodworking supplies today. His father Middleton was dying, so his last chance to be recognized was about to be lost. Adella wondered who his mother was ... upon which of the Prescott women Middleton had expended his youthful lusts. *Had she been murdered to hide Middleton's indiscretions ...?* Knowing this family, Adella wouldn't be surprised.

Adella stashed the jars and wooden slats under her bed, draped her blanket and cloak low to hide them, and sat down on its edge.

If Middleton died today, what would happen ...?

An hour later, a knock came to her door. Adella opened it to find little Rufina standing before her.

"Hello," Adella said.

"Mother wants you," Rufina said.

"You're Rufina, daughter of Winnifred, aren't you?" Adella said.

Rufina nodded.

"Tell her I'll be right there," Adella said, and Rufina ran off.

Adella strode after her, yet the child quickly

vanished in the distance before she reached the end of the hall. She paced the hallways and stairs alone, seeing no one else, not even Hallewell and Hartford in the kitchen. Everything was silent until she approached the music room, where soft murmurs of voices alerted her. She stepped into view, and every voice suddenly silenced. Every face turned to stare at her.

Adella swallowed hard and kept walking, ignoring their glares. She approached the door to the new wing, but Hayden and Harlow stood before it, blocking her path.

"The family is in private conversation," Hayden said.

"Mistress Winnifred summoned me," Adella answered.

"They're meeting in Winnifred's room," Hayden said. "They can't be disturbed."

Adella was strong, yet these boys looked stronger, and she'd ruin her pretense if she tried to push past them.

"Tell Mistress Winnifred I came, but I've returned to my room," Adella said.

"That's probably wise," Hayden sneered.

Adella turned, forcing herself not to punch Hayden for his rudeness, which is what anyone risked if they talked like that to a carpenter.

She didn't want to parade past the music room again, yet she had no choice. She kept her eyes forward and down, yet she could feel their eyes watching her.

Not a single voice spoke as she walked past.

She was halfway up the curved stair in the entrance when she heard a door burst open behind her. No one spoke, but loud, heavy shoes echoed down the hall. More footsteps joined them, and Adella startled as she saw Mitchell walking to the front door carrying two rifles, four pistols in his belt. Behind him walked all the other men of Marleigh Manor ... and each was carrying guns. They stomped into the entryway and opened the main doors.

Wintry air gusted inside as they all marched out, not wearing coats, heedless of the cold. They crunched into the thick snow, then stopped, gathered in a group.

Then the rest of the men, and the women, and even some Prescotts, crowded out onto the front steps, watching. Several women were weeping.

Guns raised, pointed at the sky.

"Marleigh ...!" Mitchell shouted.

Explosions of gunfire blasted every ear. More rifles were raised, and then pistols, a full minute of one blast after another.

The ritual Winnifred had told her about ...!
Master Middleton was dead ...!

Adella bowed her head. Open war for Lordship of Marleigh Manor had begun.

Chapter 11

While everyone watched, the men fired every gun they had. Several paused to reload. Only Adella hurried back to the new wing. Unopposed, she pushed through the door and arrived in Winnifred's room still hearing occasional gunfire.

"You know," Winnifred said, looking at her.

"It's started," Adella said.

"My brother died an hour ago," Winnifred said. "We've been arguing about what to do ever since."

"What's to happen?" Adella asked.

"Reed will be sent for the doctor, the constable, and the judge," Winnifred said. "Letitia refuses to reveal the location of his will until they arrive. Everyone but Mitchell wants the reading as open and public as possible. You will attend; I insisted you be there to represent me."

"What then ...?" Adella asked.

"Nothing good, I assure you," Winnifred said.

A day of fears and tears followed. Visitors came to see Winnifred. Adella respectfully stood back and listened.

"Grace, no one is going to kick you out," Winnifred insisted.

"Mitchell doesn't like Darbys," Grace argued.

"Mitchell doesn't like anyone," Winnifred said. "Don't worry; being in charge changes everyone. He'll have some quick growing up to do, but he will."

"Where would we go?" Grace asked.

"I couldn't live knowing you were unhappy," Winnifred said. "Come, child, give me a hug."

Grace's eyes were still wet when she left, and Charity and her husband came in shortly afterwards.

"Sister!" Winnifred said. "And Garrick! I didn't know you'd returned."

"We wrapped up the legal paperwork faster than I'd expected," Garrick said, his voice deep and slow. "The deeds are signed and payments transferred; all went according to plan."

"Glad to hear it," Winnifred said. "At least some news is good."

"My deepest condolences for your brother," Garrick said.

"Thank you."

"Winnie, we must do something," Charity said.

"Mitchell is Lester through and through."

"If Middleton left no will, he's Lord of Marleigh Manor already," Winnifred said. "He's our nephew. We must endure ..."

"We're going to end up like Everleigh," Charity said.

"Mitchell isn't going to drown us," Winnifred said.

"No, he'll harass and torment us until we want to drown ourselves," Charity said.

"I've written to my family in Wessex," Garrick said. "If needed, we'll move there."

"Please don't ... not yet," Winnifred said. "Your daughter was just in here crying about having to leave ... and I'd be heartbroken if the twins were taken."

"Reed went to fetch the judge," Charity said.

"This will all be sorted out soon," Winnifred promised. "We can hold out until then."

"They'll make this the Berkeley-Marleigh Manor," Charity said.

"We should've been Marleigh-Prescott for four generations," Winnifred said.

"You and I could run this place better than any of our brothers," Charity said.

"No court would support us against the slightest legal challenge," Winnifred said. "It will work out. I promise."

"That's a precarious promise," came a man's voice.

Rayden stood in the doorway, glaring at all of them.

Winnifred and Charity exchanged knowing glances, and Charity took her husband's arm. They departed, Rayden stepping out of their way.

"Come in, brother," Winnifred said.

Rayden walked toward her bed with a casual swagger. He stopped and stared at Adella.

"This is a private conversa ...," Rayden began.

"Adella is here for my sake," Winnifred interrupted. "I asked her to remain, and anything you wish to say to me ..."

"Exactly how do you plan to keep that promise ...?" Rayden demanded.

"By doing all I can ... and not overreacting," Winnifred said. "I'm trapped in bed; I need this family more than anyone."

"You know what Mitchell will do," Rayden said.

"We have suspicions, nothing more," Winnifred said. "Both of us could be wrong."

"Mitchell hates everyone," Rayden said.

"Yes, but he needs us, too," Winnifred said.

"He's been itching for revenge since he was denied by father," Rayden said.

"Then it's time we scratched that itch," Winnifred said. "Trust me; don't do anything rash."

"I've known lots of people like him ...," Rayden said.

"Many thought you were just like him,"

Winnifred said. "You've grown out of your youthful misdeeds ... learned from your mistakes."

"We'll all be gone before Mitchell changes," Rayden said.

"Come here again ... after the will is read," Winnifred said. "Until then, we're just wasting breath."

Rayden stared at Winnifred, glanced at Adella once, then suddenly walked out.

"It's time," Winnifred said. "Adella, I need to speak to Mitchell. Find him and ask him to come. Give him a head start, and then follow ... I need you here when I talk to him."

"What if he ...?" Adella began.

"Don't take no for an answer," Winnifred said. "Ignore bluster and threats. I have words for both of you."

"I alone choose my husband," Adella warned.

"I intend no mention of marriage," Winnifred promised.

Hayden and Harlow stood like soldiers outside the closed door to Letitia's bedroom. Adella approached them.

"Is Mitchell inside?" Adella asked.

"Only Middleton is inside," Hayden said.

Adella nodded, then turned to walk down the hall.

"Mitchell's not in his study," Harlow said as she stepped away. "I suspect he's in the master office."

"Master office ...?" Adella asked.

"Top of the entry stairs, first door to the right," Harlow said.

"Thank you," Adella said.

"What do you want him for?" Hayden asked.

"Winnifred wishes to speak to him."

Hayden and Harlow exchanged glances.

Adella nodded to both, then walked slowly away. She'd never yet fully ascended the entry stairs, yet there was no point being afraid. She was delivering a message, not confronting.

Enfield, Edwina, and several Berkeley-Marleighs stood in the music room, whispering ... until Adella walked past. Silently they watched her pass by. She knew they suspected her, yet their suspicions held no relation to the truth. In a way, their fears protected her; better they suspect she was a sent-for spy, rather than a former squatter and thief. She walked past the kitchen, saw Camden's room empty, and reached the foyer with ease. Climbing the steps, she ignored the framed, painted faces, except for Vertiline, who was rendered so beautifully Adella couldn't help but admire.

Turning right at the top, Adella knocked at the first door.

"Enter," said Mitchell's voice.

Adella opened the door to find a grand office, larger and brighter than she'd expected, with the biggest desk she'd ever seen. Flames were dancing in a fireplace as tall as she was, over which hung the Marleigh coat of arms, atop a pair of crossed swords. Adella swallowed hard; if their heraldry were a skull, their display would look like a pirate flag.

Captain Marston Ramsay Marleigh had been a pirate!

Mitchell looked up in surprise, a stack of papers in each hand.

"You ...!" he exclaimed.

"My name is Adella," she reminded him. "I bring a message: Winnifred wishes to speak to you."

"I see," Mitchell said. "What about?"

"You'll have to ask her," Adella said.

"Why should I wish to talk to her?" Mitchell asked.

Adella bit her lip; she didn't like his tone.

"The true Lord of every great house must be a gentleman," Adella said. "I assume you will be, too."

Mitchell glared as if he were going to shout, yet he set his papers aside, stood, and nodded to her.

"Things are about to change," Mitchell said. "If you feel uncomfortable, please let me know; I'll have Reed drive you all the way home."

"That would be a very long trip," Adella said.

"I'm aware of that," Mitchell said.

Mitchell followed her out into the hallway, locked the master office door with a large, ornate key, nodded to Adella as if dismissing her, and then walked toward the stair. Adella waited, then followed at a distance; no point letting him know she'd be there, too. She didn't try to keep up with his rapid footsteps, and

233

ignored the whispers about Mitchell's hurried passage coming from the music room.

As she stepped inside Winnifred's room:

"Now you may close the door," Winnifred said to Mitchell.

Mitchel looked surprised, then glanced from the bed to Adella and back again.

"She's involved ...?" Mitchell demanded.

"I'm about to share information you both need to hear," Winnifred said. "I hate to repeat myself."

Mitchell obviously objected, yet he steeled himself and closed Winnifred's door behind Adella. She went and stood between Winnifred's bed and the window, not saying a word. Mitchell stood tall at the foot of her wide bed, frowning.

"So, here we are," Winnifred said to Mitchell. "You've waited most of your life for this day, and as soon as the judge arrives, we'll see if your waiting ends."

"I never should've had to wait," Mitchell said.

"Where would we be, if my father had made you Lester's heir?" Winnifred asked. "You wouldn't be the man you are today. You were too young; either Middleton, Enfield, or Rayden would've figured out how to take advantage of you ... and made themselves your puppeteer. You'd have grown up weak and overindulged, a pawn of stronger men."

"Are you saying Grandpa Morley did me a favor ...?" Mitchell asked.

"Father did what the family needed," Winnifred

said. "He knew inheritance law; you were the rightful heir, but with a weak, immature Lord, my brothers would've ruined the family ... not for the first time. Now you're a strong young man. You're no one's fool or puppet, and you can make the family into whatever you want. The question is: what kind of a leader do you want to be? Will you be the Lord your grandfather Morley was, putting the needs of the family first, or pander to petty wants ...?"

"What has this family ever done for me ...?" Mitchell asked.

"You've got grievances ... totally justified," Winnifred said. "I remember your cousins teasing you. Yet more than a decade has passed since then, this house is still here, and our wealth has grown, because we didn't put a child in charge of our family finances. Now you're a man, able to master business affairs above the ability of any child, because you weren't given Lordship too early. But your days of plotting and planning revenges are over; those are the strategies of children. You control our family; the question is: *how will you lead ...?*"

Mitchell stared at her as if astounded, yet determined not to show it.

"What do you suggest?" Mitchell snapped. "What would you require ... and what support do you offer?"

"The courts are your support," Winnifred said. "If Middleton wills you his title, the deed to Marleigh

Manor is yours. If not, we'll go bankrupt paying lawyers ... and you'll still get the deed ... albeit at a much lower value."

"So ... you haven't seen the will," Mitchell said.

"No, but I've watched and studied my brothers longer than you've been alive," Winnifred said. "I've got a good idea what's in it. But wills can't violate the law; Middleton knew that. You've got two futures; a rich old man, alone in a huge house, friendless ... except for Harrington, or the respected Lord of a large and great family with many servants. Which future do you prefer?"

"Knowledge of my plans requires a price," Mitchell said.

"I don't need to know your plans," Winnifred said. "Everyone here will see your plans; you're smart, but no one is leaving Marleigh Manor without everyone knowing about it. Your plans will be evident with every decision you make."

"Then why am I here?" Mitchell asked.

"My support depends on what actions I see," Winnifred said. "If I see a grown man assuming the responsibilities of his inheritance, then you'll have my support. If not, if I see the revenges of a spiteful child, then you won't."

"What kind of support are we talking about?" Mitchell asked.

"Influence," Winnifred said. "I carry the opinions of many, and can sway others."

"What about Vertiline's jewels?" Mitchell asked.

"My will clearly states who I'm leaving Vertiline's jewels to," Winnifred said.

"And who is that ...?" Mitchell asked.

"Adella," Winnifred glanced at her. "I'm leaving Vertiline's jewelry to Adella."

Adella staggered as Mitchell snapped his head to look at her.

"She ... she's not family!" Mitchell argued.

"No, she isn't," Winnifred said. "But my jewels were left to me from Vertiline, and aren't part of the Marleigh estate. I can leave them to anyone I want."

"Why her ...?" Mitchell demanded.

"You keep your secrets, I'll keep mine," Winnifred said. "You may leave now, Master Mitchell; you've learned all I wanted you to know."

"But ...!" Mitchell exclaimed.

"I say no more," Winnifred said.

"You ... are dismissing me ...?" Mitchell shouted.

"Take one last word of advice," Winnifred said. "To any crisis, everyone has a 'God reaction' - an instantaneous, knee-jerk response, how they'd respond if only they could. The more unexpected the crisis, the stronger their 'God reaction'. For the powerless, it comes to nothing, as they lack any means to enforce their will; limitations force the poor to consider more reasonable options. However, for the powerful, 'God reactions' can be fatal. Reacting upon impulse denies better, more rational responses. Remember that ... when the mantle of leadership falls upon you."

Mitchell stared at Winnifred, then stared at Adella. She crumbled under his glare; she didn't know what to say. Then Mitchell turned and stormed out, slamming the door behind him.

Adella stared at Winnifred.

"You ... you lied to me ...!" Adella stammered.

"I never mentioned marriage," Winnifred said.

"You told him I'm getting your jewels!" Adella exclaimed. *"Now he'll want ... to marry me ... to get his hands on Vertiline's jewels!"*

"But he can't have you ... not unless you judge him worthy," Winnifred said. "Your parents are dead; no one can force you to marry. Mitchell has one chance; either he becomes like my father, a truly worthy man, or he loses Vertiline's jewels."

"Did you really leave me her jewels?" Adella asked.

"Will you believe me without seeing my will ...?" Winnifred asked.

Adella didn't know what to think. Winnifred was certainly stronger than she'd expected; she'd manipulated Mitchell like he was eight years old ...

... and manipulated her as well!

Chapter 12

Jewels ... if they were real, she was rich ...!
She'd only inherit after Winnifred died ...!
Winnifred might live for decades ... and she could change her will again ... at any time.

The only way she'd learn if Vertiline's jewels were real, and if she'd inherit them, would be to live in Marleigh Manor until Winnifred died.

Every man in Marleigh Manor will want to marry me ... only to get Vertiline's jewels!

"It's up to you now," Winnifred said, disturbing her from her reverie. "The future of the Marleigh family ... depends on you."

"Why me ...?" Adella asked.

"I have to trust someone," Winnifred said. "No Marleigh is trustworthy, not even my sister. Charity would take Vertiline's jewels to the Darby family and make them rich, but my responsibility is the Marleigh family. If I could leave, I would, but I can't; I've no one but you."

"You know many girls ...!" Adella argued.

"I know several spoiled, rich trollops who'd jump at the chance to marry Mitchell and inherit a fortune in jewels," Winnifred said. "Vertiline was a good girl from a poor family, and that's what Marleigh needs."

"Why not a Prescott ...?" Adella asked.

"I'd end up with the same problem," Winnifred said. "Prescotts hate Marleighs; they'd break up the household, just in the opposite way."

"What if Mitchell kicks everyone out ...?" Adella asked.

"He can't afford to," Winnifred said. "My original offer stands; in the spring, I'll get you away from here, to anywhere you want to go, with enough money to set you up for life. Mitchell won't kick you out as long as he thinks you're my heir."

"You're using me," Adella said.

"I'm also giving you the chance of a lifetime," Winnifred said. "Think about it ... you needn't decide today."

Adella didn't remember walking out of Winnifred's room. She strode out of the new wing and past the music room without looking at anyone.

What was she to do?

Winnifred could kick her out, reveal her secrets,

and leave her hunted by constables while unable to support herself, or she'd become trapped in the politics of a murderous family.

No wonder the poor hated the rich ...!

The rich married for wealth.

Only the poor married for love.

Conversations she'd heard flitted through her mind. By all reports, Vertiline had made a new man of old Morley ... unless he'd been a decent man all along, twisted by an evil father, and just needed a good woman to bring it out. Most people never change ... the idea that Mitchell could be made into a decent husband was laughable. Certainly love would never remake him; *he'd never known love.*

True or not, Mitchell thought she was going to inherit Vertiline's jewels. That made her valuable. She'd no fear he'd tell others; marriage to another man could pass Vertiline's fortune out of his reach. Mitchell would try to claim her, trick, or bully her into giving him her jewels or ... surrender to marriage, but she knew his true nature.

Could greed force Mitchell to become a better man?

Was that Winnifred's plan ...?

Why did she have to be Winnifred's pawn ...?

Hallewell and Hartford appeared in the kitchen and cooked a feast. Everything was set on a table in the music room; no formal meals tonight. Children rang bells and informed everyone where the food was, and soon the music room was crowded with Marleighs, Berkeley-Marleighs, Darbys, a Northcott, a Fulton, and several Brixtons; everyone except Reed and Winnifred.

The family carriage, drawn by all four horses, pulled up. Many crowded to the windows to see. Reed jumped down from the driving board and opened the carriage door. Three men stepped out into the snow.

"They're here ...!" Hortence cried.

Twenty minutes later, Adella filed up the stairs with everyone else. Having viewed the deceased, the judge, doctor, and constable headed the parade, and everyone filed in behind. Many of the older children, including Harrington, came. Even Reed stood in the crowd. The only adult not present was Winnifred.

They entered a room Adella had never seen. It was a huge, high-ceilinged party room, as large as a dance hall. She'd never explored above the foyer and suspected this huge room took up half of the second floor.

At one end was a low stage. The judge, doctor, and constable stepped up onto it, followed by Mitchell, Enfield, Rayden, and Charity.

From the back of the room came Letitia, eyes red from crying. Everyone moved aside to let her pass. She was carrying a thin leather case. When she reached the stage, she opened the case and held it out. The judge reached inside and drew out a single sheet of paper.

Not a sound was made as the judge quietly read

the contents of the page, front and back.

Finally he cleared his throat.

"Mistress Letitia, do you avow that this is the sole will of your husband?" the judge asked.

Letitia nodded, unable to speak. The judge looked to Mitchell and the others on the stage, then cleared his throat again.

"This is the final will and testament of Master Middleton Kent Marleigh, Lord of Marliegh Manor," the judge read. "I, Middleton Kent Marleigh, being of sound mind although ailing body, do make this will to leave behind all my worldly possessions as follows. Yet before I list my wishes, a few matters need to be announced. I attest that each of these statements is true and request each be written into law and widely published.

First I wish to apologize to my wife. I was not the husband she deserved. I've made many mistakes and engaged in indiscretions to my shame ... and my shame alone.

Second, I wish to apologize to my daughters. I was not the father they deserved. Yet I love each of my children and ask only their forgiveness.

Third, I publicly apologize to the living victims of my youthful indiscretions. These are Judith May Prescott and Abigail Orpha Prescott. As a young man, I used my position and influence to force my wills upon them ... to my everlasting shame. I now wish to make amends and pray they forgive me. Other victims of my youth include Margaret Fulton and Cynthia Dryden; although they have long passed from this mortal realm, I express my shame and sympathy to their descendants.

Fourth, I wish to apologize to the results of my youthful indiscretions. These are my illegitimate children, as much of my flesh as my recognized daughters. They are Rowena Ethel Prescott, Reed Crawford Fulton, Ettie Edwina Prescott, and Hortence Jane Dryden. I pray they forgive my weakness for not recognizing them long ago, as I should have, and I ask my daughters and family to accept them as my recognized children.

I have no personal bequests. All I own belongs to my family. I leave everything to my family. My final wish is that my family ... all my family ... stay united.

In this manner, I must refrain from leaving legal decisions to undo my final wish. Any other choice would destroy the family I've managed since the untimely death of my dear brother, Lester Hale Marleigh. For the sake of the family, regardless of personal reservations, and with a final plea that all decisions be made mindful of the benefits of the Marleigh line, and all related to them, and in accordance with the law, I name my successor and heir to the Lordship of Marleigh Manor: Master Mitchell Myerscough Marleigh."

Gasps and a muffled scream came from the listeners.

The judge handed the will to the constable, who

scanned it, then passed it to the doctor.

"As the duly-appointed judge of this district, confirmed by the governor, I declare this will legal, verified, read, and witnessed. This concludes these proceedings. My deepest sympathies to all for your loss."

Glares threatening murder flashed across the Marleighs on the stage. Mitchell never smiled, just stood as solid as Gibraltar; *his time had come.*

Finished reading the will, the constable handed it to Mitchell, who accepted it like a king handed his scepter. The judge stepped up and shook his hand, followed by the constable and doctor. Then, with nods to several others, the three again offered their condolences to Letitia, then paraded through the gathering toward the back. Yet, before they left, Mitchell stepped up to the podium. All three paused to watch.

With lordly airs, Mitchell stared across the inhabitants of Marleigh Manor. His eyes fell upon Stella first; his mother's smile was beaming. Most of the faces were frowning, and some Prescott women were already crying. Then his eyes fell on Adella.

"I hereby acknowledge and accept Lordship of Marleigh Manor," Mitchell said in a loud, clear voice. "Reed, see that our guests are comfortably returned to their homes. Thank you."

Mitchell looked like he wanted to say more, yet he stepped down off the stage, walked through the crowd, passed the judge, constable, and doctor, and exited the room.

No one spoke. Confusion masked every face. Whatever anyone had been expecting ... it hadn't happened.

Mitchell was Lord of Marleigh Manor.

No one saw Mitchell the rest of the afternoon, but everyone heard him; heavy stomps came from the master office, and once something crashed loudly, yet no one dared to investigate.

Adella hurried to Winnifred and reported all. Others came; Grace, Rowena, Hayden, and Edwina arrived to talk to Winnifred ... or hear what she had to say. Laurence also came, but he seemed concerned only by the nervous tones in everyone's voices.

Winnifred insisted that everything would be fine. She'd watched old Morley hand his Lordship to Lester, and then to Middleton. She insisted no reason to fear existed, yet her assurances calmed none.

"How will we live ...?" Grace demanded.

"What about my son ...?" Rowena asked.

"Can he throw everyone out ...?" Edwina asked.

"He can, but he won't," Winnifred assured them. "The constables will recognize his ownership, however, Mitchell doesn't cook or clean; he needs us. Besides, I own Vertiline's jewels; if he casts me out, I could buy a new house for all of us. He won't risk me taking Vertiline's jewels away. Trust me; everything will be fine."

No one seemed comforted. Slowly they excused themselves and departed to talk in secret.

"Adella, I need to speak to Phoebe," Winnifred said when they were alone.

"Phoebe ...?" Adella asked.

"Formerly Phoebe Polly Charleston, Rayden's wife, mother of Laurence," Winnifred said. "Corner room, first to the left as you enter the new wing. Please ask her to come ... and come with her. Be careful; she's a nasty drunk."

Adella soon knocked, and a momentary pause followed.

"Come in," said a woman's voice.

Adella opened the door to find the first messy room she'd seen in Marleigh Manor. Phoebe's room was cold; curtains were drawn back, shutters open, and frosty glass panes showed the wide, wooded hill, with their only road leading down from its top. No fire burned in the fireplace, yet the room smelled smoky ... and soiled, in desperate need of cleaning.

With uncombed hair, upon the bed lay an older woman, blonde turning gray, dressed only in a scarlet chemise. She looked like she'd once been beautiful, but age and the bottle tight in her grip revealed the ravages of time and drink.

"Is Mitchell ...?" she asked.

"Mitchell replaced Middleton," Adella said.

"Mouthful of crap!" she cursed, and then her eyes seemed to focus. "Who are you ...?"

"I'm Adella, a friend of Winnifred. She'd like to speak to you."

"Winnifred ...?" Phoebe asked. "Are you a Marleigh ...?"

"No relation at all," Adella said. "My grandmother was a friend of Winnifred."

"Why ...?" Phoebe asked.

Adella couldn't make out what she was asking, yet she'd seen plenty of drunk carpenters. After all this time in Marleigh Manor, Adella was surprised to see a face she'd never seen before, yet Phoebe didn't look like she left her room often. She wondered how many others were hidden in corners of the house she'd never explored.

"What do you want ...?" Phoebe asked.

"Winnifred wishes to see you," Adella said.

"No one wants to see me ...!" Phoebe insisted, yet when Adella made no reply, she sighed and forcibly climbed off her messy bed.

Phoebe seemed barely able to stand, yet she stumbled around the bed. Adella stepped into the hallway to let her pass. Harrington stepped out of his door as Phoebe crossed the hall, and he and Adella exchanged surprised glances. Yet Adella followed Phoebe all the way into Winnifred's room.

"Phoebe," Winnifred said. "Please, come in."

Phoebe was already inside, yet she made no comment on it. She staggered to the foot of Winnifred's bed and stared at her.

"Have you heard about Mitchell?" Winnifred asked.

"Estella just told me," she said, nodding toward Adella. No one bothered to correct her.

"What plans do you have?" Winnifred asked.

"Should I start packing?" Phoebe asked. "Back to the bar? Better there than here."

"Are you unhappy?" Winnifred asked.

"Why should I be?" Phoebe asked. "Wine to bathe in, food, fire ... I don't gotta do nothing."

"Has your husband said anything?" Winnifred asked.

"Rayden tells me nothing," Phoebe said. "I don't ask. No reason to."

Winnifred motioned for Adella to close the door, which she did.

"What's going on here ...?" Phoebe asked, glancing back and looking alarmed. "I know what you think of me, old woman. I'm not afraid of you."

"Mitchell is what's going on," Winnifred said.

"Mitchell ...!" Phoebe sneered. "Needs a good whipping, that upstart! Child ... thinks he's so grand!"

"What can be done?" Winnifred asked.

"Toss him out by his ears!" Phoebe snapped, staggering slightly. "I've tossed troublemakers worse than him into the street, and don't think I still can't!"

"What if he tosses us out?" Winnifred asked.

"Back to the bar, I guess," Phoebe said, shrugging. "Better than living here; lordly bitches looking down at you ...!"

"Will you take Rayden back to the bar?"
Winnifred asked.

"Who cares where he goes?" Phoebe asked. "I
don't."

"Thank you for coming to see me, Phoebe,"
Winnifred said, and she added. "Always good to speak
to a real woman."

"Damn right it is!" Phoebe said, but then she
looked confused.

"Adella, would you escort Phoebe back to her
room?" Winnifred asked. "I'm feeling sleepy."

"Yea, get some sleep," Phoebe said. "I don't
need no escort."

Adella opened the door as Phoebe approached,
and then closed it after she staggered through.

"Well, that was fruitless," Winnifred said. "I'd
hoped Rayden had told her his plans, but apparently he
has no more regard for his wife than anyone else."

"Why did he marry ... *that?*" Adella asked.

"Who knows why men do anything?" Winnifred
asked.

"Harrington saw me bringing her to you," Adella
said.

"Good," Winnifred said. "Half the household
must know by now. Go out, listen where you can, and
find out what everyone's saying."

"What should I say?" Adella asked.

"Just comment on how worried everyone looks,"

Winnifred sighed, laying back. "Get them to talk about Mitchell, if you can."

"Are you all right?" Adella asked.

"I just need rest," Winnifred said. "My condition is draining."

"Anything I can do?" Adella asked.

"I've tried every doctor in the district," Winnifred said. "I'll be fine."

Nodding, Adella stepped out, slightly worried about Winnifred, yet she knew nothing about medicine. She purposefully walked the wrong way, down the familiar hallway she used to sneak through, toward the far end of the new wing, spied several children playing in the common room near the back door. The oldest was Rufina; Adella smiled at them, yet said nothing. She circled around, walked past the privy, Mitchell's bedroom and study, and wondered if he'd keep his study locked from now on; as Lord of Marleigh Manor, Mitchell now owned the master office. Yet she kept walking, and found Lydia knitting before the fireplace in the entry room.

"Lydia, isn't it ...?" Adella asked.

"Yes, mam," Lydia set her knitting aside and stood.

"Oh, please, I'm no Marleigh," Adella said.

"You're a guest, I'm a servant ... for now, at least," Lydia said. "Can I do anything for you?"

"I was just ... going to my room," Adella said. "I'm frightened. Everyone seems so ... nervous."

"Family politics," Lydia said. "Big change today."

"Is Mitchell ready for the office?" Adella asked.

"That's not for me to say," Lydia said. "It's not even a safe question to ask, begging your pardon."

"You don't need to stand on ceremony for me," Adella said. "Why isn't it safe?"

"Nothing's safe anymore," Lydia said, a worried tone to her voice. "Excuse me, mam; I need to check on the twins."

"Of course," Adella nodded politely.

As Lydia hurried off, Adella left the new wing. She hadn't heard a cry; Lydia was lying to escape her questions, yet she couldn't blame a Prescott for being worried.

In the music room, the Berkeley-Marleighs sat with glasses of wine.

"Adella ...!" Stella called. "Please, come join us."

Adella hesitated, then walked toward her.

"I was just ... going to my room," Adella repeated her lie. "I'm frightened. Everyone seems so ... nervous."

"Change frightens some," Stella said. "Poor Middleton! He was a good man."

"I never got to know him," Adella said.

"Too bad," Stella said. "He kept this family from tearing itself apart after my first husband got killed."

"Killed ...?" Adella asked although she already knew the story.

"In a duel," Stella answered. "Harlan, let Adella sit down. She's our guest."

Her youngest son jumped up and offered his chair. Adella didn't want to sit, yet she'd been instructed to listen. As she sat, Harlan pulled up the harp stool for himself.

"You remember my sons, Barton Perry, named after his father, Barton Marlowe Quinton, and Harlan. And you couldn't forget my daughters, Bessie and Nora."

Adella nodded to each.

"Well, now that my son is Lord of Marleigh Manor, things should quiet down," Stella said. "Transfer of family title is a terrible hardship, and now we must accept and become accustomed to the new way."

"New way ....?" Adella asked.

"New leadership, of course," Stella said. "Every family leader brings a new perspective."

"A Berkeley-Marleigh perspective?" Adella asked.

"There are no Berkeley-Marleighs," Stella said. "My father insisted I take that name when I married Lester, and old Morley agreed, but Mitchell is a full-blooded Marleigh. When I married my second husband, I took his name: Quinton. When Bessie married, she appended our name to her husband's, Holton Fawcett Manley, and became Bessie Philomena Manley-Quinton. Now that the transition of title is complete, she'll be going back to her husband's family, where she lived before Mitchell summoned us."

"The rest of you will be staying?" Adella asked.

"My son Mitchell is Lord of Marleigh Manor," Stella said. "My second son, Barton, is next in line. Our place is here."

Adella nodded, secretly alarmed. She hadn't considered; the next in line for Lordship of Marleigh Manor was Mitchell's brother, a Quinton. Every Marleigh's only hope of controlling the family estate was for Mitchell to have a son and heir who was a Marleigh *... no wonder Winnifred hoped she'd marry Mitchell!* Winnifred wasn't using her as a tool to civilize Mitchell; *if she married him, her eldest son would be the next Lord of Marleigh Manor!*

"Are you all right, dear?" Stella asked. "You suddenly look pale. Harlan, pour her some wine."

Despite the wine, minutes passed before Adella regained control of herself. Bessie fanned her, although why she was carrying a fan in the middle of winter Adella couldn't guess.

"Thank you; I feel better," Adella said, after sipping half her glass of wine.

"Good, good," Stella said. "Now, tell me about your family, my dear. We must get to know you."

Adella began reciting the same lies she'd told before, yet she understood her purpose: Stella was examining her, sizing her up as a potential wife for her son, Harlan, or her younger brother-in-law, Norton. Did Stella want the house to remain in Mitchell's hands, Marleigh hands, or become a house of Quintons? Either way, she'd be mother of its Lord.

Hallewell and Hartford arrived and again placed steaming bowls and platters of food for the family on the wide table in the music room. Slowly others came in, congregating in small groups, each looking askance at everyone else. In the middle of the room, Stella and her sons celebrated as if it were a party; everyone else acted as if at a wake. Some were already planning Middleton's funeral; dates and times were debated by those who dared speak openly.

Some left silently, excusing themselves with the lie that they were deeply mourning Middleton. No one believed them.

Adella sat in the room all evening, listening to them chatter. Stella suggested that, after the dismal formalities had passed, Marleigh Manor should host a huge party to celebrate Mitchell assuming steerage of the family. She went into great detail describing the important local figures she'd insist be invited.

Adella wondered if there'd be any family left by the time the dismal formalities passed.

Reed appeared in the music room, stoic, yet glancing around as if he'd never been in it before. Several conversations failed as he arrived, yet he stepped in, walked to the table, took a plate, and began filling it. Middleton had recognized him in his will, but what did that mean?

Would Mitchell have to accept him now?

Barton walked up and shook Reed's hand, congratulating him, and welcoming him to the family.

Reed looked like he wanted to punch him; Reed was the first-born son of Middleton. Without Mitchell, Reed would've been Lord of Marleigh Manor. Yet Reed spoke politely and demurely, assuring Barton that the judge, constable, and doctor had been delivered safely to their homes.

"Safely ...?" Barton asked. "Have there been any incidents to make it unsafe?"

"Not since late fall," Reed said. "A driver was found murdered on North Road."

Adella's eyes widened.

"Murdered ...?" Barton exclaimed. "This is beastly news!"

"The murderer was never found," Reed said. "Whoever murdered him drove his cart here ... with all its lumber intact. The constables are still searching for the murderer, but he could be on the mainland by now."

Or ... the murderess could be listening to your conversation, Adella thought.

"Adella ...!" Stella exclaimed. "You've gone pale again ...!"

"I ... should go to my room," Adella said.

"Bessie, Nora; help her," Stella said. "Barton, shame on you, discussing grisly topics on such a day ... in the presence of ladies; it's too much."

"My apologies," Barton said to Adella.

"Mine, too," Reed added.

Minutes later, Adella found herself being half-carried, Bessie on one arm and Nora on the other, through halls, up and down stairs, to her room.

"Don't worry, dear," Bessie said. "My brother Barton always talks on inappropriate matters."

"So does Harlan, yet he's really smart," Nora added. "You'll like him once you get to know him."

Harlan ....? Adella sighed, certain she was being primed again.

Both girls talked pleasantly, chatting as they would to a sister, rambling on about their opinions of Marleigh Manor and how it could be improved. Both seemed overly friendly, as if working together for a previously-discussed agenda. At her door, Adella thanked them, yet they insisted on entering her room to help her undress. Adella didn't know how to refuse; she hadn't needed help to get undressed since she was five, but these girls insisted that no woman could manage alone.

Bessie and Nora were shocked by the bareness of her room, her lack of makeup, no tables or chairs, no fireplace, wardrobe, or proper bedding. Four of Winnifred's old dresses were lain across the foot of her bed, and the sisters fussed that such gowns needed careful tending. Adella was careful to insure they didn't look under her bed; she could never explain Reed's jars of resin and glue. She felt certain both these silly, frivolous girls would faint if she described how she'd sealed her windows and tightened the ropes on her bed.

Neither girl would depart until Adella was in bed, her blanket and cloak pulled up to her chin.

Adella pretended to be sleeping until she heard their footfalls vanish in the distance. Then she sighed and shook her head.

The driver's body had been found ...!

Constables were still looking for his murderer ... for her ...!

If anyone knew ... or even guessed ...!

Worries kept her awake ... or bad dreams woke her when she dared fade into oblivion. Old nightmares tormented; *prison, trial, a hangman's noose ...!*

When the bell rang for breakfast, she stayed in her bed.

Shortly afterwards, half of the women in Marleigh Manor flooded into her room. Abigail Prescott was summoned to examine her, and Stella, Edwina, Charity, Grace, Bessie, Nora, Rowena, Ettie, and Hortence acted as if the plague had arrived. Adella repeatedly explained she'd just had nightmares ... probably brought on by Middleton's passing. However, all insisted it was because of the horrible room.

Within an hour, Adella was moved to another room. This room was smaller, yet had a fireplace, padded furniture, and a carpet; it wasn't cold at all. Its bed had a feather mattress, clean sheets, and thick quilts; Adella had never lain in such luxury. Her dresses hung in a small wardrobe, and still the women seemed scandalized.

"Sending a lady to sleep in that ... storage room ... was unthinkable!" Stella insisted, and all the women agreed.

Edwina thought her shortage of dresses was inhuman, and her lack of sleeping gowns unfathomable. She promised Adella some old chemises and nightgowns, and would bring them to her before supper time. Stella sent Bessie and Nora to fetch some proper makeup, appalled to learn Adella had none.

Adella sat horrified, yet unable to show it, as six women helped her prepare for lunch. Never had she worn makeup nor imagined how tight a corset could be laced. They fussed with her hair for almost an hour, and Charity had Grace fetch her a string of pearls for Adella to wear around her neck.

Looking in a mirror, Adella hardly recognized herself. Her reflection was a true lady of wealth and breeding, like a painting of Vertiline, her hair curled and piled atop her head so not one lock touched her neck, which looked surprisingly long and thin. Charity's string of pearls probably cost more than her father's tools and everything he'd ever owned. Her pinked cheeks were caked in so much makeup she felt like mortar had dried onto her face and would crack and fall off if touched.

As she entered the dining hall, the ladies introduced Adella as if they were auctioneers peddling at public market. Exclamations described her beauty, gentility, nobility, grace, and innocence ... which Adella felt she lacked in every way. Yet the men applauded and fawned upon her as if meeting her for the first time ... even Mitchell. She sat in her usual place, yet again every eye was upon her.

Chapter 13

Lunch was delicious, and for the first time, Adella felt like the impostor she was. Gaudy, pretentious, and self-conscious, she looked like all the other ladies, a painted doll for men to play with, engaging in vacuous discussions about the weather and everyone's health. Afterwards, they adjourned to the music room, where the exact same continued.

The music room was so grand Adella had always assumed wealthy families gathered there to enjoy its beauty. Now, as decorated as every curtain and lampshade, Adella realized it was because these people had nowhere else to go. They accomplished nothing, held no lofty goals, and all they thought about was enhancing their wealth and status in the family. She doubted if one of them, save perhaps Rowena, Reed, Ettie, and Hortence, could even build an outhouse with all the wood and every tool she'd ever held.

Middleton's illegitimate children, Rowena, Reed, Ettie, and Hortence, stood like lepers by a well; the Marleighs, especially Letitia and her three daughters, blatantly ignored them, and silently glared. Quintons welcomed them with forgeries of delight, not accepting them, but delighted at how their presence humiliated the Marleighs. Prescotts, even Camden, didn't seem to know how to react to Reed and his half-sisters. Former equals made into superiors; their former-relations avoided meeting their eyes, as if they felt suddenly felt even more disgraced. Darbys avoided them, watching to see how the illegitimates' newfound status would prove ... to their benefit or detriment.

Rowena, Reed, Ettie, and Hortence had tried to engage with their newly-pronounced relations. They ended up standing together, ostracized and outcast, which only enhanced their discomfort.

Adella wished she could join them. She was more an outsider than they, although only she and Winnifred knew it. She especially liked Rowena, yet feared she might slip and say something that would reveal she'd eavesdropped on her private conversations. She liked Lydia for the same reason, yet Lydia wasn't welcomed in the music room and was openly distrustful ... of who she thought Adella was.

Adella sat between the only women she felt comfortable around; Grace and her mother, Natalie. When Natalie announced she had to feed her twins, Adella expressed a love of babies and asked to accompany her and Grace.

On their way out, Reed caught her eye; he looked envious, forlorn, and uncomfortable. He'd been denied his rightful life, and now suffered privileges and responsibilities of a bloodline which had betrayed him. His real father had to die before he'd recognize him. Adella felt sorry for Reed, yet she couldn't jeopardize her own precarious pretense.

Glad to escape the tensions of the music room, Adella smiled. As they stepped into the entry room, the clicking of needles came from the couch before the fireplace.

"Can Lydia join us?" Adella asked.

Lydia and Grace looked surprised, but Natalie smiled.

"Lydia, would you ...?" Natalie asked.

"Yes, Miss Natalie," Lydia said, and she set aside her needles.

The four of them entered the nursery. Both twins were awake yet quiet. Adella felt giddy, being included in their conversation rather than eavesdropping. She glanced at the closet door, wondering what these girls would say if they knew of her hideaway behind the wall.

"Thanks for joining us," Adella said to Lydia.

"Is there something you'd like, Miss Adella?" Lydia asked.

"It's just Adella, and no; I just ... feel like an outsider."

"Are you uncomfortable?" Natalie asked.

"Just ... homesick ... a little," Adella said.

"We're sorry to host you through such a calamitous event," Natalie said. "Poor Middleton was diagnosed four months ago, but anticipation only made it worse."

"I suspect Reed and his sisters are suffering worse than I," Adella said. "Did they know ... before the reading of the will ...?"

"Everyone knew," Grace said. "It's been horrible pretending we didn't know, and now ...!"

"Will they be accepted?" Adella asked.

"That's up to Mitchell," Natalie said.

"But Winnifred said Marleighs and Prescotts were once united by marriage ...?" Adella asked.

"We are ... were ...," Lydia said, and then she caught herself. "Begging your pardon, Miss Natalie and Grace ...!"

"We're not Marleighs," Natalie said to Lydia.

Lydia looked frightened, yet finally bowed her head.

"Prescotts are all terrified of what changes Mitchell will bring," Lydia lowered her voice to a whisper. "Mitchell hates us more than ever ... Reed especially. None of us will be here by summer."

"He can't ...!" Grace began.

"Who can stop him?" Natalie asked.

"I wouldn't worry," Adella said. "Winnifred said she's not worried."

"What can Winnifred do?" Grace whispered, glancing at the open door to her room.

"Winnifred has Vertiline's jewels ... which Mitchell wants," Adella said.

"Vertiline's jewels ...?" Grace asked. "How much ...?"

"A fortune," Natalie said. "At least, that's what I've heard ..."

"More than a fortune," Lydia said. "All Prescotts know; Vertiline loved jewelry. Old Morley spared no expense, and almost bankrupted the family, giving her gifts. My great-grandfather, Merton Kinsley Prescott, said Morley did it to infuriate his father, who hated Vertiline, but he was wrong; old Morley transferred the family treasury from cash to precious jewels to get its wealth out of reach of his murdering father, Captain Marston Ramsay Marleigh."

"I never knew that!" Grace said.

"Neither did I," Natalie said.

"Prescotts have long memories," Lydia said.

"You've every right to be bitter," Natalie said. "Prescotts and Marleighs are basically one family."

"Not when half are servants, begging your pardon," Lydia said.

"Mother married into the Marleigh family, and

father's mother is Charity," Grace explained to Adella. "Charity's brother, Middleton, is the father of Rowena, Reed, Ettie, and Hortence. They're illegitimate, but related to all of us."

"If we proclaimed that, we'll be thrown into the snow," Lydia said.

"Not anymore," Adella said. "Mitchell knows he'll never get Vertiline's jewels if he throws everyone out. Ask Winnifred."

Moments later, all four girls invaded Winnifred's room, Natalie with both of her twin sons in her arms. After a brief explanation, Winnifred stopped Grace in mid-sentence.

"Adella, you know what I'm about to say," Winnifred said. "Go to the music room and tell Rowena that Natalie needs her. Then stay there; you know what I want."

Adella nodded. Leaving the girls with Winnifred, she returned to the music room to find it unchanged. She whispered Winnifred's request into Rowena's ear. As Rowena walked away, Adella smiled.

"What's going on?" Reed asked Adella.

"Nothing I can say here," Adella whispered. "Trust me."

Adella walked away from Reed, as if dismissing him, and several Marleighs and Quintons smiled to see it. She aimed toward Stella and her children.

"Adella, please join us," Stella said, and both Barton and Harlan jumped up to provide her a place to sit. Barton's was closest; she sat on his chair.

Like Charity, Nora was an accomplished harpist, and at Adella's request, Nora gave an amazing performance. Soft notes and gentle melodies filled the music room for almost an hour. Everyone fell silent to listen; they'd discussed the transition until no opinions remained unvoiced. Near the end of her strumming and plucking, Rowena returned and silently nodded to Adella, yet her expression was grim. Adella couldn't approach her in public; her news would have to wait.

Later that evening, as Adella reached the top of the stairs on the way to her new room, a harsh voice spoke.

"Adella ...!"

Mitchell stood in the hallway, beside the top of the stairs. She paused and looked at him.

"I hope you've had a pleasant evening," Mitchell said.

"As much as possible ... under the circumstances," Adella said.

"Would you do me the honor of a brief conversation?" Mitchell asked.

Adella stared at him. Even standing alone in the hallway, Mitchell was an imposing figure, immaculately dressed, tall and solidly built. Adella feared him, yet she suspected he wouldn't act violently with so many ears close by.

"Of course," Adella said.

Mitchell gestured, then escorted her toward the

master office. He held the door and allowed her to enter first.

As before, in her brief, first impression, everything was grand, the woodwork old, yet polished and gleaming. The desk was wide and tall. Clutter was piled everywhere, stacked papers, scrolls, and pistols set aside as if absently dropped, empty flower vases, beautiful on their own, and towering bookshelves. Chairs, tables, and benches stood before the massive fireplace, which looked a hundred years old, yet all in excellent condition. Windows, red drapes drawn aside, overlooked the front of the manor, down the hill onto snow-covered lands, and across to distant hills. Another wall hosted seventeen paintings of austere old men; previous masters of this office.

Mitchell closed the door.

"May I offer you a brandy?" Mitchell asked.

"It burns my tongue," Adella said, remembering the driver's flask.

Mitchell nodded, poured himself a brandy, and took a small sip.

"May I speak plainly?" Mitchell asked.

"If you must," Adella said.

"You seemed as surprised as I when Winnifred announced you as heir to Vertiline's jewels," Mitchell said.

"I didn't know Vertiline had jewels until that moment," Adella said.

"Winnifred is using you," Mitchell said. "We've

no proof she named you in her will. She loves to manipulate ..."

"Everyone in this house manipulates," Adella said. "You invited me in here; you must want something. Yet I worry more about why someone manipulates."

"You're smart," Mitchell said. "You know why Winnifred announced her bequeathment before both of us ...?"

"To manipulate us," Adella said.

Mitchell looked surprised.

"She has ... intentions for you?" Mitchell asked.

"The same intentions she has for you, I suspect," Adella said. "Twice my father tried to force me to wed. Both suitors failed. No one will force, manipulate, or bribe me to an altar."

"We agree on something," Mitchell said, toasting her with his brandy glass. "No offense; your beauty is evident, but the Marleigh family is a cesspool of hatreds and resentments. I must resolve what matters I may."

"I agree," Adella said. "I'll retire and leave you to your duty."

"If her bequeathment is real, then Winnifred is making you integral to Marleigh," Mitchell said. "Why ...?"

"You'll have to ask her. "

"Pressuring Winnifred is pointless."

Adella nodded; *she knew that firsthand.*

"Why did your mother send you here?" Mitchell asked.

"My grandmother suggested it," Adella said. "My mother's a lot like Winnifred. She duels with secrets ... and usually wins."

"Formidable woman," Mitchell said. "You must resemble her."

"Is that a compliment?" Adella asked.

"It sounded like one, but don't mistake me," Mitchell said. "I can't allow myself to be manipulated ... by anyone."

"Isn't that why you were denied your title ...?" Adella asked.

"Only according to Winnifred," Mitchell said. "I questioned Enfield and Rayden. If that was Grandpa Morley's intent, they knew nothing of it."

"Winnifred alone knew ... or someone's lying," Adella said.

"Uncle Middleton may have known, yet he never spoke of it," Mitchell said. "Middleton liked being patriarch; he may have believed my knowledge of Grandpa Morley's intent a threat to his position."

"You've achieved your goal," Adella said. "What will you do with it?"

"Winnifred's speech was painfully accurate," Mitchell said. "I'd hoped to restore peace by removing the most calamitous elements."

"That would leave you alone," Adella said.

"This family enjoys vengeance," Mitchell said. "Prescotts, Darbys, and even Quintons hate each other. You can't extinguish a house-fire by allowing part of it to keep burning."

"You can't extinguish hate by adding more, or by favoring one hate over another," Adella said. "You've inherited a house afire. I pity you."

"I'm hated by everyone," Mitchell said. "My younger brothers, the Quintons, are strangers to me. Marleighs hate whoever's in charge. Prescotts hate all Marleighs ... for decisions made before any of us were born."

"No Marleigh's ever amended those decisions ... despite countless opportunities," Adella said. "What's your plan? How will you make peace?"

"By any means necessary," Mitchell said.

"I hope I'm not one of your means," Adella said.

"Winnifred's involving you, not I," Mitchell said. "That's why I asked to speak to you. If you wish, I can provide you escape from her manipulations. If you prefer to stay, I welcome your suggestions as to how I should proceed."

"My suggestions ...?" Adella asked.

"You're the only one here no one hates," Mitchell said. "You've no ancient resentments or ... hidden agendas ... except what Winnifred just gave you ... and we don't even know if her promise is real."

"I'll ... have to think upon it," Adella said.

"Thinking is always best," Mitchell said. "If at any time, day or night, you wish to offer suggestions, I'd be delighted to hear them."

"Thank you," Adella said. "I'll certainly inform

you ... should any possibilities occur to me."

"I look forward to talking with you again," Mitchell said.

Adella nodded.

Mitchell bowed, then opened the door and again held it for her. Adella stepped out into the hallway.

"Good night, Lord of Marleigh Manor," Adella said.

"Good night, guest of Marleigh Manor," Mitchell said.

Adella had to force her feet to walk slowly. She recognized manipulations; Mitchell had presented himself as a gallant young Lord facing an impossible challenge, vainly seeking to do good for everyone. If she were innocent of eavesdropping, he might have elicited her sympathy. Yet he was the same brigand who'd plotted with Harrington to steal three hundred silver coins from Enfield. He'd arranged for future meetings under the guise of listening to her advice, yet once Mitchell had Vertiline's jewels, he'd need her no more than Captain Marston had needed his young wife, Sarah.

Adella wondered if Mitchell's first wife would suffer the same untimely death.

She turned the corner to step down the curving stair, only to find Rayden standing there, at the top of the stair, leaning against the wall ... as if he'd been pressing an ear to it. Adella startled, and his cold eyes met hers.

"Master Rayden!" Adella exclaimed.

"Miss Cumberbatch," Rayden nodded to her.

She looked down; Rayden held an empty glass cup in one hand ... and the wall he'd been leaning against was adjacent to Mitchell's master office. *Had he been eavesdropping on her conversation with Mitchell ... through the wall?*

"So lovely to meet you ... here, of all places," Rayden said. "Do you and Mitchell meet ... in private ... often ...?"

"Sir, were you spying upon us?" Adella demanded.

"Spying ...?" Rayden chuckled. "What an interesting term! You should take care before you go spouting such words. Some might wonder what service drew you to this house ... right before an important death ... at a tragic moment in family politics. Just when a new ear and set of young eyes might prove ... so useful ...? And such a pretty pair of eyes ... meeting in secret with the new Lord of a wealthy family ...? Is that why you were brought here ...?"

Adella stared, yet didn't reply. Furious, she pushed past Rayden, rushed down the stair, and fled from his suspicious eyes.

Why had he laughed at the word 'spying'?

Did he think she'd been sent here to seduce Mitchell?

How many of her conversations had he spied upon?

She hurried to her new room, delighted to find it warm, a small fire brightly burning in her little hearth.

Her new room was a proper guest room, worthy of this elegant manor, small, yet decorated similar to Winnifred's room. She could live happily here, warm and contented.

Yet, had the ladies really given her this new room? Could they have done so without Mitchell's approval? Or had this room been Bessie's or Nora's room, and they gave it to her to curry her favor? Or had Mitchell secretly put her in that dreadful room just so he could later gift her with better accommodations? Had Winnifred arranged all of this to trick her into marrying Mitchell ...?

Too many plots, too many motives, and too many agendas; she couldn't trust anyone. Even if Winnifred hadn't willed her Vertiline's jewels, someone thinking she had might threaten her. She was now a barrier preventing others from gaining Vertiline's jewels. Winnifred was placing her life in jeopardy.

Yet, as she undressed and slipped into the warm, lacy nightgown Edwina had provided, the comforts of her new room relaxed her.

Whether or not old Morley had been twisted by his father, Mitchell had certainly been twisted by this hateful house. Growing up angry, constantly teased about his stolen inheritance, Mitchell must've endured a painful, friendless childhood.

Yet, despite his devious nature, he could act civil and politely when he needed to, which showed a strength of will seldom achieved. His manners today had been impeccable. With the proper molding, could he be transformed into a man only of his better half, noble, casting off his bitter resentments?

The Lady of Marleigh Manor: did everyone want her to have that title? Mitchell, Winnifred, Stella ... well, she wanted her to marry one of her sons, but only because she believed her to be of a wealthy family. Yet she owned nothing, not even the clothes she was wearing, just an old box of tools hidden in a secret room.

What would happen if she married Mitchell ... and then they discovered the truth?

She laid back on the thick mattress, rested her head on its soft pillows, and pulled clean sheets and plush quilts up to her chin. She loved her new, warm bedroom; *could she really give this up and go back to begging, penniless on icy streets?*

Would she succumb to the irresistible manipulations of comfort?

Mitchell was handsome ... and natures could change.

All night she dreamed of him ... of the life she could have. Matron of a wealthy family, she could manipulate others for the good of many. Perhaps she could even shut down their workhouses; horrors of those places haunted the stories carpenters told around campfires. She saw herself not as a penniless orphan, but as a noble benefactress, a lady of wealth and standing to remake a whole district into a wonderful place.

What kind of life would her future children have

if she left? If she did have children, how could she tell them, raised in a hovel, that they could've inherited Marleigh Manor ...?

Then her dreams turned dark. Mitchell towered over her, threatening to crush her. His face became that of the cart driver on North Road, chasing her across the rugged countryside. Thorns clung and ripped her skirt. She couldn't escape ...!

She lifted her adze ...!

Adella awoke sweating, biting back a cry.

She'd killed a man; was she any better than those who lived here ...?

As the noises of the manor alerted her to the coming of breakfast, Adella dressed in a new gown she'd found in her wardrobe, possibly from Nora, as it was too thin for Bessie. A knock came to her door, then it opened. A young Prescott girl entered holding a wide bowl of steamy water. Her eyes widened as she looked up at Adella.

"You ... you're dressed!" she exclaimed.

"Well, yes ...," Adella said.

"I was sent to dress you ...!" the little girl said.

"Who are you?" Adella asked.

"Ginny," she said. "Virginia Rhody Prescott, mam."

"A pleasure to meet you," Adella said.

"Thank you, mam," Ginny said. "If they knew I'd arrived too late ...!"

"I won't tell them," Adella promised. "Now, let's

have a talk."

"Prescotts aren't allowed to talk to Marleighs," Ginny said.

"I'm not a Marleigh," Adella said.

The young girl couldn't be more than seven. She appeared to think this over, then set her bowl of water on the small table.

"What a pretty little thing you are," Adella said. "Where's your room?"

"In the Prescott wing ... I mean, the servants quarters," Ginny said. "We're not allowed to call it the Prescott wing."

"I won't tell," Adella smiled at her. "Maybe you could show me your room someday."

Ginny shrugged.

"Do you like my room?" Adella asked. "You can play in here ... if you're careful."

"Really ...?" Ginny looked around.

"Yes, but first you must be my friend," Adella said. "Who told you to come help me dress?"

"Hortence," Ginny said. "She was a Prescott, but Middleton made her a Marleigh."

"I see," Adella said.

"I wish I was a Marleigh," Ginny said.

"Why would you want to be a Marleigh?" Adella asked.

"No chores," Ginny said.

"I understand that," Adella said. "I used to have chores, too." Ginny gave her a funny look. "My parents believed everyone needed to work, and I was given lots of chores."

Ginny was a delight, and when the bell rang for breakfast, Adella walked beside her as she carried her cooled bowl of water all the way to the end of the hall. Their paths split; Adella noted the door to the right which Ginny walked through, headed to the Prescott wing. Adella determined to investigate it soon, yet hurried in the other direction.

At breakfast, Mitchell sat before them at the head of the table. After grace, he rose to gain their attention.

"We received confirmation from Father Gresham this morning," Mitchell said. "He'll arrive this afternoon at 3:00. Services for Master Middleton will immediately follow."

He sat down, and eating proceeded, yet no one spoke. Few glances exchanged, each hoarding private thoughts.

Adella rose after eating and walked straight to Winnifred's room. To her surprise, Winnifred had already learned Adella was in a better room. She related to her everything Mitchell had said.

"Mitchell's not stupid," Winnifred said. "He can't act the tyrant in front of you, not if he wants Vertiline's jewels."

"How badly does he want them?" Adella asked.

"All rich men crave more wealth," Winnifred said. "So, he thinks I manipulate him?"

"He seemed worried you were manipulating me,

too," Adella said.

"You should've seen his father act innocent when our sister was found dead in the well," Winnifred said. "Everleigh Esther Marleigh; she was a soft, timid girl ..."

"Like Ginny?" Adella asked. "She arrived at my new bedroom this morning; she'd been told to help me dress, but I was already dressed. She was carrying a bowl of hot water; I'm not sure why."

"That was for you ... for washing," Winnifred said. "Expect it from now on; cleanliness is required, and most Marleigh women couldn't pull on bloomers without Prescott help. Have you bathed since you've been here?"

"*Bathed ...?*" Adella asked. "*In a tub ...?*"

"You've never bathed ...?" Winnifred asked.

"Only in streams," Adella said. "I've installed bathrooms, sanded and waxed floors, nailed ... "

"*Not while the door is open!*" Winnifred hissed. "I'll send Ginny to fetch you soon. You should bathe before the funeral. Tell Lydia I need her."

The twins were bawling. Lydia walked them back and forth, Rowena and Natalie attending ... helpless to silence their cries. Adella fetched Lydia for Winnifred, then went back to her room to wait. Not long after, a knock came to her door.

"Bath time," Ginny said.

Ginny led Adella into the older section, between the wing she stayed in and the main house. One steamy room held a tub. Ginny closed the door and wasted no

time unlacing and undressing Adella, then helped her
into the hot water. Adella loved the feeling of soaking in
hot water, yet she kept silent and let Ginny go about her
routine; she couldn't tell Ginny she'd never bathed
before. Soap bubbles amused her, as did the perfumes
Ginny added to the water. She played with the bubbles
until she saw Ginny look at her strangely. When Ginny
added fresh hot water, Adella almost jumped out of the
tub, fearing she'd boil, yet she soon sank into its
unfamiliar, delightful comfort.

Ginny dried and redressed her, and then led her
back to her room.

"It's almost lunch time," Ginny informed her.
"Then we go to the chapel."

"Where's the chapel?" Adella asked, and she
added as Ginny looked at her funny, "Don't forget, I
haven't been here long."

"The white pathway leads to it, on the other side
of the barn," Ginny said.

As she headed to lunch, she saw others doing the
same. Bessie and Nora walked beside their mother, yet
she whispered to them, then paused and waited while
her daughters proceeded onward.

"Good afternoon, Adella," Stella said, eyes
running up and down, scanning every inch of her dress.
"Why, look at you! So pretty, and for once, all your
bows are tied!"

"Bows ...?" Adella asked. "Oh, yes; Ginny
helped me dress."

"Ah, that explains it," Stella said, and she motioned to her, and together they approached the stair toward the main hall. "You're probably not accustomed to having to dress yourself. I'd almost assumed you'd never worn fancy clothes before."

"Of ... of course I have," Adella lied.

"Without makeup ...?" Stella asked.

"I've been ... out of sorts," Adella said. "My family ... has its own problems."

"What a terrible predicament for a young lady!" Stella exclaimed. "Nothing worse than an unsuitable suitor ... who causes arguments between parents. Did your mother inform your father before she ... spirited you away?"

"No," Adella said.

"Has your father pledged you to marry this abominable suitor?" Stella asked.

"I hope not," Adella said. "He hadn't ... before mother sent me here."

"Sent ...?" Stella asked. "I was wondering, if she and Winnifred were such good friends, why didn't she come here herself?"

Adella bit her lip, struggling to invent more lies.

"She ... knew ... knows a lot of people," Adella stammered. "She's well known ... in our district ... and was sure father would find her. If she'd come here, so would father."

"Do you suspect your father has followed her to France?" Stella asked.

"I wouldn't be surprised," Adella said.

"Such a pity," Stella exclaimed. "Of course, there's only one certain way of avoiding an unhappy marriage ...!"

"What's that?" Adella asked.

"A different marriage," Stella said. "If you married into a proper family, especially to a wealthy prospect, before your father finds you, he couldn't force you to marry another."

"Marriage ...?" Adella exclaimed. *"But ...!"*

"We should talk about that later," Stella insisted. "Privately, just the two of us. You will find I make as thoughtful a confidant as Winnifred, and my sons are perfect gentlemen. Arrangements could be made, if you were willing. Yet let's speak no more of this now. As you well know, the walls of Marleigh Manor ... have many ears."

Walls have many ears ...?

What did she suspect ...?

Praying she would never have another conversation with Stella, Adella walked silently beside her all the way to the dining room.

Lunch was another quiet affair, respectful of the solemn activity about to occur. Afterwards, she walked beside Bessie and Nora as they trooped out into the chilly outdoors, wrapped in warm cloaks, and followed the trail of footprints over snowy flagstones Ginny had described as white, but which couldn't be seen. Their path led around the barn to the top of a small hill.

The chapel was a small building, only slightly bigger than Winnifred's bedroom, and it had tight benches that they squeezed onto. The coffin was set before the altar, its lid propped open, holding the mortal remains of Middleton. The elderly priest, Father Gresham, arrived early, yet waited until 3:00 out of respect.

In the chapel, for the first time, Adella saw Marleighs, Prescotts, Darbys, and Quintons crowded together into the cramped space, and many stood for lack of room. Each seemed more nervous of their political enemies than the coffin.

Letitia sat in the front beside her daughters, Vivian, Jennie, and Isabell, on one side. On the other side sat Rowena, Reed, Ettie, and Hortence, and not one glance swapped between legitimates and illegitimates. Mitchell sat between them, pretending not to notice either side.

Father Gresham finally began the ceremony. The tiny chapel started out cool, yet as long minutes droned, it grew uncomfortably warm. Cloaks were shed as quietly as possible, and Father Gresham glared at the noisiest. He paused at the slightest sound so no one missed one word of his readings. Yet this funeral was little different than any Adella had attended. Most of the women wept, some loudly, which also irritated Father Gresham. Men stared silently, as stoic as statues.

When the service concluded, six men, Mitchell, Enfield, Rayden, Acton, Hayden, and Harlow arose, closed, and lifted the coffin. Reed attempted to join them, but at a harsh word from the priest, he subsided. Instead, Reed followed directly behind them, trailed by Letitia, who'd stopped crying. She was followed by her three weeping daughters.

On the far side of the hill rested a graveyard, looking down into a small valley where trees grew around a huge, bare, flat circle; Adella assumed a large lake lay there, frozen solid and covered with snow. A grave had already been dug, and after a brief, second ceremony by Father Gresham, they lowered the coffin into the bitter, frozen Earth.

A cold wind was blowing, and after the first sprinkles of earth, no one stayed to watch the coffin be covered. All hurried back to the warm main manor, avoiding reentering the tiny chapel. They entered through the door beside Adella's first bedroom, tromped up the hall, and divided toward different corners of the house. Adella followed the thinning crowd all the way into the music room.

Harlow was pouring wine for everyone, hoping to ease both their chills and nerves. Adella accepted a glass, then drank standing near Grace and Natalie.

Raised, angry voices echoed through the walls. A silence fell, making the voices seem louder. All strained to listen. No one knew where it was coming from, yet no one commented on it.

The shouting finally stopped. The house grew quiet, and every eye looked nervous.

"Nora, play something," Stella whispered.

Nora looked shocked, yet she silently walked to the harp, sat upon its stool, and began to play. Her fingers strummed a sad hymn, which seemed to soothe those who looked offended at her first note, yet the religious harmony seemed appropriate. Music alleviated the tension ... save for those few actually mourning.

Slowly whispered conversations began, protected by the gentle music. Stresses settled, and the music room resumed its normalcy, except for the presence of three illegitimate daughters, who looked terrified.

Hallewell and Hartford retired to the kitchen. Half an hour later, they wheeled in a cart laden with cold appetizers, assuring everyone a big dinner was cooking and would be ready shortly.

The mingling of families ended when dinner was served. No table in Marleigh Manor could seat everyone, so each went to their usual place in the Marleigh dining room, the Prescott dining room, or the kid's dining room. Rowena, Ettie, and Hortence sat across from Adella, yet none looked happy to be there.

For the first time since the funeral, Mitchell appeared. He stood at the end of the table, even during grace, and then he lifted his wine glass and held it aloft.

"To Middleton Kent Marleigh, beloved Lord of Marleigh Manor," Mitchell said.

Everyone stood, raised their glass, and repeated his toast.

Dinner was roast pork, a thick vegetable stew,

and fresh bread. Conversations broke out, each complimentary of poor Middleton, now in Heaven with the angels. However, his newly-named son, Reed, wasn't there. Adella wondered where he was ... and with which family he'd be dining from now on.

As dinner was winding down, a small Prescott child came in and handed Adella a note. She opened and read it.

'Come at once - Winnifred.'

Excusing herself, Adella hurried to the new wing. Winnifred was sitting up in her bed, glaring and frowning.

"What is it?" Adella asked.

"Reed," Winnifred said. "Mitchell just kicked him out."

"But ...!" Adella argued. *"But Mitchell said ...!"*

"Don't wait!" Winnifred said. "Stop him, if you can, or find out where he's going!"

Adella ran from the new wing, through the main rooms, up the stair, crossed into the old wing, down the stair and the length of the hall, and finally burst out into the snow-buried outdoors. She hadn't fetched her cloak; the cold stung, yet she was no weak Marleigh daughter. She ran through the crushed snow to Reed's door. She didn't wait to knock but threw it open and stepped inside.

"Adella ...!" Reed exclaimed.

"I just heard," Adella said, slightly panting from her exertions. "You mustn't leave."

"His Lordship says otherwise," Reed said.

"You're just as much a Marleigh as he," Adella said.

"I was a Marleigh from the reading of the will until one hour ago," Reed said. "Mitchell's letting me take a horse and saddle, nothing else."

"You can't go ...!" Adella argued.

"Mitchell gave me until tomorrow noon to be gone," Reed said. "After that, if I'm here, or if I take anything with me more than my clothes, one horse, and saddle, then he'll summon the constables and have me jailed."

"At least stay the night ...!" Adella pleaded.

"One night won't make any difference," Reed said, and then he paused and looked at her. "I'm a good stable-hand. Do you think your parents would hire me?"

"My parents are dead," Adella said.

"What ...?" Reed exclaimed.

Adella gasped; *she wasn't supposed to say that!*

"My ... parents ... are dead," Adella repeated, thinking fast. "That's why I was sent here. A house-fire ... I lost every penny and every relation. My family's holdings matched our debts; nothing was left. Mother had named Winnifred my god-mother when I was born; I had no one else to rely on. Winnifred invented the story of my mother going to Paris. Please ... don't tell ...!"

"I'm sorry," Reed said, and then he added.

"Losing your family ... I know how you feel."

"Please, don't leave yet," Adella said. "Stay the night."

"I can't," Reed said.

"Then ... don't just leave," Adella said. "Go to Winnifred. Talk to her first."

"Why ...?" Reed asked.

"I don't know," Adella confessed. "I don't know if she can do anything. But she's rich, and has something Mitchell wants ..."

"I know about Vertiline's jewels," Reed said.

"Maybe she can do something ... get Mitchell to change his mind," Adella said. "Please ...! Just talk to her ...!"

Reed stared at her.

"Very well," he said. "Because you asked ..."

"Come with me," Adella said. "We'll go talk to her ..."

"If you're seen walking through the house ... with me ... you could be the next one Mitchell tosses out," Reed said.

"I'll wait here," Adella said.

"We've been expecting this most of our lives," Reed said. "The Prescotts and I."

"You're not a Prescott ...?" Adella asked.

"My mother was Margaret Fulton," Reed said. "She was a barmaid in the village; she worked with Phoebe before she got Rayden drunk and married him in the middle of the night. I was born in the tavern ...

Middleton's first son. He took me on as stable-hand when she died."

"I didn't know," Adella said.

"It doesn't matter," Reed said. "Mitchell's hated me and every Prescott since the day he was born. Not one of us will be living here by spring."

"He ... he said he'd changed ...," Adella said.

"He must've wanted something from you," Reed said.

"He still does," Adella admitted, "but I won't give him what he wants."

"Then you'd best pack your bag," Reed said.

"I know," Adella said.

Reed looked at her, bowed his head, and headed out into the snow. Adella couldn't see him go; his only window was thickly shuttered, his only light coming from an oil lamp and vents of his small stove. Yet she stared at his rough workshop and tiny bedroom... *a servant's quarters.*

Reed was Mitchell's first cousin. He deserved everything Mitchell had ... and now he owned nothing. He'd ride until he had to sell his horse for food, and either find another job or beg. The idea that he could end up in a Marleigh workhouse was sickening.

He was a good man.

Good men don't last long in Marleigh Manor.

She sat on a bench and waited.

An hour later, Reed returned.

"What'd she say?" Adella asked.

"A lot," Reed said. "She's mad as a mother bear in a snowstorm. She gave me ten silver coins, enough to support me for months, and we agreed on where I'm to go."

"Where ...?" Adella asked.

"She asked me not to tell," Reed said. "I'm to leave tonight, now, and stay there until she sends word."

"Why ...?" Adella asked.

"She wouldn't say," Reed said. "But she made me promise to stay in touch; she might make Mitchell change his mind."

"Do you believe her?" Adella asked.

"I believe she'll try," Reed said. "Yet even she admitted I'm only the first. Mitchell will likely start weeding out everyone he doesn't like as soon as I'm gone."

"I'm sorry," Adella said.

Reed picked up his bag of clothes and slung it over his shoulder.

"Farewell, Adella," Reed said.

"I pray we meet again," Adella said.

Reed went out his door and around to the barn. Adella followed, unwilling to let him go, yet helpless to stop him. He grabbed a fancy saddle and blanket, some reins, and strapped them to the big red horse in silence. Shivering against the icy chill, Adella silently watched him.

"Go inside," Reed said as he mounted. "You mustn't catch cold."

"Thank you," Adella said. "Take care."

With a mastery Adella seldom saw, Reed rode off, hooves kicking up snow. She watched him ride across the path in front of the manor, up the long hill, and vanish over its crest.

Tears leaked as she hurried back to her warm room ... and burst their floodgates as she closed her door.

Chapter 14

Noise awoke her. Yawning, Adella heard rapid footfalls and voices raised in alarm. She was still wearing her dress from last night; she opened her door.

"What is it?" she asked the first person she saw.

"The ghost ...!" Harlow shouted as he hurried past. *"The ghost is back ...!"*

Adella followed as the whole household hurried through the manor and crowded into the new wing. Unable to get near enough to see, Adella asked what had happened.

"Another line of silver coins!" Camden told her, crowded against the back. "It goes across the hall, from Mitchell's bedroom to his study door."

"What does it mean?" Adella asked.

"No one knows," Camden said.

"Everyone, be quiet!" Rayden shouted. "There has to be a reason ...!"

"Another hidden treasure ...?" Harlow asked.

"We don't know," Rayden said. "The study door is locked."

Suddenly Hayden appeared behind Adella.

"I can't find him," Hayden shouted over everyone's heads. "He's not in the master office."

"He's not in his bedroom," Rayden said, and he pounded on the study door. "Mitchell ...! If you're in there, open up!"

No one answered.

Others were sent, but all returned with the same report; Mitchell wasn't to be found.

"Find the key," Enfield said.

"I already did," Rayden said. "The key is in the lock ... on the inside."

"Kick in the door," Enfield said.

"Don't destroy the door," Rayden said. "I might be able to get it open."

Rayden went into Mitchell's room, then returned with a large scroll and a long metal pin. He unfurled the scroll: it was a map, and he slid it through the wide gap under the study door. Then he stabbed the pin into the keyhole, and everyone heard the key fall. Rayden pulled out the map, upon which rested the key.

Without hesitation, Rayden slipped the key into the lock and opened the study door.

A cry came from Rayden ... and a scream from

Charity. Rayden and Enfield rushed inside ... and slammed the door behind them.

"What is it ...?" several voices demanded.

Charity's face was pale; *she couldn't speak.*

Moments later, Rayden and Enfield came out of the study and locked the door behind them.

"Acton, we need the constable," Rayden said. "Someone has to get him ... as fast as possible. Will you ...?"

"Of course," Acton said. "What's wrong?"

Enfield stammered some sounds, nothing intelligible.

"It's Mitchell," Rayden said. "He's been murdered."

Gasps and screams burst from the crowd.

Adella paled.

Murdered ...?

Mitchell ...?

It couldn't be ...!

"This room is sealed," Rayden announced. "Enfield has the key and no one is to go near this door until the constable arrives."

"I'll get him," Acton said.

"I'll ride with you," Garrick said.

The crowd parted just enough to let both men pass. They tromped down the hall and around the corner. Few eyes followed them.

"There's nothing we can do until the constable gets here," Rayden said.

"I demand to see ...!" Barton shouted.

"You'll stay here with us," Rayden said. "Hayden, Harlow, Enfield, and I; we'll make sure no one touches anything until the constable arrives. The rest of you, find someplace else to be. I want this hallway cleared. Don't leave the house."

No one moved.

"Please, do as he says," Enfield said. "We'll keep everyone informed ... as soon as we know anything."

"Why can't I see ...?" Barton demanded.

"Because we're suspects," Rayden said. "As his brother, you're a motivated suspect. Since I've been in prison, I'm sure to be suspected, and I don't want anything upsetting the constable's investigation until my name is cleared."

"Are you sure?" Letitia asked.

"I don't need a doctor to tell he's dead," Rayden said. "Whoever did this knew their business."

"*Who ...?*" Letitia asked.

"That's the constable's decision," Rayden said. "The more we interfere, the more suspect we'll be."

"Yes, we must leave it to the constable," Enfield said.

Charity had to sit down; someone brought a chair out of Letitia's bedroom for her. The rest were shooed away.

Adella went straight to Winnifred's room.

"What happened?" Winnifred asked.

"Mitchell," Adella said, barely able to believe it.

"They say ... he's been murdered. "

"What ...?!?" Winnifred screamed. *"Who says ...?!?"*

"Rayden and Enfield," Adella said. "Acton and Garrick are riding to fetch the constable."

"Oh, dear God!" Winnifred gasped, and she seemed to wilt upon her sheets.

Adella ran around and grasped her arm. *She'd sprung the news too quickly ...!*

"I'm sorry," Adella said.

"My heart ... my poor old heart," Winnifred gasped. "I don't know if I can take this."

"It's terrible," Adella said.

"Who ...?" Winnifred asked.

"We don't know," Adella said.

Adella finally sat on the bed beside her. Neither spoke; *what could they say?*

Others came to talk to Winnifred, yet they only asked the same unanswerable questions.

"Rayden's right; we must wait for the constable," Winnifred said.

The doctor arrived with the constable, Acton, and Garrick. At their command, the new wing was emptied of all but Winnifred, and they unlocked the door and examined the scene. Adella waited with the rest, in the crowded music room.

Several hours passed ... and Adella grew more fearful with each.

They'd found the cart driver's body ... and now

*the constable was here ... beginning a murder
investigation ...! He was sure to have been involved in
the dead driver's discovery ...!*

Hallewell and Hartford wheeled another cartload
of food out of the kitchen, sandwich makings, but few
had stomach for eating. Wine was sipped, yet little was
said.

Each glanced nervously at the others.

Someone was a murderer ...!

Enfield, Rayden, Charity, and Barton were
summoned to the new wing. An hour afterwards,
Rowena was sent for. Many gasped when her name was
announced. She looked as shocked as any as Rayden
escorted her into the new wing.

Another hour passed. The constable was seen
through the window, walking around the outside of the
house, Rayden and Barton behind him. Every eye
watched as they trudged through the snow, pointing at
every footprint, examining the grounds. When they
walked out of sight, a dozen voices began speaking.

Finally all of them, the constable, the doctor,
Enfield, Rayden, Charity, Barton, and Rowena came into
the music room.

The constable stepped forward, then eyed each
of them carefully.

"Master Mitchell has been murdered," the
constable said. "The line of thirty-one silver coins ran
from his corpse to the locked chest at the foot of his bed,
atop which was a strange pattern. Eight silver coins

stretched in a line across the top of the chest, and the seventh silver coin had four others stacked atop it. Searching Mitchell's pockets, we found the key to his chest and opened it. Many things lay in it, including a considerable amount of gold and silver, several loaded pistols, a knife, and a few other items. The only thing there of eight ... was his diaries. I've scanned all of them, but paid close attention to his seventh diary. Each was filled with comments, mostly derogatory, of the members of this house, many directed at Master Middleton, whom Mitchell greatly resented. However, I don't believe in ghosts. Somewhere in this house, or recently fled from it, is the murderer. I intend to reveal that person."

Several looked alarmed at this pronouncement. The constable surveyed them all again, long and silently, and then resumed.

"Inside Mitchell's seventh diary was one revelation ... on the fourth page," the constable said. "Between his many elaborate drawings, Mitchell chastised himself dozens of times for an indiscretion he committed two years ago. It seems Mitchell forced his affection upon a young lady of this household and later regretted it. His regret grew when he learned she was bearing his child. It's my duty to report that the child, Paxton Hayes Prescott, is Rowena and Mitchell's son."

Gasps, and a scream from Stella, filled the music room. Stella looked as pale as snow.

"This changes nothing in my investigation," the

constable said. "I will find out who murdered Master Mitchell."

"How ... how could they?" Harlan asked. "The door was locked ... from the inside!"

"When I find that out, the culprit will be arrested," the constable said.

"It was the ghost ...!" Letitia said.

"Enough of that!" the constable raised his voice to shout down the exclamations that followed. "There's no such thing as ghosts! Anyone who suggests Mitchell was murdered by anything but a human being will be marked as suspect."

"How ... how was he killed?" Hayden asked.

"Master Mitchell was stabbed ... the exact details are not to be discussed," the constable glanced back at Enfield, Rayden, Barton, and Charity. "Those who saw the body have been warned, and will be arrested for interference if anyone but they appears to know more details than I've described. None of you will leave this house. I'll send for Mr. Reed Fulton and have him returned. You'll each make yourselves available for questioning at any time I wish, and the slightest lie to me will be punished with instant imprisonment. Is there any question about that?"

No one spoke. Stella looked like she was about to faint.

"That's all I have to say," the constable said. "Master Mitchell's bedroom and study are locked. If anyone has duplicate keys to those rooms, I require them immediately. If anyone is found to have opened or entered either of those rooms, they'll be arrested. I'll remain inside this house until the guilty person is identified. Nothing is to be carried away, thrown out, or buried while I'm here. Nothing is to be burned except coal and firewood. Destruction of any evidence shall be severely punished. You've all been warned. Capital crimes are a hanging offense ... and anyone who aids or conceals the murderer shall also hang."

With a cry, Stella fainted.

Adella fled to her room.

Many thought the ghost of Marleigh Manor had murdered Mitchell ...!

She was the ghost ...!

If they found her secret door in the closet then they'd find her father's tools, her old blanket, her bowl, lantern, and everything! They'd find the charred remains of the clothes of the cart driver and link both deaths! If they suspected her of one murder surely they'd pin the other on her!

Mitchell's study had been locked! Had someone else found her secret room? If they had, they'd have found both secret doors ... and known how to pass secretly out of Mitchell's locked study!

Who could've found her secret doors ...?

Had they murdered Mitchell ... and planned to pin it on her ...?

Mitchell had more enemies than friends. Even

Harrington had plotted against him ... and he seemed closer to Mitchell than anyone.

When Lester had died, and Middleton taken his place, Stella had abandoned her only child to grow up motherless ... to escape death threats made against her. But that didn't make sense. *Why hadn't she taken him with her? What kind of mother abandons her only child?* Were there really death threats ... *or were the threats just another invented lie?*

Reed hated Mitchell, but he'd departed before the murder. Adella couldn't imagine he'd murder; Reed didn't seem the type. Of course, she hadn't known him for long, and deceptions were common in Marleigh Manor.

Barton had thought he was next in line. Stella had thought the same. Could one, or both of them, have murdered Mitchell? Were they seeking to make this house Quinton Manor?

Enfield didn't seem a murderer, yet his elevation to Lord of Marleigh Manor would leave Hayden, Harlow, and Harrington in line. Any of Enfield's sons could've planned this, not realizing Barton would be next if Mitchell was murdered after assuming patriarchy of the clan.

And that assumes they didn't know who'd fathered Rowena's son ...!

Had Harrington murdered Mitchell ...?

Rayden was the cleverest of the brothers. He could've done it, hoping to become Enfield's chief advisor.

And this was just the list of enemies who might inherit. Every Prescott wanted Mitchell dead, to save them from being kicked out like Reed. The number of people she'd heard complain about Mitchell tripled the total of possible murderers.

Mitchell could've been murdered not for personal gain, but simply by someone who loathed him.

Anyone could've found her secret doors in Mitchell's study and the nursery.

Anyone could be using her as their scapegoat to get away with murder.

The locked room ... *she was the ghost ...!*

Only one hope of not getting blamed for the murder existed; *she had to find and expose the real killer.*

Yet that wouldn't be easy. Using her hideaway, the murderer could have easily locked the door from the inside. Yet, would the murderer want the her hideaway to be found? Had they found it, then they'd have found traces of her ... someone ... living there. Wouldn't they have left some pointer to it? Or, maybe they didn't know about her hideaway. Could they somehow have locked the door from the outside ... and made it look like it was locked from the inside?

The line of silver coins, the same trick she'd used to lead them to the stolen coins, linked this murder to the ghost.

The disappearance of the baby; anyone who was

truly inquisitive, and didn't believe in ghosts, must've known there must be a secret entrance to the nursery. She'd last escaped through the nursery; her secret door wasn't braced. If anyone had searched the nursery closet they'd have found it.

Yet they didn't know she'd been the one hiding in there ... so they couldn't prove it was her.

But someone had found her hideaway ... and removed her nail-pegs. Then they killed and snuck out of Mitchell's study, leaving his door locked.

The ghost of Marleigh Manor was being framed ...!

Perhaps this wasn't about her. Perhaps they'd found another way to lock the room from the inside, hoping it'd get blamed on the ghost ... not knowing the ghost wasn't dead!

She was still a fraud ...!

If her identity was revealed, would anyone believe her ...?

Ever since she'd first arrived, Adella had wanted to flee. Now she was trapped; no one could depart. Her absence would begin a search of every road and village in the district, and point the murder investigation toward her. She'd no hope of escaping without being recaptured, and escape implies guilt.

The constable would eventually interview her. *What could she tell him?* He could check on her story of being the goddaughter of Winnifred, learn she was fake, and her pretense could be undone.

She'd killed the cart driver with an adze; a carpenter's tool. That adze was in her father's toolbox. Revelation of her true identity would land suspicion of both murders on her.

No matter what she did, she was in danger ... *facing a hangman's noose ...!*

Chapter 15

Adella hadn't eaten anything all day, yet when the bell rang for dinner, she wasn't hungry. Shortly afterwards, someone knocked on her door. Adella peeked out to find Bessie standing there.

"The constable wants everyone at dinner," Bessie said.

"I'm not hungry," Adella said.

"No one is," Bessie said. "Less than half showed up in any dining room. People were sent to gather the missing. The constable says he'll personally collect anyone who doesn't obey."

Adella wasn't surprised; the constable wouldn't want people hiding in their rooms ... less chance of the guilty person revealing themselves. Those who refused would look guilty. Grudgingly she followed as Bessie went to knock on her younger brother's door.

Harlan took a while to convince, but finally relented. As they trooped back, Camden emerged from the door to the Prescott wing, leading half-a-dozen followers, each shuffling reluctant feet.

The constable sat in Mitchell's chair. Soon Letitia, Charity, Grace, Natalie, and Acton arrived, each looking less excited than she.

"Excellent," the constable said. "Now we can begin."

Grace was said and dinner began. Yet most put nothing on their plate, and sat looking nervous, hands in their laps. Finally Barton sighed loudly, and reached for a serving spoon, and then everyone reached for something.

Worried glances, accusing stares, and suspicious looks swapped back and forth, all observed by the constable.

"I'm sorry," the constable finally said. "I know this is a terrible time, and I'm sure you all want it resolved quickly. We know the tragedy happened in the middle of the night. Was anyone outside their room last night, visiting the kitchen ... or the privy?"

No one spoke. *Adella hadn't expected anyone to.*

"Come now, some of you are older than I am," the constable said.

"I ... visited the privy," Letitia said. "I don't know the hour I went, but I didn't see anyone."

"Did you hear anything?" the constable asked.

"Nothing," Letitia said. "Snores, I suppose, but I paid no attention."

"What about you, Enfield?" the constable asked.

"Not last night," Enfield said. "Sometimes, not always. The only thing I ever see is the Prescott boy who cleans the privy."

"What's his name?" the constable asked.

"I'm not sure," Enfield said.

"Byron," Grace said.

"What's his relation?" the constable asked.

"Lydia's younger brother," Grace said.

"That would make him the son of Sarah and Carlton Brixton?" the constable asked.

"Yes," Grace said.

"He's just a boy," Enfield said.

"Yes, and that does concern me," the constable said. "Master Mitchell wasn't a small man. Had Mitchell ever been in a real fight ... a fist-fight?"

"Not since we were kids," Hayden said.

"Whoever murdered him, Master Mitchell knew them," the constable said. "Mitchell wasn't the trusting type, yet he let them stand behind him."

"How do you know ...?" Rayden asked.

"No sign of a struggle," the constable said. "Surely Mitchell would've defended himself if he'd known he was being attacked."

"My son wasn't a man to trust an enemy," Stella said.

"He didn't trust a known enemy, to be sure," the constable said. "This implies a high level of trust, however misplaced. Who was closest to Mitchell?"

"No one," Enfield said.

"Harrington often spoke to him," Rayden said.

"Harrington is fourteen years old," Enfield defended his son.

"No one is accusing anyone," the constable said. "I merely need to know Mitchell's daily habits. Did Harrington speak to Mitchell alone?"

"Yes," Enfield said. "I wouldn't say they were friends."

"Were they enemies?" the constable asked.

"Harrington is impressionable," Enfield said. "I suspect my nephew wanted Harrington to think they were friends. Harrington occasionally ran errands for Mitchell, sending messages and fetching others."

"Did Harrington have any other close friends?" the constable asked.

"My son isn't a murderer," Enfield said.

"No, but if Mitchell was using him for unknown purposes, might not his murderer have used him, too?" the constable asked.

"We keep a close eye on our brother," Hayden spoke up. "He's not bright ... tends to find trouble."

"He always gets caught," Harlow said. "If anyone was using him, we can get it out of him."

"Do nothing to interfere with my investigation," the constable ordered. "I will question him before you do."

Hayden and Harlow nodded.

"Constable Kendall, I barely knew Mitchell," Garrick said. "I've been living here almost thirty years. I recall the day he was born. Yet I can't recall Mitchell ever having a friend, not even a playmate, since his father died."

"Felled in a duel, wasn't he?" the constable asked.

"He was drunk, insulted the wife of Lord Oakley Ramsey, who was the wealthiest landholder in the Foreholm district," Garrick said. "He refused to apologize. They met right out front and settled the matter that night."

"Where might I find Lord Oakley Ramsey?" the constable asked.

"He died six, no, seven years ago," Garrick said. "Thrown by his favorite horse. I watched as they buried him."

"That's an unbreakable alibi," the constable said.

"Unless he's the ghost," Letitia said.

Several scoffed, but the constable smiled.

"You believe in ghosts?" the constable asked.

"Certainly," Letitia said.

"Have you ever seen a ghost?" the constable asked.

"I'd be scared into the next life if I had," Letitia said.

"I heard about the former appearances of the

ghost," the constable said. "He ... or she, since she stole a woman's nightgown ..."

"My chemise," Letitia said.

"Yes, and the ghost also borrowed a baby, which few men would do," the constable said.

"Are you saying the ghost is a woman?" Garrick asked.

"I don't believe in ghosts," the constable said. "I don't think there is a ghost. Strange things happen, and it's often easier to blame ghosts than deduce true causes. However, belief in ghosts is a powerful thing. Just because ghosts don't exist doesn't mean a ghost can't be accused ... for a crime committed by the living."

"So, you're saying someone in this house is the murderer?" Rayden asked.

"Not at all," the constable said. "Whoever committed this act was in this house at the time, yet they may not have lived in this house, or may have departed afterwards."

"Constable Kendall, are you referring to Reed?" Acton asked. "Forgive me, sir, but I know him well. He's a good man. "

"Reed has an alibi, yet I'm obligated to confirm it," the constable said. "Winnifred has also vouched for him, and from her I obtained his whereabouts. He'll be brought back ... for questioning only."

"I still say it was the ghost," Letitia said.

"I hope not, Widow Letitia," the constable said. "Ghosts are exceedingly hard to handcuff."

Adella kept silent; she didn't want the conversation shifted to her. She nibbled at her food, trying to appear focused on eating, innocuous to the discussion. Out of the corner of her eye she spied most doing the same. She wondered if any of them could be the murderer. Yet she finished eating, and was one of the first to leave the table.

Another knock rapped upon her bedroom door. She opened it a crack. Rowena stared anxiously through the gap.

"Adella, can I come in?" Rowena asked.

As Adella opened the door, Rowena pushed inside carrying a small child, little more than a year old, in her arms.

"Is this your son?" Adella asked.

"Yes, Paxton Hayes Prescott," Rowena said. "Winnifred wants him rechristened to Paxton Hayes Marleigh-Prescott."

"Heir to Marleigh Manor," Adella said.

"No!" Rowena insisted. "Do you think they'll let a Prescott child live to lord over them?"

"You're afraid," Adella said.

"Marleighs have murdered Prescotts before," Rowena said. "Some just vanished in the night ... or were sent on distant errands and never returned. I can't let Paxton suffer their fate. I need your help."

"What can I ...?" Adella began.

"Take me with you," Rowena begged. "I'll be your friend, your servant; I don't care. I need to get out of this house ... before my baby and I are both ...!"

"Rowena, calm down," Adella said. "Nothing's going to happen while the constable's here."

"Local laws have never served Prescotts," Rowena said. "My grandparents ... and great-grandparents ... all turned to the law when a Prescott mysteriously died. They've never listened to us."

"Your baby is the only thing keeping Marleigh Manor from the Quintons," Adella said. "No Marleigh wants that."

"Quintons are just Marleigh-offshoots," Rowena said. "Some think Stella murdered the son she abandoned to pass Lordship to the son she raised."

"Who thinks that?" Adella asked.

"I can't say," Rowena said. "Every Prescott is terrified. If a Marleigh is arrested, it will be a dishonor on the family. Some think they'd rather see a Prescott unjustly blamed than a Marleigh justly hung."

"Not all of them, surely," Adella said. "Relax. I won't leave without you."

"Thank you ...!" Rowena exclaimed. *"Thank you, Miss Adella ...!"*

"Just Adella; I don't want anyone thinking I'm putting on airs ... or related to anyone here."

"Do you mind ... if I hide here ... for a while?" Rowena asked.

"Hide here as long as you like," Adella said.

"I need to feed Paxton," Rowena said.

"By all means," Adella said.

As Rowena nursed her son, Adella sat beside her on the bed.

"What do the other Prescotts think of Lord Paxton?" Adella asked.

"Most think it's a death sentence," Rowena said. "Camden hates the idea of rechristening; this was originally Prescott Manor."

"Winnifred hopes to mend the bond between families," Adella said. "With a Marleigh father and a Prescott mother, Paxton could do that."

"I won't let them take my baby," Rowena said.

"Tell me about Stella," Adella said. "I've been wondering how a mother could abandon her only child."

"That's why I'm so scared," Rowena said. "After Lester got himself shot, Mitchell was the obvious heir. I think old Morley made Middleton the Lord of Marleigh Manor just to keep one of his children from murdering the boy."

"Well, someone will have to manage the family until Paxton grows up," Adella said.

"Mitchell had just become of age," Rowena said. "If Middleton hadn't died, we'd be in court right now. A few, mostly Prescotts, tried to get Middleton to step down for years, ever since Mitchell was fifteen, but Middleton planned to keep the Lordship for life."

"Middleton did keep his Lordship for life," Adella said. "In the end, he gave in to the law ... to keep the transference out of the courts."

"Our families have too many skeletons in our

closets to risk standing before a judge," Rowena said.

"What about Mitchell?" Adella asked. "Did you ever love him?"

"He told me he loved me," Rowena said. "I told him I couldn't ... not unless he made our relationship public. He forced himself on me ... I was older, but he was stronger."

"He raped you ...?" Adella asked.

"I wasn't his first ... or last," Rowena said. "Two girls from the village claimed to be carrying his child; both vanished and were never heard from again. He also slept with Lydia; she believed his love-lies, and cried for months afterwards. When he refused to make their love public, she threatened to tell everyone. He threatened to kill her. She's been terrified of him ever since."

"The more I learn about Mitchell the less I like him," Adella said.

"After Lester's duel, Stella shielded Mitchell," Rowena said. "There were several incidents ... accidents, they said. A banister railing Mitchell liked to slide down suddenly gave way and dropped him. A huge planter fell out a window and almost crushed him. A gun rack fell over; several of the rifles had been cocked; their bullets sprayed his wall ... while Stella was in his room."

"How horrible ...!" Adella exclaimed.

"Mitchell wouldn't leave," Rowena said. "He threw a fit, demanding they give him his father's title. Marleighs wouldn't let anyone with a claim to family

Lordship leave their control. In the end, Stella fled for her life, leaving her son to Winnifred's care. But Winnifred couldn't control him. He threatened her. Then she got sick and was condemned to her bed ... she's been there ever since. Stella never wrote or came back, not even for a visit, until Mitchell called her to support his claim. Why she came is still a mystery."

"Stella came to support her son, didn't she?" Adella asked.

"She hadn't spoken to Mitchell since she abandoned him," Rowena said. "Whatever she came for, it wasn't love."

After several hours of small talk, a loud voice called for Rowena. She paled as Adella peeked out.

Camden stood at the end of the hall. Several doors opened and faces peeked out.

"Constable Kendall wants Rowena," Camden announced to the wing.

"What for ...?" Nora asked from the door next to Adella's.

"Constable Kendall is questioning everyone," Camden answered. "He wishes to speak to Rowena now."

"You'd best go," Adella whispered behind her door.

"Not yet," Rowena said. "I don't want them to know I'm here."

Receiving no answer, Camden departed. The other doors closed. Adella watched until it looked safe.

"Can I leave Paxton here?" Rowena asked.

"I can't feed him," Adella said.

"He'll sleep now," Rowena said. "The constable can't question me long; I don't know anything."

Adella doubted if it worked that way, yet she took Paxton in her arms and let Rowena slip out.

Adella stared at the sleeping child. She'd always loved babies, yet the last time she'd played with one had started the 'ghost' nonsense. She had no fear; Rowena had always seemed nice. She wouldn't risk leaving her son in danger ... which meant she couldn't leave him with a Marleigh ... but why hadn't she left him with a Prescott? Would members of her own family harm her child?

Two hours passed, and Paxton slept the whole time. Then Rowena returned.

"What did he want?" Adella asked.

"To talk about my relationship with Mitchell," Rowena said. "I told him everything; no point protecting Mitchell's reputation now. He's going to look into the missing village girls, although if they were killed, then Mitchell's the likely suspect, and only God can bring him to justice. He also made me describe everything I could about the night Mitchell died, where I slept, who I talked to, and what was said. He's very forceful."

"He wants you to feel scared," Adella said. "He's pressuring you ... seeing if he can make you confess."

"I didn't do anything ...!" Rowena exclaimed.

"He's spoken to Winnifred, Enfield, Rayden, and

Charity. He's talking to Stella now ... and Barton next."

"I hope I'm not on his list," Adella said.

"Everyone is ... but you're probably on the bottom, with Grandma Preshea," Rowena said.

"Who ...?" Adella asked.

"Grandma Preshea," Rowena said. "She's a Prescott, lives in our wing, but she's old, trapped in her bed ... like Winnifred ... only her mind wanders."

"I've never been in the Prescott wing," Adella said.

"It's a lot like this wing ... except most of the paint has peeled," Rowena said. "Reed would've painted, but Middleton refused to buy us paint. We didn't dare ask Lester; he would've beaten us for asking."

"Fairness isn't a Marleigh trait," Adella said.

"No words truer than that," Rowena agreed.

Rowena spent the night, sleeping in the bed beside Adella, Paxton nestled between them. Adella was awakened several times, yet each time Rowena was already caring for her son, nursing or changing a diaper. Adella didn't know why she trusted her, yet she did. It felt good to have someone to talk to.

A knock on the door proved to be Ginny, again holding a bowl of hot water.

"Good morning," Ginny said.

Adella looked at her through the crack.

"Ginny, can you keep a secret?" Adella asked.

Ginny nodded. Adella opened her door and

pulled Ginny inside.

"Rowena and I fell asleep talking last night," Adella said. "You mustn't tell anyone!"

"I won't," Ginny promised.

Adella washed her face and hands in the hot water, which felt wonderful, and then stood like a statue. Rowena helped Ginny, and soon Adella was wearing her dark green dress again, this time with a ridiculous amount of underclothes. Being dressed by others felt weird; no wonder rich daughters couldn't do anything for themselves. Adella wondered if they were trained to be helpless to keep them dependent upon fathers, who preferred to select their own son-in-laws.

The four of them, Rowena holding Paxton, went to their separate breakfasts, the Marleigh table, the Prescott table, and the kids' table. They said good-bye in the hallway, winking shared trust. Then Adella steeled herself and walked into a room where she trusted no one.

Constable Kendall stood in the dining room, talking to Enfield and Stella. Rayden and Charity arrived a minute later. Everyone took seats, and Hartford carried in a platter of steaming kippers, set it upon the table, then carried in a plate stacked with scones and bowls of chilled butter. He snagged two empty teapots and returned them filled and steaming. From behind the door, Adella heard Hallewell yell something, and Hartford vanished back into the kitchen.

After grace, they ate. The constable flipped

open his notebook.

"Today I wish to speak to Hayden, Harlow, and Harrington," Constable Kendall announced. "Then I'll need to speak to Acton, Natalie, and Grace. This afternoon I'll need to speak to Ettie and Hortence. Please don't be hiding; interviews take longer if I have to search for each ... person."

Adella felt certain he meant to say 'suspect'.

No one spoke, and the usual silent war of suspicious glances waged uninterrupted. Adella tried not to look at anyone, yet occasionally caught someone staring at her ... and their eyes didn't always look away when she noticed.

"How goes the investigation?" Barton asked suddenly.

Constable Kendall stared at him before answering.

"This investigation has only begun," Constable Kendall said. "Once everyone has had a chance to tell me their version of the situation, then I'll compare versions. That should greatly reduce my list of suspects, which currently includes everyone."

"And if any versions conflict ...?" Barton asked.

"Then those suspects aren't cleared," Constable Kendall said. "My list will soon shorten considerably, and then interviews begin again. I compare claims with facts until one remains."

"That seems a sound practice, but is it proof?" Barton asked.

"Proof is rare in murder," Constable Kendall said. "Unlike theft, a murderer doesn't carry much evidence from the scene of the crime."

"Much evidence ...?" Barton asked.

"In this case, evidence exists to identify the murderer," Constable Kendall said. "I only need to find it."

"What evidence ...?" Barton asked.

"You'll know that when I choose to reveal it," Constable Kendall said.

"And then ...?" Barton asked.

"Then I arrest the suspect the evidence points to ... and take them to trial," Constable Kendall said. "In my district, only judges declare guilt or innocence. I carry out the sentence of the court."

"How did you become a detective?" Barton asked.

"Asking questions is my job," Constable Kendall said. "If I finish with the Marleighs and Darbys today, you and your brothers are next on my list. I hope you're as forthcoming with answers."

"I've nothing to hide, and Mitchell was my half-brother," Barton said. "I want this murderer found as much as you do."

"Why ...?" Constable Kendall asked.

"Wha ... I beg your pardon?" Barton stammered.

"Why do you want the murderer found?" Constable Kendall asked.

Barton fumbled, then seemed to regain his balance.

"Quintons always seek justice," Barton said. "Criminality is an offense against every law-respecting gentleman."

"No child committed this crime," Constable Kendall said. "Either the killer is a man who only pretends to be a gentleman, or they are a woman."

"Surely that knife ...!" Barton began.

"*I said the details of the murder would not be discussed!*" Constable Kendall snapped. "I allowed you to witness the scene as he was your brother. You may present your thoughts during our interview."

"No Quinton has anything to do with this ghastly crime," Barton said.

"Are you a judge ...?" Constable Kendall asked.

"No," Barton answered.

"Then by what authority do you make that statement?" Constable Kendall asked.

"I ...!" Barton started.

"What do you think of Barton's claim, Enfield?" Constable Kendall interrupted.

Enfield looked startled. His mouth opened, but no words spoke.

"I share Barton's feelings," Rayden spoke up. "I'm equally certain no Marleigh could commit an act so heinous. Surely every man in Marleigh Manor would say the same of their close relations, even Prescotts. Yet one of us is wrong. Your duty is to tell us which."

"A duty I intend to fulfill," Constable Kendall promised.

"Could you debate these matters when not in the presence of ladies?" Charity overspoke all of them. "Are there no gentlemen here?"

"I beg your forgiveness, Mrs. Darby," Constable Kendall said. "My duty requires I delve into the unpleasant."

"Breakfast is hardly the proper place," Charity said. "My dreams were awful, and I've yet to recover."

With all dignity, Charity rose and departed. Grace and Edwina rose to follow her, and Adella took advantage of their defiance to rise and leave. She'd eaten all she could stomach and desperately wanted to see Winnifred.

Chapter 16

To Adella's surprise, she arrived at Winnifred's door to find her deep asleep.

"She took some medicine," Lydia said from the nursery door. "All this terrible news, poor Middleton, and now Mitchell; she needed rest. Charity made her drink a sedative the doctor gives her."

Adella stared at Winnifred's peaceful face. She couldn't talk to her, which she desperately needed to; the constable was sure to interview her and she needed to know what to tell him.

"Are you unwell ...?" Lydia asked.

"No, I'm fine," Adella said. "Well, I wouldn't call myself happy. This isn't a good time to be a guest."

"I'm sorry, 'mam," Lydia said.

"I told you, I'm not family," Adella said. "I've spent my life working, not being pampered."

"But ... your family ...?" Lydia asked.

"My father believed work makes people strong, wise, and compassionate," Adella said. "Spoiled children make spoiled adults, and my father had no patience for anyone who couldn't pitch in when chores needed to be done."

"What a wonderful family you must have," Lydia said.

"What about you?" Adella asked. "Paxton Prescott is the next heir ..."

Lydia's eyes filled with tears.

"You didn't see what they did to Mitchell," Lydia said. "They tormented him, twisted him. What they'll do to that poor baby ...!"

"Who tormented him?" Adella asked.

"Hayden and Harlow used to beat him up ... the way they do with Harrington," Lydia said. "They brush it off as games all kids play, but they bullied him mercilessly. Middleton's daughters called him 'The Robbed Heir'."

"You loved him ...?" Adella asked.

"I ... thought I did ... for a while," Lydia said. "I pitied him."

"And how did he return your pity?" Adella asked.

"Who've you been talking to ...?" Lydia asked.

"Rowena," Adella said. "The day before he died, Mitchell invited me into his master office. He held the door for me, spoke honestly and politely ... every bit the dashing gentleman."

"He was a master of pretense ...," Lydia said.

"I was luckier than you ... or Rowena," Adella said. "Mitchell was ... charming ..."

"He could be ... when it suited his purpose," Lydia said.

"Winnifred warned me, but as I left him, I had dreams ... fancies that she was wrong," Adella said.

"Fancies of wealth torment worst of all ... because the poor desire riches so badly," Lydia said.

Adella shook her head, reached out, and pulled her in close. Hugging tightly, Adella could feel shudders of tears Lydia was fighting not to show, yet she gripped Adella and clung.

"We can't let anyone turn Paxton into another Mitchell," Adella whispered. "Both families deserve better."

"He's the same blood as Mitchell and Lester ... descendant of Captain Marston ...," Lydia sobbed.

"Every man needs a Vertiline," Adella said. "Treat him with the love his father should've known."

"Thank you, 'mam ... Adella," Lydia said.

Tears finally came, and Adella held Lydia while she had a good cry. Mitchell had preyed on her servitude; *her love was real, even if his wasn't.*

While Lydia cried, Adella glanced at the closed

closet door. If she could, she'd slip inside her hideaway and remove every trace that anyone had ever lived there. With time and tools, she could permanently seal both secret doors, fill their cracks with glue, layer telltale grooves with sawdust, then lightly sand and paint over the stained wood with hot, diluted wax to fully conceal her work. No one would find her doors without knocking holes in the walls.

Yet the slightest noise would be investigated ...

Soft knuckles rapped on the nursery door. Natalie opened it.

"Oh ...!" Natalie exclaimed, seeing Adella with Lydia. "When I saw the door closed ..."

"Please, come in," Adella said.

"Talking ...?" Natalie asked. "I can go ..."

"She knows," Lydia said. "Rowena told her."

Natalie dropped her eyes a moment, then stepped inside and reclosed the door. Her hands were slightly shaking ... trembling ... and she crossed her arms to hide them.

"Everyone's talking ... in whispers," Natalie said. "Quintons are in the music room, pretending innocence, and everybody else is hiding, trying to figure out who killed Mitchell."

"Pretending innocence ...?" Adella asked.

"No one needs to look as innocent as the guilty," Natalie said.

"Do you think they're guilty?" Lydia asked.

"I just finished my interview with Constable Kendall," Natalie said. "I don't know what to think."

"What did he ask ...?" Lydia and Adella demanded together.

"My conversations with Mitchell, memories of him, my opinions of him, my opinions of his elevation to patriarch, and where I was and what I was doing every minute of the night he was murdered," Natalie said. "Never have I been so intrusively questioned."

"Did he seem ... satisfied?" Lydia asked.

"The only thing that will satisfy him is finding the murderer," Natalie said. "He forced me down and fed me wine. All I did was talk ... and I've never felt so helpless and exhausted. His eyes ... bore into me ... left me blushing."

"Does he have any chief suspects?" Adella asked.

"Constable Kendall doesn't answer questions," Natalie said.

"What questions didn't he answer?" Adella asked.

"I asked how he thinks I could overpower Mitchell," Natalie said, looking exhausted. "He replied to my questions cordially, yet never said anything except what everyone knows."

"You need some wine," Adella said firmly.

"I'll get it ...," Lydia began.

"No, I'll go," Adella said. "I couldn't eat much breakfast."

"I'll go with you," Natalie said. "Hallewell and

Hartford are preparing to serve lunch."

"I'll wait here with the twins," Lydia said to Natalie.

"Very well," Natalie said. "I won't be long."

On the way to the kitchen, Natalie and Adella passed Ginny, who was carrying the bell to ring for lunch. They heard silvery tinkles behind them before they reached the kitchen, so they headed to the dining room instead. Two open bottles lay on the table. Adella poured for both.

"Here we go again," Natalie said. "Silent meals."

"It's understandable," Adella said.

"Mitchell's murder didn't change our meals," Natalie said. "Marleigh dinners are fencing or fisticuffs, depending on who's angriest."

"As long as they're not angry at us ...," Adella said.

Each took their places and sat, awaiting the others, who slowly arrived, approaching like mice suspecting a trap. Almost every seat was filled when Constable Kendall walked in, and Enfield arrived last.

Harlow said grace, and as soon as it was finished, Hallewell and Hartford carried in steaming dishes. Hallewell returned to the kitchen for a plate of pastries while Hartford poured a glass of wine for the constable.

Lunch was pasta in a cheesy sauce sprinkled with spices. Adella loved it, yet refrained from speaking even to compliment the cooks. The few times she raised her eyes from her plate, she spied searing glances darting back and forth. She lowered her gaze to keep from becoming involved in their silent accusations.

"How go the interviews ...?" Enfield asked suddenly.

Everyone seemed shocked.

"Informative," Constable Kendall said. "After lunch, I'll need to speak to Grace, Ettie, and Hortence again, briefly, just to confirm a few facts, and then the Quintons. Tomorrow I'll start on the Prescotts."

"You should've started there," Stella said. "They hated my Mitchell."

"So you said," Constable Kendall said. "Begging your pardon, Mrs. Quinton, but I've uncovered no one who claims to be a friend to Mitchell."

"Marleigh Manor has never been a friendly house," Stella said.

"Do you hope to change that?" Constable Kendall asked.

"*Me ...?*" Stella asked.

"You are Paxton's grandmother, even if he was born illegitimate," Constable Kendall said. "I'd think you'd want to insure his ... proper upbringing."

Stella paused before responding.

"I ... will consider that," Stella said.

Silence resumed. Adella ate her lunch and several small pastries, each of which tasted of honey and vanilla. Grace rose first, and Adella ceased eating to flee the hall.

She checked back on Winnifred to find her still

sleeping, then wandered about, and finally decided to hide in her room. However, as she reached the top of the foyer stairs, a familiar noise drew her attention, a familiar click-clacking; *someone was using tools ....?*

Adella followed the click-clacking. A wide hallway led into a side of the second floor she'd never explored. There she found a narrow stair rising up to a third floor, and at it's top, in a doorless room near the foot of the stair, stood Enfield tapping a chisel with a small hammer.

Adella peeked inside; Enfield was using his chisel on a large, smooth stone; a river stone, which he was reshaping into a bust. Finished statues stood around him, each magnificently displayed, and on every wall hung framed paintings. Each colorful painting was of the same colorful style; by the same artist. Yet the style was ... crude, almost childlike. The statues were equally ... not terrible, but inexpert, with obvious flaws.

"Adella ...!" Enfield exclaimed, seeing her in his doorway. "Come in! Come in!"

Adella stepped inside and Enfield stepped away from his project.

"Like it ...?" Enfield asked, pointing to his carved stone. "Well, you can't really tell ... I haven't done the face yet."

"Who will it be?" Adella asked.

"Mitchell," Enfield said. "He was the patriarch of the Marleigh family, if only briefly. We need to commemorate every head of our family ... keep our history accurate."

"Perhaps you should carve him screaming," Adella said.

"He did like to shout," Enfield smiled. "Do you like painting ... or poetry?"

"Always, but ... perhaps not now," Adella said. "Two deaths ... I'm quite overcome."

"My apologies," Enfield said. "I hope you'll visit us again in better days. I'm trying to stay busy ... to keep from dwelling upon it."

"I keep escaping to my room," Adella said.

"Can't blame you," Enfield said. "I hide up here whenever I can. Nothing calms me like making art."

"It's beautiful," Adella said to be polite.

"Thank you, but I'm no master," Enfield said. "I just create what makes me happy."

"Best reason I can think of," Adella said. "Please ... don't let me stop you."

"Oh, I'd much prefer conversation," Enfield said. "It's so nice to have someone new to speak to. So many strange things have happened lately, besides your arrival."

"Strange ...?" Adella asked.

"All this business started with the ghost," Enfield said. "Baby stealing, dropping a silk chemise, and leaving lines of silver coins."

"Winnifred told me of those," Adella said.

"Yes, but the incident I find most interesting is the line of empty bottles in Mitchell's bedroom," Enfield said. "He walked into them in the dark ... just after a failed attempt to reveal the ghost."

"I didn't hear about that one," Adella lied. "Empty bottles ...?"

"Yes," Enfield cocked an eye at her. "Right before you arrived here. It was almost as if someone knew that he'd been planning to reveal them ... had been spying on him ... and set out to make a fool of him."

"I don't believe in ghosts," Adella said.

"If it wasn't a ghost, it had to be a real person," Enfield said. "Someone who could enter the Marleigh wing and eavesdrop on Mitchell in his study."

"I wouldn't know," Adella replied. "As you said, I hadn't arrived."

"Yes, so I did," Enfield said. "However, you may be interested to know, I have considerable resources, if you should suddenly desire to depart. I have friends all over England. If you find yourself in need of a friend, and a place to go, with money in your purse, these things could be provided."

"Constable Kendall forbids anyone from leaving," Adella reminded him.

"True, but he doesn't have the resources to prevent someone from leaving, does he?" Enfield asked. "My services wouldn't cost a thing ... except maybe a few honest answers."

"I always try to be honest," Adella said.

"Don't we all ...?" Enfield smiled.

Enfield set his chisel point against a penciled line

on his rough stone and rapped it with his hammer. Frowning, Adella watched for a minute, wondering what he knew ... and suspected. Then she strode back and crossed the wings, hoping to avoid any more private conversations. She descended the stair into the old wing.

"Adella ...!" Barton called.

She stopped in her tracks. Barton stood before her, in the middle of the hallway, blocking all passage ... as if awaiting her.

"Mr. Quinton," Adella acknowledged him.

"Barton Perry Quinton, at your service," Barton said. "I was hoping we could speak ..."

"I'm very tired," Adella said.

"My family has contacts in Sheffield," Barton said.

Adella paused, trying to hide her nervousness.

"Do you know my family?" Adella asked.

"No, but I hope to ... soon," Barton said, and he stared at her accusingly.

"I'm sure they'll ... be delighted to meet you," Adella said.

"What church does your family attend?" Barton asked.

"Sir, as I said ...!" Adella began.

"Very tired," Barton said. "I'm sorry to bother you. I merely wished to ask a few questions."

"Such as ...?" Adella asked.

"Such as, if your mother and Winnifred were close correspondents," Barton said. "If so, she must've

335

known the unsettling circumstances she was sending you into ..."

"I'll have no accusations made against my mother," Adella said.

"None intended," Barton said. "I simply wonder if she could've had ... concealed intentions ... for placing you here."

"My mother seldom shared her intentions ... even with me," Adella said.

"I see ...," Barton said.

"Are you the constable now, performing your own interrogation ...?" Adella asked. "Does Master Kendall know ...?"

"I hope we can keep this just between us," Barton said.

"I expected Quintons would treat guests with greater civility than Marleighs," Adella said.

"I pray I haven't given the wrong impression," Barton said.

"Interrogations give one impression," Adella said.

"Please forgive me," Barton said. "My family didn't arrive expecting to become suspects for a murder."

"Then we should both pray the constable does his job ... and not try to do it for him," Adella said.

With determined steps, Adella strode forward. Barton stepped aside to avoid a collision. She marched as if angry, yet inside she was shaking.

Concealed, he'd said. *What did he suspect ...?*

Adella marched straight into her room, hoping not to be ambushed again. To her surprise, upon her bed sat Rowena nursing Paxton.

"You said you wouldn't mind ...," Rowena reminded.

"I don't," Adella smiled, although for the first time she missed the months she'd spent in seclusion, unseen and not speaking to anyone.

How many private conversations must she endure ...?

"Everyone stares at me," Rowena said. "No one spoke during lunch except to toast Paxton."

"Your family hopes to restore the Prescott name," Adella said.

"More than that," Rowena said. "Some hope to turn the tables, to make Marleigh's pay for forcing us to be servants."

"Resentments die hard," Adella said.

"He's my baby ...!" Rowena sounded exasperated. "Mitchell took after Lester ... *I don't want Paxton to become ...!*"

"I just had this conversation with Lydia," Adella said. "She fears ..."

"So do I," Rowena said.

"Lydia really loved Mitchell, didn't she?" Adella asked.

"More than most of his conquests," Rowena said, and when Adella stared at her. "More than me. Servants and superiors ... a kind voice, a soft touch, a strong hand lifting you up ... out of desolation ..."

"Rich men have their ways," Adella said.

"Like breathing fresh air for the first time," Rowena said. "Suddenly you feel ... like a person ...!"

"Do all Marleigh men ...?" Adella asked.

"I've never met a man who was different," Rowena said.

"My father was," Adella said.

"How do you know what your father was like before you were born?" Rowena asked.

"My mother told me," Adella said.

"Well, that's one," Rowena said. "Adella, hiding here isn't working. Paxton cried ... everyone in the wing must've heard."

"I'm sorry," Adella said.

"I need to get away," Rowena said. "Can't your mom send you home ...? Say it's an emergency ...? Say you're homesick ...?"

"My father would force me to marry a man like Mitchell," Adella said, thinking. "Wait, ... there is a place we can hide ...!"

"Where ...?" Rowena asked.

"Reed's room," Adella said. "He's gone, and no one will hear Paxton except the horses."

"Can we ...?" Rowena asked.

"We won't know until we try," Adella said.

Rowena was already warmly dressed. She wrapped a thick blanket around Paxton and Adella threw on her cloak, then checked the hallway. Seeing no one, they stole out of her room and hurried to the door at the end. With worried backward glances, they snuck outside, then raced across the snow toward the barn.

Suddenly both girls stopped in their tracks; hooves thundered. They stood, trapped, halfway between the house and barn. They turned to run back, but ...

It wasn't one horse; five horses trotted rapidly into view, headed toward the barn. The girls paused to stare, and received curious stares. The first two were constables, the next pair Acton and Garrick, and the last was Reed.

"They found him ...!" Rowena whispered. *"We'd best go back ...!"*

Reed stared at Adella, his red face wind-chapped, and hair wild, sprinkled with frosty flakes.

"No, let's go see," Adella said.

All five men rode inside and dismounted. Adella led Rowena into the barn through the small door. The men were tending the sweating horses.

"They'll get sick if you give them icy water," Reed told Acton.

"Fetch water from the house," Garrick said to Acton, and his son nodded and turned toward the manor.

All five stopped as they saw Adella and Rowena standing inside the door.

"We found him," a constable said.

"I've been cleared," Reed said to Adella. "Mr. Galstrom spoke for me, told them I was at his inn from dusk until nearly noon ... long after Mitchell was killed."

"Our orders were to bring you here," the other constable said. "Once Constable Kendall has talked to you, I'm sure you'll be free to go."

"I hope so," Reed said. "Beastly place ... even without Mitchell."

With a nod, Acton hurried past the women, headed to the kitchen. Reed began unsaddling the horses, shaking out and hanging their damp blankets.

"Can't someone else do that?" a constable asked.

"Not as well or quickly as Reed," Garrick said.

Within ten minutes, Acton returned with two buckets of warm water. All five horses were settled and penned. The wintry cold was starting to chill her feet, yet Adella stood waiting. As the men started toward the house, Reed stopped and looked at her.

"I'm glad you're back," Adella said.

Reed nodded to her, his frown set ... and she couldn't blame him. Then he glanced at Rowena, Paxton's shape clearly visible under his blanket. Reed must've heard about him ... *everything* ... since Acton and Garrick knew.

"You ladies should come inside," Garrick said.

Chapter 17

They marched inside the hall, boots heavy on floorboards. Doors opened and faces peeked out. Stella's third son, Harlan, glanced at them, and suddenly he laughed.

"Be quiet!" Bessie scolded him from her doorway.

The crowd paraded past, Reed in the center. Adella and Rowena followed discretely, several steps behind. As they reached the end of the hall, Rowena leaned against Adella and whispered.

"I'll see you later."

Rowena slipped through the door which led to the Prescott wing.

The men turned left and marched up the stair into the main manor. Adella followed them. She caught Reed's eye as he glanced back at her several times, yet neither could speak.

Faces stared from the kitchen, music room, and entry room. In the new wing, the men turned left toward Mitchell's room. Adella turned right.

"Winnifred ...?" Adella shook her arm.

Adella thought her efforts were futile, yet a soft hiss filled Winnifred's breath, and her head rolled from side to side. Slowly her eyes opened.

"It's me ... Adella."

Winnifred blinked several times.

"Adella ...?" she asked. "Oh, damn. My sister ... made me drink ...!"

"Reed's back," Adella said.

"Reed ...?" Winnifred asked. "My head's a whirl. Fetch some tea, will you? It takes a while for my medicine to wear off."

Neither Hallewell nor Hartford were in the kitchen, yet the old woman washing dishes helped her, although she never spoke, not even when Adella thanked her profusely. Soon Adella was pouring for Winnifred, and handed her a fresh cup.

"Oh, I hate those potions," Winnifred said, sipping the hot tea. "Reed is back, did you say?"

"Yes, the constables forced him back," Adella said. "Reed said he's not a suspect, that Mr. Galstrom hosted him all night."

"Thank the Divine!" Winnifred said. "I feared his absence would make the constables suspicious."

"I'm sure it did," Adella said.

"Help me sit up, dear," Winnifred said, and Adella pulled her up with ease and stuffed pillows behind her. "Careful of my tea. Well, this is the first lucky break we've had. No one will question Mr. Galstrom's word, and that should satisfy the constable."

"We still don't know who the killer is," Adella said. "However, I was ambushed by Barton ..."

Adella related their conversation ... and stressed the word *concealed*.

"Be careful around Quintons," Winnifred said. "Obviously they suspect you."

"I won't feel safe until the real murderer is arrested," Adella said.

"Since Reed has an alibi, it must've been someone already in the house," Winnifred said. "We must trust Constable Kendall to do his job ... not interfere."

"I've been wanting to ask you," Adella dropped her voice to a whisper. "What should I tell Constable Kendall? He's interviewing everyone."

"He interviewed me," Winnifred said. "I told him what you told Reed ... that your family died in a house-fire, and you're my god-daughter. Constable Kendall promised me he wouldn't reveal your secret; he expects deceptions, so I gave him one."

"But what if he checks?" Adella asked. "Is there

a Castleford Manor north-east of Sheffield?"

"I haven't the foggiest," Winnifred said. "If there is, it probably didn't burn down ... not recently. However, London may have a telegraph that reaches Sheffield, but no town in this district has one, I assure you."

"He could send a letter," Adella said.

"Mail travels slowly in winter," Winnifred said. "To get to Sheffield and back, at this time of year, will take far longer than Constable Kendall has. I know he hasn't sent any letters since he got here, and even if he learned you're a carpenter's daughter, no letter could confirm you murdered anyone."

"News that there's no Castleford Manor would make him suspicious ...," Adella said.

"You didn't murder anyone, so someone else did," Winnifred said. "Once the constable finds the murderer, all inquiries will end."

Adella couldn't argue, yet she was still worried.

"Some still think it was the ghost," Adella whispered. *"I'm the ghost ...!"*

"Letitia believes in spirits and fortune-telling, and Constable Kendall actually chuckled when I told him that," Winnifred said. "You needn't worry. If you were implicated, I'd be assumed to be involved, so I'm doing everything I can to shift attention away from you."

"That's the first good news I've heard in days," Adella said.

"Just remember what you told Reed," Winnifred

said. "Recite it in your mind until no distraction can dislodge it."

"Will the constable try to trick me?" Adella asked.

"Undoubtedly ... and he's a master of deception," Winnifred said.

Noticing the outfit Adella was wearing, Winnifred had her fish through her wardrobe again. This time Adella chose a wider variety of gowns and undergarments. Adella blushed to admit she didn't know what some of them were.

"If I hear aright, Ginny has been assigned to help you wash and dress," Winnifred said. "She knows what they are."

Carrying her new gowns in her arms, Nora and Bessie ran up to look at them as she passed the music room. Both fawned over the brightly-colored gowns, seeming truly excited. Nora suggested they help carry the gowns to Adella's room, yet Stella called them back; their brothers were being interviewed by Constable Kendall and both needed to be at hand when they were called.

Adella walked back alone, glad to have escaped yet another conversation. All these rich people did was talk. Didn't they ever actually do anything? Every one of them could benefit from a few hours sanding ceilings, straightening bent nails, painting walls, or waxing floors. Sadly, she doubted if any of them were capable of accomplishing even the simplest task using any tool other than their mouths.

She turned a corner ... and stopped. Harlan
Mark Quinton, Stella's youngest son, stood whispering
in the hallway, with Harrington, who startled as she
appeared. Both fell silent as they spied her, watching
them. Adella stared at them, then slowly walked past,
her eyes accusing, their eyes guilty, yet no one spoke.

Adella wondered what secrets they were sharing,
or plotting, yet her days of eavesdropping were over.
She left them behind and descended the stair.

To her relief, her small, warm bedroom was
empty. She hung her new dresses in her tiny wardrobe,
then flopped onto her bed in a most unlady-like manner.
Like every carpenter, she'd dreamed of being rich and
enjoying the comforts she now had, yet she couldn't be
gladder that she wasn't as weak and helpless as a
Marleigh girl.

She didn't need her quilt in this room. She fell
asleep against feather pillows and dreamed of her father.

He was mighty proud of her!

The dinner bell awoke her, and she smoothed
out her dress and joined the crowd winding their way to
the dining rooms. As she sat down, Nora blushed and
avoided meeting her eyes.

Constable Kendall arrived and informed Stella
that he wished to interview her step-brother, Norton,
after dinner. He also announced that her niece and
nephew, Dalton and Clare, whom Adella didn't know, as
they sat at the children's table, weren't required at this

time.

Conversations were attempted, yet each attempt failed. Everyone ate in silence, yet tensions screamed. Dinner was a chicken stew with biscuits and gravy. Adella had to admit she'd never known cooks as good as Hallewell and Hartford. Either could be the chief cook at any construction site, and they'd quickly become the toast of the workers. Yet she didn't say anything, and left as soon as others started to rise.

As she reached the foot of the stair, she saw Reed halfway up. She called to him, and he stopped and waited for her; they walked toward her room together.

"How did your interview go?" Adella asked.

"Not well," Reed said. "Constable Kendall is demanding, meticulous, and accusing. He repeatedly questioned me on if I'd returned to Marleigh Manor."

"But ... Mr. Galstrom ...?" Adella stammered.

"Mr. Galstrom said I arrived at the inn before sunset and stayed there until almost noon ... hours after Mitchell was killed," Reed said. "Constable Kendall seemed to think I could've waited until Mr. Galstrom was asleep, snuck my horse out in the dark, without waking the stable boy, ridden back to Marleigh Manor, killed the man who'd just kicked me out, ridden back, snuck my horse back into the stable, again without waking the boy, and snuck back into bed before Mr. Galstrom woke up."

"That seems highly unlikely ... if not impossible," Adella said.

"It's worse than that," Reed said. "Constable Kendall also thought I might've hired someone to avenge being kicked out."

"That's impossible," Adella said.

"There's no shortage of Prescotts who hated Mitchell," Reed said. "I grew angry. We yelled at each other."

"That's dangerous," Adella said.

"I accused him of trying to invent a suspect since he didn't have one," Reed said.

"Reed, you mustn't anger him," Adella said.

"He angered me," Reed said.

"The person he names will go to trial," Adella said.

"And he'll look like a fool if he sends the wrong man," Reed said.

"The judge may agree with whoever the constable sends," Adella said.

"I won't be called a liar," Reed said. "If I'd killed Mitchell, it would've been in an open duel with witnesses. I'd never stab someone from behind."

"Did he believe you?" Adella asked.

"I'll never know," Reed said. "He's unscrupulous; never says what he's thinking."

They walked down the next stair in silence.

"Are you staying ...?" Adella asked.

"Once the investigation is over, I don't know," Reed said. "Enfield and Rayden begged me to stay. Winnifred called me her nephew, and said every family here needed me. She promised to move me into the manor ... or have my room fixed up as nice as hers."

"Is that what you want ...?" Adella asked.

"There's no point deciding now," Reed said. "No one can leave; Constable Kendall not only ordered me to stay, I'm not to help anyone leave without his permission."

Adella stopped before the door to her room.

"Reed, please stay," Adella said.

"I must ... for now," Reed said.

"Promise me you won't leave without saying good-bye," Adella said.

Reed stared at her, then nodded.

"Good-night, Adella," Reed said.

Without another word, Reed walked to the end of the hall and exited into the snow. Adella watched until he vanished, then went into her room and spent the night thinking.

All the next day, except at mealtimes, Prescotts were paraded into the new wing to be interviewed. Adella had thought the interviews were being held in the study, yet she learned the study was sealed; the interviews were being held in Mitchell's bedroom.

"It's a ploy," Grace said. "Most of the family never entered there; I hadn't. It was like being asked about Mitchell while being surrounded by him. His clothes, his bed ...!"

Natalie sat before them feeding her twins.

"It was horrible," Natalie said. "I've never been spoken to that way before. His manners are shameful. He made me answer questions I'd never ask ... personal things."

"He's no gentleman," Grace agreed. "He demanded to know every feeling I've ever had about Mitchell. I've never felt so ... so ..."

"Exposed," Natalie finished for her.

"Exactly," Grace said. "The way he stared; I blushed and covered myself."

She crossed her arms over her chest.

"I hope he finds the murderer before my interview," Adella said.

"Unlikely," Natalie said. "While I was there, they carried a coffin into the study, and as far as I know, Mitchell's still in there."

"I try not to think about it," Grace said. "Mitchell ... on the other side of a locked door."

"What about his funeral ...?" I asked.

"Constable Kendall will allow none until the culprit is arrested," Natalie said.

The music room sat empty. Not a sound echoed; Marleigh Manor seemed deserted, everyone hiding in their rooms.

The next morning, Ginny awoke Adella early, led her to another hot, delightful bath, then returned her to her room. Ginny chose for her a white dress, yet before Adella could put it on, Ginny layered her in voluminous layers with half the undergarments Winnifred had given her. When she laced up the white dress, Adella felt as stuffed as a cook's wagon.

"Winnifred insisted," Ginny told Adella. "After breakfast, you'll be summoned ... for your interview."

Despite her dress' bindings, a shiver ran down Adella's spine. Yet Ginny forced her to sit still while she applied several layers of make-up.

Adella met and walked to breakfast beside Stella, who seemed haughty and angry.

"That Kendall is a scoundrel," Stella scowled. "To accuse my sons is madness, but to imply my daughters ...!"

"He's trying to intimidate ... frighten people into saying things they normally wouldn't," Adella said.

"Quintons aren't Marleighs," Stella said. "We don't lie."

Barton, Harlan, and Nora must be exceptions, Adella bit her tongue and didn't reply.

Hallewell and Hartford served a fruit, a strange melon Adella didn't recognize and didn't like. Stella declared they'd sat too long since harvest and all their sweetness was gone. The scones had currants and were tasty even before covered with butter and jam. Yet Adella couldn't eat much.

As she rose to leave, the dreaded voice spoke.

"Adella Cumberbatch, if you're done, I can escort you to Mitchell's room," Constable Kendall said.

Adella reluctantly nodded, then waited as he

351

rose, took a long, last drink of tea, and finally came around to stand before the doorway to the hall.

"If you'd please ...," Constable Kendall said.

Adella felt like a caged antelope in a zoo, or a monkey on a leash, as Constable Kendall paraded her into the new wing. She walked nervously into Mitchell's bedroom. He closed the door behind them.

Mitchell's room looked exactly as it had; messy, cluttered, but not filthy. One of his shirts, probably the last one he wore, was thrown over the foot of his bed to await whoever collected his laundry. His wardrobe door hung open, blankets still crumpled and pushed back.

A single chair sat center before the chest at the foot of his bed. Constable Kendall motioned for her to sit. He poured a glass of wine and offered it to her, but she declined it.

"Adella Hubert Cumberbatch ...," Constable Kendall began, looking at his notebook.

"Hester," she corrected him. "Adella Hester Cumberbatch."

"Ah, yes; Hester," Constable Kendall said, making a mark on his notebook.

Adella didn't believe for a moment that he'd mispronounced her name by accident.

"You're a guest here, not related to anyone ...?" Constable Kendall asked.

"Winnifred is my god-mother," Adella said.

"So she said," Constable Kendall said. "Odd, isn't it? God-mothers are usually appointed by the parents, but your grandmother chose yours."

"I ... never thought about it," Adella said.

"You never met Lady Winnifred before you came here ...?" Constable Kendall asked.

"No ... not that I recall," Adella said.

"And your mother's in Spain ...?" Constable Kendall asked.

"France," Adella corrected another attempt to deceive. "Well, that's what I told everyone."

"So, your first act as a guest was to lie to your hosts," Constable Kendall said. "Why did you lie?"

"Families ... men of wealthy families, don't marry poor girls," Adella said.

"I see," Constable Kendall said. "So, you came to find a husband ...?"

"No," Adella said. "That was Winnifred's idea. I ... I just had nowhere else to go."

"Yes," Constable Kendall said. "My condolences on your family. It must've been a great loss."

"Thank you," Adella said although she doubted if he really cared.

"Suddenly poor, lost, and alone," Constable Kendall said. "How did you pay for your transportation ...? For your coaches and drivers ...? For the inns you stayed at ...?"

"I ... don't know," Adella said. "I followed the instructions in Winnifred's letter."

"Do you still have that letter?" Constable Kendall asked.

"I ... think it got lost," Adella said. "I ... don't know where ..."

"How convenient," Constable Kendall said. "How do I know such a letter existed?"

"I swear ...," Adella said.

"You lied before," Constable Kendall said. "How do I know you're not lying now?"

"Sir, I was instructed to lie," Adella said.

"Where are you really from ...?" Constable Kendall demanded, leaning close and raising his voice. "Were you a barmaid ...? A courtesan ...?"

"Sir ...!" Adella exclaimed, and her brows furrowed.

Constable Kendall stood back up and eyed her suspiciously.

"You're the first girl in this house who didn't scream when I asked that," Constable Kendall said.

"Marleigh girls are porcelain dolls," Adella said. "In my house, everyone worked."

"Prescott girls screamed ... and so did Stella's daughters," Constable Kendall said.

"Not all women are delicate flowers," Adella said.

"Most wealthy daughters are," Constable Kendall said.

"My father believed that ... and took steps to insure his children weren't," Adella said.

"I see," Constable Kendall said. "The day you arrived, did you meet Master Mitchell?"

"Yes," Adella said. "Mister Camden met me at the door and was taking me to meet Winnifred. On the way we met Master Mitchell; Camden introduced us."

"Did Master Mitchell seem pleased at your unexpected arrival?" Constable Kendall asked.

"Certainly not," Adella said. "At the time I had no idea why. Later I learned he was focused on the upcoming family transition; I suspect he didn't like surprises."

"Why didn't Winnifred tell him you were coming?" Constable Kendall asked.

"You'll have to ask her," Adella said. "I suspect ... she wanted to use me ... in some way."

"In what way ...?" Constable Kendall asked.

"I'm not sure," Adella said. "At first I thought she was protecting me. Then I feared she was using me to upset Mitchell. Later I found out ... she wanted me to marry him."

"Marry Mitchell ...?" Constable Kendall asked.

"She knew I was strong-willed, which few women are," Adella said. "She ... hoped I'd calm Mitchell."

"Then his death must've been a great relief," Constable Kendall said.

Adella raised her head to look at him.

"Sir, what are you saying ...?" Adella asked.

"No Mitchell, no forced marriage," Constable Kendall said.

"That's terrible ...!" Adella exclaimed.

"His death spared you ...!" Constable Kendall

said.

"I never would've married him ...!" Adella insisted. "He was rude, arrogant ...!"

"So his death saved you from a terrible fate," Constable Kendall said.

"My parents are dead," Adella said. "No one can marry me without my permission."

"You never wanted to marry him ...?" Constable Kendall asked. "A poor girl from a dead family refuses to marry the patriarch of a financial empire ...?"

"Please don't speak of my family so," Adella said. "I thought about it, yes. I even felt I owed it to my future children. Yet I never could've gone through with it. Did you ever speak to Mitchell ...? Do you know how he treated women ... everyone ...?"

"I've come to know a great deal about the failings of Master Mitchell," Constable Kendall said. "He had affairs with at least six women, two of whom were afterwards reported as runaways. He had at least one bastard. He had a bad temper. Several women say he hit them."

She glanced up at his face. Constable Kendall's eyes blazed as he stared at her, but she knew he was just trying to intimidate. She'd seen real carpenters fight; Constable Kendall didn't seem nearly as menacing as angry carpenters. Yet she understood why the other girls had blushed before him.

"I hadn't heard Mitchell had hit anyone, but from my few experiences with him, I can't say I'm surprised," Adella said.

"Who have you spoken with about Mitchell ...?" Constable Kendall asked.

"Natalie, Grace, Rowena, and Lydia," Adella said. "I overheard them talking. Then they told me to ... warned me ... not to be alone with him."

"Were you ever alone with him?" Constable Kendall asked.

"Only once ... right after he'd been elevated," Adella said.

"Why did you speak to him?" Constable Kendall asked.

"His uncle had died," Adella said. "He seemed to be ... acting as a gentleman. He invited me into his office."

"What did he want?" Constable Kendall asked.

"Vertiline's jewels," Adella said.

"Ah, a fortune in jewelry," Constable Kendall said. "Quite a motive for murder, isn't it?"

"I didn't have them," Adella said. "I've never seen them. I don't even know if they're real."

"Do you believe them to be real?" Constable Kendall asked.

"Prescotts do, and if they have any reason to lie to me, I don't know it," Adella said. "Besides, even if they were left to me, that would be a reason for someone to kill me, not Mitchell."

"I've considered that," Constable Kendall said. "Vertiline's jewels are a motive for murder, but not for the murder of Mitchell."

"I had no reason to kill Mitchell," Adella said.

"You had a perfect motive," Constable Kendall said. "He would've married you to get Vertiline's jewels."

"I didn't have them ...," Adella said.

"Yet they were left to you in Winnifred's will," Constable Kendall said.

"So I was told," Adella said. "I never saw her will."

"I haven't, either," Constable Kendall said. "Yet, someone could be hired to come posing as a guest, kill a man for another, and accept a payment delivered to them by a will."

Adella stared at Constable Kendall, aghast. *What a horrible accusation! Was she about to be revealed?*

Then she realized it.

"No, that doesn't make sense," Adella said.

"What ...?" Constable Kendall asked.

"No killer would agree to that," Adella said. "A hired killer could break in, or slip in through any open door. They wouldn't want everyone seeing them ... be able to identify them. Also, anyone hired would want to get paid right away; the only way your scheme pays off would be if the person who hired them died ... and no employer would die to pay off an employee."

"Very astute," Constable Kendall said. "You're smart."

"My father thought so," Adella said.

"Whoever murdered Mitchell was also smart," Constable Kendall said. "Killed in a locked room, leaving a trail of silver coins; they left a ghost to be blamed."

"I never saw a ghost, either," Adella said. "And I've no silver coins to leave."

"If you had to guess the murderer, who would you blame ...?" Constable Kendall asked.

"I'd never ...!" Adella started. "I ... yes, I've wondered how it could've been done. I know less than you, I'm sure."

"Flattery doesn't work on me," Constable Kendall said. "Have you thought up any way it could've been managed?"

"I don't believe in ghosts ... not even in locked rooms," Adella said. "However ... Master Rayden was able to get the key out of the locked room easily. If I were you, I'd ask him."

"So, you are ...?" Constable Kendall began.

"I'm not accusing anyone," Adella said. "I just never saw anyone do that before. He must know a lot about locks ..."

"Indeed," Constable Kendall said. "In fact, I did ask him about it. He learned that method in prison. We both think there's several ways it could've been done. However, the fact that it could've been done fails to answer the question of why."

"I ... beg your pardon?" Adella asked.

"Why pin the blame on a ghost ...?" Constable

Kendall asked. "Mitchell had plenty of enemies. Why not pin it on one of them?"

"I ... don't know," Adella said.

"You see my concern," Constable Kendall said. "Killers have motives. This killer knew exactly what they were doing. The line of silver coins ... the killer must've been rich and planned it carefully."

"I suppose so," Adella said.

"Did you know about Rowena's child ... who the real father was?" Constable Kendall asked.

"I knew she had a child, but I hadn't even seen Paxton until after Middleton's funeral," Adella said. "I've learned since that no one, well, Natalie, Grace, and Lydia, also didn't know who Paxton's father was ... and they seem friendly with Rowena."

"Have you ever been in prison ...?" Constable Kendall asked.

"What ...?" Adella exclaimed. *"Certainly not ...!"*

"You finally raised your voice," Constable Kendall said. "I've been waiting for that."

"Sir, I will not be slandered ...!" Adella snapped.

"My apologies," Constable Kendall said. "I was testing you, nothing more."

"It was inexcusable," Adella said.

"So is murder," Constable Kendall said. "Very well, Adella. You may go."

"Go ...?" Adella asked. "Where ...?"

"Anywhere within the house, not off the grounds," Constable Kendall said. "I don't know if I believe your complete story; the matter of Vertiline's jewels complicates everything. Yet you're a good girl, or I'm no judge of character. You've no motive. You're not being fully honest with me, I know, but you don't seem the type who could murder for gain."

"I'm not," Adella said.

"Yet ... the murder of Mitchell may have been for purposes other than gain," Constable Kendall said.

"I haven't been here long enough to hold grudges," Adella said.

"Thank you for seeing me," Constable Kendall said. "If you think of anything odd or suspicious, please tell me right away. Again, my apologies if my accusations offended. The truly guilty are often revealed by forceful allegations."

Adella withheld a hundred insults, a string of blue fire that would scorch his ears, and a hundred questions she dared not ask. Constable Kendall was smart and clever; she enjoyed talking to smart men more than vacuous girls who giggled and squealed. Yet the longer she stayed in his presence, the more she might let something slip.

"Thank you, Constable Kendall," Adella said.

Without another word, Adella rose and left Mitchell's bedroom. She walked straight to Winnifred's room. An older Prescott woman was serving her breakfast, scones and tea, and Adella waited until she left. Winnifred sipped at her tea as Adella told her everything.

"You were his last interview," Winnifred said. "Now we'll see what he says."

"But ...!" Adella began.

"As an unrelated guest new to Marleigh Manor, you've the least reason to hate him," Winnifred said. "He's interviewed every adult, even those he knew were innocent."

"Why ...?" Adella asked.

"Just because someone would never commit murder doesn't mean they might not have seen or heard something suspicious," Winnifred said. "Constable Kendall's leaving no stone unturned ... in case his investigation reveals nothing."

"I hope he finds them," Adella said.

"I won't sleep easy until he does," Winnifred said.

"So ... what happens now?" Adella asked.

"Enfield and Barton want to hold a family meeting," Winnifred said. "Paxton won't be old enough to inherit his title for nineteen years; someone must run things in his stead."

"Is Paxton in danger?" Adella asked.

"Constable Kendall assured Enfield and Barton they'd both be arrested if anything happens to Paxton," Winnifred said. "I believe he means it. Legally, Barton is Paxton's rightful heir, but the death of the child would pin the blame of two murders on someone, and neither seems excited about facing a judge. However, I insisted the question of governorship be delayed until Constable

Kendall finishes his investigation."

"We can't afford to have the murderer be placed in charge," Adella agreed.

Winnifred smiled brightly.

"You said *'We'*," Winnifred beamed. "You've come to think of us as family."

"You know how I feel," Adella said.

"I feel you'd make a wonderful wife and mother ... and there's nothing this family needs more," Winnifred said.

"Only until the snows melt," Adella reminded her.

"Or, at that time, only if you still want to go," Winnifred grinned.

Chapter 18

Two days passed in unnerving anxiety. Constable Kendall spent much of it alone in Mitchell's room, yet he toured the house and grounds, poked his nose into every bedroom, and even searched Reed's room and the barn. He claimed he'd reduced his list of suspects to five, but he refused to identify them.

Everyone debated who his five suspects might be. Letitia still insisted it was the ghost, which troubled Adella. She avoided the nursery and the hallway to Mitchell's study. She wanted to distance herself as much as she could from the scene of his murder.

By request of the family, Mitchell's funeral was held. It was an exact repeat of Middleton's funeral, only with even less weeping. Adella sat through it frowning.

Could she have been a second Vertiline and calmed his anger ... made a decent man, husband, and father out of Mitchell? If it could be done, she was sure she could've done it. Yet she still wasn't sure if Mitchell could've been cured of resentments.

Before the funeral ended, unwanted tears welled in her eyes. She wondered why, yet she couldn't stop them.

They buried Mitchell not far from the grave of Middleton. No stones marked either of their graves; Enfield promised they'd be erected as soon as Constable Kendall ended his investigation. Yet the snowy ground looked empty without them.

The family heads held a meeting. Winnifred was the eldest Marleigh, so it was held in her room. Adella couldn't attend, but Winnifred told her all about it behind her closed door.

"Everyone insisted Constable Kendall attend, as his investigation is ongoing, and we wanted everything open and legal," Winnifred said. "Enfield, Rayden, Edwina, Charity, Garrick, Stella, and Barton attended. As elder Prescotts, Hallewell and Hartford attended, and Camden joined them. Rowena also attended. Reed insisted on attending. Several argued against his presence, yet Constable Kendall supported his attendance."

Adella felt glad Reed had been there.

"With a murder investigation hanging over our heads, it was a relatively calm meeting. Everyone agreed Paxton is the rightful heir. Some felt Rowena alone could speak for her son. Stella argued that Barton, the next heir, should manage the family until Paxton comes of age. As this was how Middleton was given the title, and considering his many failings, few supported this. Rowena suggested I and Charity be appointed her governesses, as we were the only Marleighs she trusted. However, our signatures on legal documents ... well, some judges don't consider contracts signed by women unbreakable, so that would cause unwanted troubles. In the end, it was agreed; to be valid, all Marleigh contracts had to be signed by all three governors of Paxton Marleigh-Prescott: Enfield, Rayden, and Barton."

"They'll rechristen the child ...?" Adella asked.

"Yes, right away," Winnifred said. "In exchange, Rowena has been named as the Patriarch-Mother, a title she'll always carry. Legally, this places her alongside Charity and I in family lineage. She'll be present at every family meeting and able to speak with an equal voice."

"Will Prescotts be made equals?" Adella asked.

"Hallewell and Hartford, certainly," Winnifred said. "Both are older than I, and both will be able to retire as honored elders. Camden wished to be included, but our finances can't support replacing every Prescott with hired servants."

"Sell your workhouses," Adella said.

"They're our only real source of income,"

Winnifred said. "Besides, their profits feed all of us ..."

"Sell Vertiline's jewels," Adella said.

"I can't," Winnifred said. "Vertiline's jewels are my only hold over the rest of the family. Without them, my support of Rowena and Paxton would be worthless."

"You eat like kings," Adella said. "Limit your lifestyle and you could afford ...!"

"Prescotts will eventually be freed of chores," Winnifred said. "When Paxton inherits ..."

"That won't happen for nineteen years ... if at all!" Adella argued. "Many Prescotts alive today will never know freedom ...!"

"This problem took generations to create," Winnifred said. "It won't be solved overnight."

Adella stared at the old woman. She was complicit in everything wrong in Marleigh Manor. She was using Adella ... nothing more.

"As soon as the snow melts, I expect my reward," Adella said.

"You don't have to leave," Winnifred said.

"I can't stay and hold my tongue," Adella said. "This is wrong."

An angry week passed. Constable Kendall stayed for all of it, yet he never named the murderer. Then a deputy arrived with a telegram, and within the hour, Constable Kendall had Reed drive him back to his office. He claimed that another crime had been committed and required his presence, but that he'd return soon; he wouldn't rest until the guilty person or persons had been brought to justice.

Inside Reed's carriage, Constable Kendall rode away without solving the crime.

Each day that week, Adella received a summons to visit Winnifred. Adella never went. Winnifred couldn't reveal her now, not without implicating herself, and Adella had no desire to speak to her again.

She spent most days alone in her room. When she did come out for meals, she overheard gossips about her refusals to see Winnifred. Many wondered what argument had divided them. Rowena, Grace, and Lydia each came to visit, imploring her to come out and rejoin the family, yet she refused.

Mitchell had suggested she had *'hidden agendas'*. She didn't like the word *hidden*. If anyone could've found out about her secret doors, Constable Kendall might've discovered the one inside Mitchell's study. Yet he hadn't killed himself. Barton's use of the word *'concealed'* bothered her just as much ... and he had every motive, and the strength, to kill his half-brother.

Near dusk the next evening, a firm hand knocked on her door. Adella opened it, intending to send whoever it was away, but then she looked up into the face of Reed.

"Am I disturbing you?" Reed asked.

"Oh ... no," Adella said.

"I was asked to come see you," Reed said. "Winnifred ..."

"I've no desire to see her," Adella said.

"I don't ask that you do," Reed said. "I've left you alone ... as you apparently desired."

"My isolation was never to avoid you," Adella said.

"Regardless, I didn't wish to intrude," Reed said. "I can't blame you; you arrive as a guest and are forced to endure two funerals ... and a murder still unsolved."

"Thank you for understanding," Adella said.

"Winnifred said you wish to leave Marleigh Manor," Reed said.

"I do," Adella said.

"She asked me not to allow it," Reed said. "Under no circumstances am I to drive you anywhere."

"Then I'll walk," Adella said. "Once the snow melts ..."

"I don't answer to Winnifred ... or anyone ... anymore," Reed said. "I'm grateful to her for all she's done for me, yet I needn't obey orders. Whenever you wish to depart, I'm at your service."

"Won't you get in trouble ...?" Adella asked.

"I'm not a servant anymore," Reed said. "However, until they find someone competent, I'm the only one I trust to care for my horses."

"I respect that," Adella said. "When ...?"

"Don't misunderstand me," Reed said. "I don't want you to leave."

Adella blushed.

"I'll miss you, too," Adella said.

"Enfield, Barton, and Rayden all want you to stay," Reed said.

"They do ...?" Adella asked.

"Each wants you to marry a different person," Reed said. "Enfield wants you to marry Hayden. Barton wants you to marry his younger brother. Rayden wants you to marry Laurence."

"Laurence ...?" Adella exclaimed.

"Rayden wants Laurence to have a smart wife ... to raise smart grandkids," Reed said.

"I hope he finds someone willing," Adella said.

"There're plenty of poor girls that would do anything to live in a mansion," Reed said.

"I'm not one of them," Adella said.

"I'm glad to hear it," Reed said.

"Why ...?" Adella asked.

"I've spent most of every day hiding in my room, too," Reed said. "I've no one to talk to."

"I'm sorry," Adella said.

"Would you ... like to come see my horses?" Reed asked.

"Your horses ...?" Adella asked.

"They miss you, too," Reed said.

Adella could feel her cheeks blushing, yet she forced herself not to smile.

"Wait here," Adella said.

Adella's hands trembled as she fastened her cloak clasp around her neck. She struggled to remain calm. She took a long, deep breath, relaxed her face, then reopened her door.

"I'd love to see your horses," Adella said.

Together they walked to the end of the hall, through the door, and outside. The sun was shining brightly ... and it was definitely less cold.

"Winter is ending," Reed said.

Adella looked out at the snow, which looked hard and crusty, slightly less than she remembered. Icicles hanging from the roofs and trees dripped a rainstorm. Then she saw an alarming sight.

"Smoke ... in the barn ...!" Adella warned.

"I know," Reed smiled.

Inside the barn stood a large braiser, a wide, raised iron pot, on which a hot fire was burning. The area around it had been raked clear of straw.

"I didn't want you to get cold," Reed explained.

"Thank you," Adella said.

They walked inside. The barn looked as it had the last time she'd seen it, when Reed had been brought back by Acton, Garrick, and Constable Kendall's deputies. The four horses were locked in their separate pens, cows in theirs, and a few goats and sheep stood about, most standing out in the sun. Chickens clucked noisily.

Adella went to look at the horses. Reed followed her.

"I'm glad you like my friends," Reed said.

"I've always liked horses," Adella said. "I've driven a wagon a few times, yet I've never driven a carriage."

"I'd be happy to ...," Reed said.

"Reed, I can't stay," Adella said. "I wish I could, but ... I can't abide staying in this ...!"

"Marleigh Manor has always been horrible," Reed said. "Before my mother died, I never heard a kind word about it."

"It's not the place ...," Adella admitted.

"I know," Reed said.

"That's never going to change," Adella said.

"Prescotts hope otherwise, but it's a faint hope," Reed said. "Paxton will be the first Marleigh-Prescott since Sarah married Captain Marston ... and you see how that worked out."

"I pity Paxton," Adella said. "They'll torture, tease, and torment ...!"

"He'll be another Mitchell," Reed said. "Winnifred may claim they'll free the Prescotts, yet we both know it will never happen. The powerful never surrender power."

"That's why I must leave," Adella said. "No one can force Marleighs to ..."

Adella froze, staring blankly.

"Adella ...?" Reed asked.

She waved a hand for silence and continued to stare blankly.

Long moments passed.

"Reed, do you trust me ...?" Adella asked.

"Trust here is dangerous, but I've no reason to

doubt you," Reed said.

"I'm going to Enfield," Adella said. "I'll tell him something is wrong with the horses ... have him send for you. You must speak to him privately. Make something up; a bruised ankle ... any excuse. Make it a brief conversation. Then, after you've talked to Enfield, come back here and ready the carriage to ride out first thing in the morning."

"To where ...?" Reed asked.

"If this works, by morning, you won't need to go anywhere," Adella said.

"If what works ...?" Reed asked.

"I dare not say," Adella said. "Reed, I need you to trust me."

Reed stared at her.

"All right," Reed said. "Because you asked."

Adella nodded, staring into his face. He was so handsome she wanted to kiss him, yet she turned and ran from the barn.

She knew what she had to do!

As she entered Marleigh Manor, Adella struggled to calm herself. She was certain she was right, yet her only hope of proof would be if this worked.

She was taking a great risk ...!

The powerful never surrender power, Reed had said.

He was right!

Surrender only happens when force is applied.

What Adella needed ... was force!

With slow steps and a dignified manner, Adella walked to open her bedroom door. She deposited her cloak on her bed, and then proceeded toward the stair. However, rather than turn left, Adella turned right ... and opened the door to the Prescott wing.

She'd never been inside the Prescott wing before. Her first view stopped her; a long hallway with many doors, a wide section in the middle which looked like a kitchen, and more doors in the hallway behind it. This style of architecture was common but old. Ancient, crumbling facades were falling off paint-peeled walls, not tended for decades, which carried the hallmarks of a building over a hundred years old. No other part of Marleigh Manor, not even the barn, was as old as this section.

Several Prescotts, sitting at tables in the kitchen, rose from their benches to face her. Most bore shocked expressions, as if no one but a Prescott ever entered their domain. Several elderly faces Adella had never seen before paled.

Camden stepped toward her.

"Miss Adella ...?" Camden asked.

"I need Ginny," Adella said.

Camden nodded, a woman's voice called, and soon Ginny came out of a back room, wiping wet hands on her dress. Adella waited for her to approach, then led her out of the Prescott wing.

Glancing around to make sure no one was watching, Adella lowered her voice to a whisper.

"Ginny, I need you to run an errand for me," Adella said.

Ginny nodded.

"I need you to find Enfield," Adella said. "I need you to tell him something very quietly, without anyone else hearing. Can you do that?"

Ginny nodded again.

"Tell Enfield I'm in Mitchell's bedroom," Adella said. "Don't worry, that's where I'm headed now. Tell Enfield he must come talk to me in Mitchell's bedroom. Give him a minute to start walking to meet me, then follow. Wait outside Mitchell's bedroom until I come out."

"As you wish," Ginny said.

They started off together, climbed the stairs into the main manor, and then Adella descended the stair to the foyer while Ginny hurried toward Enfield's studio.

Stella and several others called to her as she passed, yet she excused herself and hurried into the new wing. Lydia was knitting before the fire again, yet Adella just nodded to her, passed through the entry room, and walked down the far hallway. No one was in it; she opened the door and slipped inside Mitchell's bedroom.

She didn't wait long. Minutes later, Mitchell's bedroom door opened and Enfield entered.

"Adella!" Enfield said. "I got a message ..."

"It's about Reed," Adella said.

"What about him?" Enfield asked.

"I'm not sure," Adella said. "I heard him say ...

he sounded very upset ... that something was wrong with the horses. It sounded important."

"No Marleigh knows as much about horses as Reed," Enfield said.

"I know," Adella said. "I just wanted you to know. It sounded urgent ... like something Marleighs should know about."

"I'll be sure to ask him," Enfield said.

"Please, don't tell him you heard of it from me," Adella said. "I don't want Reed mad at me. That's why I asked you to meet me here. It's the one place I knew no one would be."

"Of course," Enfield said. "I'll go talk to him ..."

"It might be best if you wait here," Adella said.

"Here ...?" Enfield asked.

"I'll send someone to fetch him," Adella said. "Please ...?"

Enfield shrugged.

"Very well ... if you think it's important," Enfield said.

"Thank you ...!" Adella effused, and she stepped close and kissed Enfield's cheek.

Enfield looked delighted, yet Adella didn't wait for comments. She exited Mitchell's bedroom to find Ginny just coming around the corner.

"Ginny, I need you to run out to the barn," Adella said. "Find Reed. Tell him Enfield needs to talk to him ... in Mitchell's bedroom ... right away."

Ginny looked surprised, yet she obediently

reversed her course and hurried to find Reed. Adella watched her go, waiting to give her time, and then walked slowly back, through the entry room, smiling brightly to Lydia, yet saying nothing, and she proceeded into the music room.

In the bright candlelight, Stella, her youngest son, Harlan, and her two daughters stared at Adella.

"What is it ...?" Stella asked.

"I don't know," Adella said. "Apparently, Enfield went into Mitchell's study. He said he found something ... a clue. I think it was hidden under Mitchell's body. He's relocked the study. Enfield wants Reed to fetch the constable first thing in the morning."

"Constable Kendall ...?" Stella exclaimed. "I never want to see that horrid man again!"

"We may need to," Adella said. "Whatever Enfield found, it may point to the murderer."

"It would be nice to see the guilty hung," Harlan said.

"Yes," Stella agreed. "I'll be happy to see my grandson grow up without a murderer in his home."

Minutes later, Reed came walking past. He glanced into the music room; Adella looked away as he spied her. Without a word, Reed kept walking toward the new wing.

"He's going to meet Enfield ...!" Harlan whispered.

"When he comes out, follow him," Stella instructed her youngest son. "I need to know what he's doing."

Adella smiled. Within an hour everyone in Marleigh Manor would be talking about Reed meeting Enfield in Mitchell's room ... and then preparing the carriage to depart.

Ten minutes later, Reed passed them by again. This time he didn't even look into the music room, but walked swiftly, stoically.

As soon as Reed vanished from view, Harlan started after him.

Adella excused herself, then reentered the new wing.

"What's going on ...?" Lydia asked her.

"I don't know," Adella said. "Something about Mitchell's murder. A new clue has been found."

"Why was Reed here?" Lydia asked her.

"I'm not sure, but he left in a hurry, and Stella's youngest son is chasing after him," Adella said. "That's all I know. I need to tell Winnifred."

Adella hurried out of the entry room and straight toward Winnifred.

"Adella ...!" Winnifred exclaimed. "Who's stomping up and down the halls?"

"Reed," Adella said. "He was summoned."

"By who ...?" Winnifred asked.

"I don't know," Adella said. "I was in the music room. Stella said it was something about a new clue, something Enfield found in Mitchell's study. He locked its door and told Reed to fetch Constable Kendall first thing in the morning."

"What kind of clue ...?" Winnifred asked.

"I've told you all I know," Adella said. "Winnifred, I'm scared. I want to leave now!"

"Go back to your room," Winnifred said. "Say nothing to anyone. But promise me you'll come back here first thing in the morning. Then we'll settle all this."

"I will," Adella said. "I promise."

Adella hurried out, turning as if headed out of the new wing, but she crossed the short hallway, circled the entire new wing, and entered the nursery. The twins were sleeping in their crib, yet Adella only glanced at them. She quietly opened the closet door and crawled into her hideaway.

Her secret door closed behind her, and she didn't brace it. In the dim light from the hallway, filtering through the cracks, she found her father's tools, and by feel she closed her hand on what she needed; her covered lantern and the handle of her hammer. She hoped she wouldn't need either, but ...

She struck a match and lit the lantern, then slid its covers closed. The brightness of her flame vanished, and she listened carefully for any clue that her light had been seen. However, only the twins were in the nursery and Mitchell's study was still locked.

When she'd moved the wall three feet away from the back of the fireplace, she'd also moved the nursery closet. Behind the closet was a small gap. Adella slipped inside the gap and stood there, covered lantern in one hand, hammer in the other, concealed by darkness. She'd have to wait until things settled down.

Hurried footsteps filled the wing. Peering through her crack, out the nursery door, she saw Lydia, Grace, and Natalie enter Winnifred's room. Each stayed only a minute, and then departed with equally furtive steps. Adella wondered what Winnifred had told them but her replies meant nothing; only their missions concerned her.

All these rich families did was talk and plot. Seldom did any seek the truth.

Adella stepped back into the hidden gap and waited.

Hours later, in the deep silence after midnight, soft footsteps crept into the nursery. Wide awake, Adella tightly clutched her hammer, squeezing back into the gap behind the closet.

She heard the closet door open ... and then her secret door rose up.

Someone was climbing into her hideaway ...!

Adella froze, and tightened her grip on her hammer, determined not to make a sound. Someone crawled inside, not a foot from her knees. Quietly they closed her secret door behind them. Then they stood up, a shadowy outline in the thin streaks of dim light beaming through the cracks from the candlelit hallway outside the nursery.

For the first time, Adella wasn't alone in her hideaway!

Adella uncovered her lantern. The bright light illuminated the tall, thin figure, who loudly gasped, startled.

"Hello, Winnifred," Adella said.

With a shocked expression, Winnifred stood there, able to stand, to walk, and to crawl; *she wasn't an invalid!*

"*H-h-how ...?*" Winnifred stammered.

"There's only one way to get into the study when it's locked, and only you and I know it," Adella said. "Anyone could've faked the ghost by leaving coins, but it had to be someone with access to lots of silver, and that limited the suspects to a handful. No one in this house could've stabbed Mitchell without him putting up a struggle; Mitchell trusted no one, certainly not behind him. He had to be sound asleep. You only slept when you took a sleeping potion, and Mitchell always drank brandy when he sat at his desk."

"*You've no proof ...!*" Winnifred argued.

"You crawled inside, poisoned his brandy, and then hid here, in my hideaway, waiting for him to come in, to write or draw," Adella said. "He would've poured himself a brandy ... not suspecting your medicine poisoned it. When he fell asleep, you crawled into his study and stabbed him. You laid the coins on the floor, from his body to the locked door, which you left the key in ... from the inside. Then you came around and set the coins from the locked door across the hall into Mitchell's room, to the locked chest containing his books. You wanted Paxton to be named his heir, to keep the patriarchy of Marleigh Manor on a son with Marleigh blood, and you pointed Constable Kendall to the only proof of Paxton's parentage."

"Everyone said Mitchell was the spitting image of his father," Winnifred said. "Actually, Mitchell was an amalgamation of his father and uncles; as angry and impulsive as Lester, as randy as Middleton, as artistic as Enfield ... and as conniving as Rayden. All my brother's worst qualities; that was Mitchell."

"You faked your illness ... after old Morley died," Adella said.

"I've lain in that cursed bed for thirteen years, knowing someday I'd need an unbreakable alibi," Winnifred said. "Who would've guessed a lame old woman could murder a grown man ...? Yet I had to ... to control who ruled the Marleighs ...!"

"Why ...?" Adella asked. "You don't know Paxton will grow up a better man than Mitchell ...!"

"He's been rechristened a Marleigh-Prescott," Winnifred said. "He can mend the family tie broken by Captain Marston eighty years ago. Rowena's a good girl; she'll be a good mother. Her son will grow up, not teased and twisted as Mitchell was, with full knowledge that the mantle of leadership will someday be his."

"You succeeded too well," Adella said. "Paxton will inherit whether you go to jail or not ..."

"I failed entirely," Winnifred said. "When Stella left, I tried to be a mother to Mitchell. I did my best, yet he refused to listen to me, trusted no one, and he was so angry! He hated everyone, even those who'd supported him. Finally I recognized my failure, and knew I had to atone for it.

"Mitchell had to be removed; legally, there was no other way. At first, I'd wanted the Lordship to pass to Reed. I pressured Middleton to legally recognize him, but he refused to cooperate, and then he got sick. I hadn't considered the claim of Barton Perry Quinton; Mitchell hadn't seen his mother since she'd abandoned him; he wasn't supposed to bring them here. By the time I learned of it, they were already coming. I tried to get Mitchell to send them back, but he wouldn't."

"So you tried to get me to marry Mitchell, and when I wouldn't ...!" Adella said.

"You were smarter than I'd thought," Winnifred said. "Most young girls would've jumped at the chance to become Lady of Marleigh Manor. Your son would've been my next best hope ... after Reed was no longer an option."

"But I knew too much about Mitchell," Adella said.

"That left Paxton as my only hope," Winnifred said. "Paxton can mend the family rift, hire new servants, and make us all one family."

"In nineteen years, when he's old enough," Adella said. "Your plan leaves the Prescotts as servants for two more decades ..."

"What else can be done?" Winnifred asked.

"Vertiline's jewels," Adella said. "Give them to Rowena ... or sell them yourself. Hire enough servants to free the Prescotts from labors."

"If I do that, you won't report me ...?" Winnifred asked.

"You're a murderess," Adella said. "If I let you go, I'll share your guilt."

"If you send me to a noose, no one will ever find Vertiline's jewels," Winnifred warned. "No one will get them ... nothing will change."

"I won't hang beside you," Adella said.

"I'll write a confession ... and give it to you," Winnifred said. "I'm already old; you can read it at my funeral ... or if I'm ever arrested. If you don't report me now, then the Prescotts will be free of their chores right away. Otherwise, they stay servants ... for the rest of their lives. You, Adella, you have the power to spare me ... and them ... or condemn us all."

Adella stared at Winnifred, holding her shining lantern and squeezing the grip of her hammer.

The fate of all the Prescotts, for the next twenty years, depended on her ...!

No one in this family did anything until they were forced to ...!

The powerful never surrender power.

She held all the power.

"You will send Hayden and Harlow to search your family's workhouses," Adella said. "Most of those poor souls would jump at the chance to escape your hellholes ... even to be servants in this house."

"I will ... right away," Winnifred promised. "But ... that leaves you with nothing. There must be something you want ... something I can ...!"

"I want what you promised," Adella said. "Horses ... and a carriage, and enough wealth to support me somewhere ... anywhere else."

"Will you leave alone?" Winnifred asked.

"No," Adella said. "I'm taking Reed."

"You can't," Winnifred said. "Reed's a good man, one of the few in this house, and I need fathers like him to keep our next generation from becoming as spoiled and twisted as our last. But ... I can give you and him my blessing. He needn't be a stable-master anymore, and he'll want a strong, smart young wife to mother his children. You can stay here ... marry ...!"

"Live with the guilt of letting a murderess go free ...?" Adella demanded.

"I'm not free," Winnifred said. "You can't lie in bed for thirteen years with impunity; my health is failing, and if I'm ever seen walking, then I'll be suspected ... and hanged. Besides, you can't escape guilt by running away. But which guilt is worse; the guilt of keeping my secret, of letting the ghost of Marleigh Manor be Mitchell's murderer ... or keeping Prescotts slaving for Marleighs for the next nineteen years ...?"

Adella stared at her, Winnifred, *a murderess who deserved a noose ...!*

Yet ... Adella had murdered, too.

Sometimes you had no choice ...!

Winnifred had many choices. *She'd made the wrong choice ...!*

Adella had chosen to walk the length of North Road alone. She'd exposed herself to danger. Yet she couldn't leave every Prescott doomed to slavery ... *who knew what would happen in nineteen years, if they'd ever really be set free?*

Adella silently cursed blue fire.

"I want Vertiline's jewels," Adella said. "Now. I can't trust you. I'll present them to the whole family, see they're sold and the money is used right."

"I'll give them to you as a wedding present," Winnifred promised. "You and Reed ... with my blessings."

"Prescotts must be treated as equals," Adella said.

"I'll do what I can," Winnifred promised. "I'll talk to Hayden and Grace; the younger kids look to them. It may take a while, but that's the goal I've always wanted ... to undo the mistake my Grandmother Sarah Ann Prescott made ... marrying a thieving pirate."

"Very well," Adella scowled, and she sighed deeply. *"Mitchell Myerscough Marleigh was murdered ... by the ghost of Marleigh Manor."*

"It will be our secret," Winnifred promised.

Chapter 19 - Epiloge

Reed and Adella's spring wedding was the highlight of the season. Everyone in the district attended. Prescotts, in their new status, greeted everyone in new suits and gowns. Ten local carpenters were hired to restore all the aged parts of Marleigh Manor ... and Adella personally oversaw their work. Under her expert guidance, each repair was done correctly.

Barton Perry Quinton departed long before the wedding to return to his wife, and he took Bessie back to her husband. Stella and Nora remained to assist in Paxton's upbringing. Harlan desperately attempted to court Rowena, yet she refused his every effort.

Glad to be freed from their workhouses, the new

servants made the restored Marleigh-Prescott Manor more pleasant than anyone alive could recall. Camden was placed in charge of every servant. Prescotts taught them their chores, and everyone seemed happy.

Vertiline's jewels proved more numerous and valuable than anyone except Winnifred knew. Adella walked through Marleigh Manor wearing more riches than her father and mother had ever dreamed of, and she walked with Reed beside her.

Paxton grew up regarding them as his favorite aunt and uncle.

Much later, in the middle of the night, Adella secretly sealed both doors to her hideaway permanently. No one ever found either entrance.

To Adella's delight, the ghost of Marleigh Manor was never seen again.

Well ..., almost never ...!

THE END

All Books by Jay Palmer

The VIKINGS! Trilogy:
> **DeathQuest**
>
> **The Mourning Trail**
>
> **Quest for Valhalla**

The EGYPTIANS! Trilogy:
> **SoulQuest**
>
> **Song of the Sphinx**
>
> **Quest for Osiris**

Souls of Steam

Jeremy Wrecker, Pirate of Land and Sea

The Grotesquerie Games

The Grotesquerie Gambit

The Magic of Play

The Heart of Play

The Seneschal

Viking Son

Viking Daughter

Dracula – Deathless Desire

Murder At Marleigh Manor

JayPalmerBooks.com